The Shade Under the Mango Tree

Evy Journey

Sojourner Books

BERKELEY, CALIFORNIA

Book Layout ©2013/ BookDesignTemplates.com
ISBN: 978-0-9962474-8-1

Love consists in this, that two solitudes protect and touch and greet each other.

Rainer Maria Rilke

Talent develops in quiet places, character in the full current of human life.

Johann Wolfgang von Goethe

Prologue

February, 2016: Luna

Ov's thin upper body is slumped over his crossed legs, his forehead resting on the platform. His brown, wiry arms lie limp, the right one extended forward, hand dangling over the edge of the platform. Dried blood is splattered on his head, and on the collar, right shoulder, and back of his old short-sleeved white shirt.

It seems fitting that he died where he used to spend most of his time when he wasn't on the rice fields—sitting on a corner of the bamboo platform in the ceiling-high open space under the house. It's where you get refreshing breezes most afternoons, after a long day of work.

The policeman looks down at Ov's body as if he's unsure what to do next. He lays down his camera and the gun in a plastic bag at one end of the platform untainted by splatters of gelled blood.

He steps closer to the body, anchors himself with one knee on top of the platform, and bends over the body. Hooking his arms underneath Ov's shoulders and upper arms, he pulls the body up, and carefully lays it on its back. He straightens the legs.

He steps off the platform. Stands still for a few seconds to catch his breath. He turns to us and says, "It's clear what has happened. I have all the pictures I need."

He points to his camera, maybe to make sure we understand. We have watched him in silence, three zombies still in shock. Me, standing across the bamboo platform from him. Mae and Jorani sitting, tense and quiet, on the hammock to my left.

Is that it? Done already? I want to ask him: *Will he have the body taken away for an autopsy?* I suppose that's what is routinely done everywhere in cases like this. But I don't know enough Khmer.

As if he sensed my unspoken question, he glances at me. A quick glance that comes with a frown. He seems perplexed and chooses to ignore me.

He addresses the three of us, like a captain addressing his troop. "You can clean up."

The lingering frown on his brow softens into sympathy. He's gazing at Jorani, whose mournful eyes remain downcast. He looks away and turns toward Mae. Pressing his hands together, he bows to her. A deeper one than the first he gave her when she and Jorani arrived.

He utters Khmer words too many and too fast for me to understand. From the furrowed brow and the look in his eyes, I assume they are words of sympathy. He bows a third time, and turns to go back to where he placed the gun and camera. He picks them up and walks away.

For a moment or two, I stare at the figure of the policeman walking away. Then I turn to Jorani. *Call him back. Don't we have questions? I can ask and you can translate, if you prefer.* But seeing her and Mae sitting as still and silent as rocks, hands on their laps, and eyes glazed as if to block out what's in front of them, the words get trapped in my brain. Their bodies, rigid just moments before, have gone slack, as if to say: What else can anyone do? What's done cannot be undone. All that's left is to clean up, as the policeman said. Get on with our lives.

My gaze wanders again toward the receding figure of the policeman on the dirt road, the plastic bag with the gun dangling in his right hand. Does it really matter how Cambodian police handles Ov's suicide? I witnessed it. I know the facts. And didn't I read a while back how Buddhism frowns upon violations on the human body? The family might object against cutting up Ov—the way I've seen on TV crime shows—just to declare with certainty what caused his death.

I take in a long breath. I have done all I can and must defer to Cambodian beliefs and customs.

But I can't let it go yet. Ov chose to end his life in a violent way and I'm curious: Do the agonies of his last moments show on his face? I steal another look.

All I could gather, from where I stand, is life has definitely gone out of every part of him. His eyes are closed and immobile. The tic on his inanimate cheeks hasn't left a trace. The tic that many times was the only way I could tell he had feelings. Feelings he tried to control or hide. Now, his face is just an expressionless brown mask. Maybe everyone really has a spirit, a soul that rises out of the body when one dies, leaving a man-size mass of clay.

I stare at Ov's body, lying in a darkened, dried pool of his own blood, bits of his skull and brain scattered next to his feet where his head had been. At that moment, it hits me that this would be the image of Ov I will always remember. I shudder.

My legs begin to buckle underneath me and I turn around, regretting that last look. With outstretched hands, I take a step toward the hammock. Jorani rises to grab my hands, and she helps me sit down next to Mae.

Could I ever forget? Could Mae and Jorani? Would the image of Ov in a pool of blood linger in their memories like it would in mine?

I know I could never tell my parents what happened here this afternoon. But could I tell Lucien? The terrible shock of watching someone, in whose home I found a family, fire a gun to his head? And the almost as horrifying realization—looking back—that I knew what he was going to do, but I hesitated for a few seconds to stop him.

8

Part 1:

Luna's Journal

Luna

August 2007

I am home.

I stand on the sidewalk, somewhat lightheaded from the six-hour flight between Los Angeles and Honolulu. I breathe the plumeria-infused air deep into my lungs. Relish the crisp warm breeze that blows my hair on my face. As I grab the handle on my luggage, I scan the neighborhood. Nothing much has changed since last summer.

I roll my luggage across the concrete entryway, pass the hibiscus hedge, and stop to pluck a bouquet of its flaming-red flowers. Its home is a vase on the coffee table in the living area. To signal I'm back. While visitors surf, tan on the beach, don flowery muumuus and shirts, and slurp maitais or Hawaiian punch while ogling hula dancers, I look forward to domesticating with Grandma.

Grandma's house—a two-story of stained wood in Waipahu, Hawaii—is where I left my innocence.

I pause at the foot of the six steps to the trellised porch. A tinge of sadness never fails to temper the joy of arriving. Two months are never enough. Just when I'm getting used to the pace and pattern of languid days with Grandma, I must leave again. Back to the modern stucco in the burbs of Los Angeles I left nine hours ago.

Life keeps going forward, like Mom says, and I must march along with it. This summer will wane. It's reassuring to know, though, that another is sure to come.

Gripping the handle on my luggage, I drag it up the porch. The house has been home to Grandma since the mid-sixties when she married my grandfather. Grandpa's parents had built it before sugar plantations dating back to the 1850s were transformed into a town, their history and artifacts ensconced in a museum and a park a couple of miles or so from here. Before streets—including where Grandma's house stands—were sucked into housing subdivisions of cookie-cutter stuccos like my parents' California home. Before mango and papaya trees and an occasional lychee tree replaced sugar cane.

The Kamakas have lived here for four generations, two more than other families in the neighborhood. Yes, time marches on. And I must march along with it.

Before I can press the buzzer, the door opens, releasing a familiar scent much like the Lady Emma Hamilton rose in Grandma's garden. A rose fragrance with an undertone of lemon. It wafts past me to blend with the salty open air.

"Green mangoes?" I say, as Grandma's petite frame emerges from behind the door. I have grown half a head taller than she is.

Her mouth turns up ever so slightly at the corners in that familiar little smile. Her hazel eyes beam their welcome at me. It's Grandma's eyes, more than her mouth, that have always revealed her emotions.

"Here I am again."

"Luna, my little keiki! Right on time."

"Big keiki, Grandma." I stoop to receive her kisses and hug and kiss her back.

I pick up traces of the scent of green mangoes from her hair, mixed with the lingering bouquet of jasmine. Grandma has never worn perfume or cologne. Instead, she picks jasmine from her garden every morning and tucks it under her long hair, pulled back and twisted into a bun above the nape of her neck. The first few years of my summer visits after returning to my family in California, I slept with Grandma on her king-sized bed for a week or so. I often fell asleep, snuggled close to her, inhaling the hint of jasmine from her loosened hair.

"Go, take your bags to your room and come to the kitchen. Lunch is almost ready."

My bedroom on the second floor was carved out of a bigger one Mom had shared with her sister, Auntie Juanita. As in previous visits, it's much like it was when I went back home last September. The same red-and-green-striped spread on the bed, its padded headboard lined in cotton printed with a Ti-leaf Haku lei—a crown of green leaves from the ti plant—large enough to span the bed's width. The wooden desk by the window that belonged to Mom, bare now except for a couple of children's books on top. The old, dark-brown, wooden chair where my three dolls sit. I place them there on the last day of every visit and imagine them waiting for my return.

Minutes later, I sit on a high-backed bar stool at Grandma's long butcher block work table. The same stool Grandma fitted with a child seat when I was a toddler. The kitchen-dining room with its high, sloping ceiling is bathed in early afternoon sunshine by a skylight above it. She hands me a tall glass of fresh iced coconut water.

She continues blending some sauce with a whisk. When she's not in her garden, she spends her waking hours at this table, sitting on a chair of cane and wood, preparing meals and snacks, managing her now-reduced household, writing cards or letters, and reading magazines she stashes on open corner shelves that—along with cabinets—line an outside wall.

The chunky butcher block is the hub around which everything happens when the Kamaka family get together. It's cleaned, adorned with flowers from Grandma's garden, and outfitted with as many chairs and dinner settings as required by the expected number of visitors.

I gulp a mouthful of coconut water, trying to chase away the unease creeping up my chest as I watch Grandma. She's graying faster every year, and becoming a little more bent.

"Mango salad?" I force myself to focus on her twirling hand as she whisks lime juice, fish sauce, sweet chili paste, and garlic. The sauce releases a pungent aroma, making my mouth water.

With a small spoon, Grandma scoops a few drops of the mixture for me to taste. The sauce tingles my taste buds and I nod in approval. Her green mango salad is legendary.

She stirs the sauce into a bowl of peeled and julienned light-green mangos and scatters torn leaves of mint and Thai basil on top. She takes a pinch of the salad and tastes it.

She passes the bowl to me and I put it on the breakfast table in the dining area. "Are these Tanaka mangos?"

"Maggie came by early this morning and gave me a few. I think they fell from her tree."

"Are they okay?"

"Oh yes. Firm. Fresh. Good lemony green mango smell. Knowing Maggie, she couldn't have left them on the ground an hour. Anyway, I peel them. How was your flight?" She glances at me.

"Good. Good. Nice summer weather for flying. I'm starved. What are you serving with your mango salad?"

"A bit of grilled tuna and some poi." Her eyes twinkle, lips pursing to suppress a smile.

I crinkle my nose. I never liked poi and she knows it.

Ten minutes later, we sit at the breakfast table by the window. She doesn't serve poi. She has dug a few potatoes and picked zucchini from her garden, and grilled chunks of them along with the tuna.

From where I sit, I see the mango tree in the front yard rising above the rooftop of her house. Its lowest branches dip below the first story—a lush green canopy of waxy leaves that protects anyone looking for shelter from rain or sun.

But this mango tree has a problem: it doesn't bear fruit. It soars, sprawls and flowers, promising a bountiful harvest. But in the first thirteen years I lived here with Grandma and two aunts, I've never seen those flowers morph into yellow kidney-shaped fruit. Even one mango hanging on one of its branches would have given cause for some celebration. The last four summers I've returned on vacation, nothing has changed.

Grandma and Grandpa never doubted the mango tree would fruit. They planted it thirty years ago, a few years before he passed away. It had been grafted from another tree that bore large green mangoes speckled with red and yellow.

But something had gone awry. The mere twelve feet of a semi-dwarf tree they expected grew more than twice as high. They waited for it to bear fruit, but ten years later, it gave great shade but not a single fruit. They would have settled for the speckled green ones from the stock into which the yellow mango was grafted. On a street where every house has at least one fruitful mango tree, the fate of Grandma's tree is a small tragedy.

"Tanakas' mango trees still bear fruit?" I ask Grandma before I shove another big bite of mango salad into my mouth. The Tanakas live two houses up the street.

"Oh, yes, lots. Maggie takes care of them like they're her kids, now that they've all moved away, like your mom and your aunts. Especially, the big one with yellow fruit."

"That's a beautiful tree when it's got lots of bright yellow-orange fruit. Like large nuggets of gold in a sea of dark green. I've seen passersby take pictures."

"She keeps all the yellow mangos for her family. I can't blame her. They're as soft and sweet as custard. Juicy and fragrant. A hint of tartness to tease the taste buds."

I see and taste a succulent yellow mango in my mind and wish I had one to sink my teeth into. Instead, I ask, "Can you make salad out of them when they're green?"

"You can, but why? They're better eaten ripe out of hand. You can peel them like a banana. But I'm grateful she shares a lot of the fat green, speckled ones with me and your aunts."

"Generous of Mrs. Tanaka," I say.

"Keeps your aunts from complaining about my tree. Anyway, the speckled kind makes a better salad."

My aunts grew up with the Tanaka children who gave them more mangoes than they could eat. Grandma made good use of leftover mangoes, cutting and freezing them for smoothies or mango bread when the season was over.

By the time I changed residences the summer before ninth grade—when my parents took me back to send me to the same public school my brothers went to—my grandmother had become philosophical about her barren tree.

"It's beautiful, your tree. Lush. Can cover the three Tanaka trees put together."

Grandma smiles, pleased. "You can sit under it even when it showers. I've had many restful hours under its cool shade. Besides, it might surprise us yet."

So far, though, no surprises. But every year, Grandma and I thrive under its protective spread of large waxy leaves. We sit on the beautiful Adirondack-style wooden bench one of Maggie's brothers—who's a craftsman—built for her.

Grandma's mango tree does have a distinct function for the neighborhood. It's a landmark you can't miss. It's on a corner of the main street, is taller than her house, and you can see its wide umbrella of green luxurious leaves from afar. Locals use it as a reference point when giving directions to the area.

Years ago, my aunts tried to persuade Grandma to cut the barren tree down. She smiled but told them to "leave my tree alone."

Grandma lives by herself. During the day, she tends her chickens and a garden while opera music soars out of her decades-old boom box. She gets help every Monday from a large and pretty Japanese Hawaiian house cleaner who's been coming since I was little. By now, she must be almost sixty. When her chores are done, she stays for another hour to chat with Grandma over iced tea, wasabi nuts, or rice crackers.

*****

A knock wakes me up on my first weekend morning in Waipahu. Grandma doesn't knock; she tiptoes in, lets me sleep as long as I need to, at least for the first two weeks of my stay. So I know it must be Auntie Celia. Auntie Juanita never comes into my room.

Though my two aunts are supposed to alternate visiting Grandma, I hardly ever see Auntie Juanita. My aunts have families, each with two children, and a joint dental practice in Honolulu.

"Come in." My voice is soft, slurred by sleep.

19

"Get up, sleepy head. I need a kiss and a big hug. It's past ten, you know." Auntie Celia sits on my single bed and bumps me with her hips. Old family friends say she reminds them of Grandma when she was young. She's taller, though, and has naturally curly hair that must come from Grandpa.

My eyelids are still too sticky to open fully, but I push myself up to my butt, hug her, press my lips to her cheeks, and rest my head on her shoulders. I let my body go slack against hers.

She hugs me back and returns my kiss. "Ugh. Morning breath. Get up, you little slug. I brought you some manapua, and they're still warm. Got some malasadas, too. Come down and tell me about your exciting year. I want to hear what you intend to do, now that you're close to being declared an adult."

The prospect of biting into warm pillowy steamed bread and savoring its char siu pork filling perks me up. I lift my head off her shoulders and give Auntie Celia a wide smile. "From your favorite bakery?"

"Where else?" Auntie Celia scowls, feigning annoyance at my question.

Grandma makes manapua, too, but she fills hers with chicken meatballs and Chinese sausage. Auntie Celia's favorite bakery stuffs its buns with tender pieces of saucy red char siu. I like both kinds for different reasons but only when the buns are still warm.

Later, after a simple lunch of chicken ramen and more grilled zucchini the three of us prepared together, Grandma leaves us to finish the dessert. Warm malasadas she'll roll in powdered sugar

Auntie Celia says, "Big changes this year, huh? Breaking free from family. Got your first driver's license. Going to UC Berkeley this fall. Settled on a major yet?"

"Interdisciplinary studies. Sort of liberal artsy."

"I thought you might do that. No interest in the physical or biological sciences, eh?"

I shrug. "Got nothing against them but mixing chemicals or poking into a mouth full of teeth ain't my thing."

Auntie Celia laughs. "Don't knock it. Tooth cavities have bought me luxury. You're more like Mom than any of us. You have her idealism, her sensitivity."

"That's good, isn't it?"

"It is except when it's not. What does your mom say? If I know her as I think I do, she would be unhappy with your choice."

"She's not objecting too much. Tries to stick to the principle we're old enough to decide what we want to do."

"Typical Louisa. Ever sensible."

"I guess." I pause, mulling for a moment. "Actually, you're right. She's unhappy but tries to hide it."

"Ahhh. Let's hope she gets over it. Or at least, gets used to the idea."

Waving a hand, she ends further talk of Mom's unhappy reaction. "Anyway, from now on, you can take Mom to the grocery. I don't have to do it anymore when you're here."

"I'd be happy to, but I don't think she trusts me with her car. I already offered, but she told me to wait and see what you say."

"In that case, let's go in fifteen minutes. You drive. She won't take much to convince. Look confident, and most of all, observe the speed limit."

Auntie Celia was right, of course. Once we're back home from the supermarket and we've put away the groceries, Grandma says, "Thank you, keiki. You did well. Observed the speed limit and did all your signals. I don't need to wait for Celia to take me shopping. Not this summer, anyway."

Among the three sisters including my mother, I believe Grandma trusts Auntie Celia the most although she's the youngest. I don't think Mom and Grandma are close. I've often wondered why but I've never asked.

Auntie Celia usually returns to her home in Honolulu at sunset. Before that, she and I water Grandma's vegetable garden in the backyard, feed the ten or so chickens in their coop next to the garden, and harvest their eggs. She'll take the eggs and the vegetables we pick to her home in Honolulu.

*****

The halcyon days of my too-short summer visit whizz by. Before I could persuade Grandma to let me take her on an afternoon outing to Hanauma Bay, one of her favorite spots, two months have gone by. I find myself packing, making sure I'm leaving my room the way I've always done the last four summers. I drag my rolling luggage once more, but this time, it's down the steps to where Grandma waits.

I kiss Grandma goodbye, and she kisses me back, both of us trying to hold back tears. "Time goes by quicker than you think, keiki. You'll see. I'll be here, waiting for you next summer."

"Bye, Grandma. I love you." I turn and run down the steps to Auntie Celia's car, wiping my wet cheeks with my fingers.

Auntie Celia hands me some tissues before I can buckle myself on the front passenger seat. She says, in a jaunty voice, "Forecast for metro LA weather is sunny and polluted; San Francisco Bay Area, foggy, cool, and good air. Cheer up. You're off on a fresh adventure."

Lucien

Tuesday February, 2013

"Hi, Lucien!" A quartet of voices greets me from the service bar as I saunter into the local Peet's three blocks from my office. I play along. Smile. Wave.

I've come to this coffeehouse every weekday afternoon at half-past two. I come for the coffee. The ambience. Customers minding their own business. The absence of music to lull you into a false sense of ease while subdued conversations warble along with hissing frothing machines. Familiar, predictable, comforting.

I stand in line for café mocha. Stick earphones into my ears. Play a Bob Dylan song in my iPad— "Like A Rolling Stone." When I was a boy, Gramps often played Dylan on his stereo and sang along with it. This song was his favorite. It takes six minutes to play. Enough to entertain me while I wait.

The song finishes and I'm still fourth in line. I take off my earbuds, as if in doing so I could speed up the line. By the time I reach the service bar, I'm a little irritable. Time standing in line is time lost from my short break.

Aaron, the server, turns his undivided attention to me. Unleashes his toothy charm. He does have beautiful straight teeth.

"The usual?" It's not really a question. He's been at this Peet's off and on for a year and knows it's the only drink I order. When he's not at Peet's, he toils on art installations using junk automotive parts, dreaming of fame.

I suppress my irritation at having waited ten minutes and trade a word or two with Aaron. He punches my order into the register. I hand him a five-dollar bill. "How's the art project going?"

"Close to finished. I need a couple more pieces I haven't found yet." He gives me coins in exchange for my bill. Another toothy smile. When no one else is in line for coffee, we talk more. We're both unattached. Two guys who've chosen to devote our lives to our passion—art and design. For Aaron, art installations using junk and other discards. For me, dwellings which fit the vernacular aesthetic of the local culture where the building I designed would be located. We are only two among many like us in this revitalizing city.

Today, several customers are still waiting. Vacationers to the San Francisco Bay Area. Conference attendees staying at nearby hotels. Families visiting sons or daughters going to universities in the area.

Aaron looks past me to the next person in line.

"Good luck," I say. After a robotic nod, he turns on his sixty-second charm for the next customer. I move to the side to wait along with a few others.

The fifty minutes I spend in this place are sacred to me. The only break from work I allow myself besides the half hour I eat a sandwich at my desk, delivered around noon by a nearby deli. They give me much-needed respite from the intense, creative work that consumes the hours of my day.

I'm the first to admit: My social life consists of coffee breaks and occasional visits to a kava bar, infrequent casual dates, and talking shop with colleagues at the architectural firm where I work and with technicians in the building industry.

The café has been a big part of my regular social milieu since I graduated three years ago. I look around, see familiar faces. We don't say a word to each other but we nod, bonding in some way. Together, yet apart. You could say I am a solitary soul, like many in a tech or design business. Like most of the regulars in this café.

But I'm not complaining. I am quite comfortable with my life. My social goings-on mesh well with my work—nothing to distract me from projects that usually require my undivided attention. Every one of them can present an unforeseen problem demanding an inventive solution. I thrive on the challenges. The exchange of ideas. The rowdy, contentious discussions we have about solutions. The highs from solving design problems.

I always learn something new. And I can boast about how well concepts or proposals I've submitted to various projects have been received.

In a few years, I mean to be my own boss. So, right now, work is my focus. Build a portfolio. Capitalize on my experience at the firm and at Habitat for Humanity. Use ideas inspired by nature and indigenous structures in my travels. Design dwellings and furniture reflective of the setting and the character of people who use or inhabit them. Be a hybrid Frank Gehry and Frank Lloyd Wright somewhere in the world.

I hear the barista call my name. My café mocha is ready. Seconds later, cup in my right hand, iPad clutched in my left, I stand for a moment, looking for a free table. The usual café crowd sit at little tables lining the long banquette. A few regulars squinting at cell phones, their coffee drinks getting cold. Earnest university students bent over homework. A couple of gray-haired couples gazing past each other.

One small table is free and I rush to claim it as my temporary territory. A small cube of space I'll own for the next half hour or so. No one bothers to look up as I pass their tables. So engrossed are they in what they're doing that the outside world is but a distant image. I may be blasé, but I'm not cynical. I don't think people are inherently suspicious or fearful of strangers.

Still, I would have perked up at a small smile. Some recognition from you, fellow coffee shop habitués, that we share the same space and time, even in our treasured solitude. Solitude we hope an email or a message on our cell phones would interrupt. Once in a while.

I put cup and iPad down on the eighteen-inch round table and push it some inches from the banquette. There, where I intend to park my bottom, a thick black notebook lies. My irritation goes up a notch.

I adhere to this unspoken café rule: You need a clear marker to stake claim to a chair and table. The owner should have placed his black notebook in clear view of anyone walking by. I swipe the notebook off the seat and plop it on the table, where it belongs. When its owner returns, I'll move to the stand-up bar until another table opens up.

I take my first sip of café mocha. An indulgence. A legacy from Mom and Dad. Since age four, I'd go with them to the first Peet's Café every weekday morning. Built more than two decades earlier, it took over the life on a block of Vine Street in Berkeley.

This Emeryville branch is on the edge of a voluminous structure, a once-upon-a-time warehouse repurposed five years ago as a market of food stalls and restaurants. Its cave-like space nurtures college-educated solitary souls lured by a gentrifying city dense with one-bedroom condominiums and upscale apartments. And yes, if anyone wants to stereotype me, I'm well-aware I'm one of those. The difference is, I didn't buy readymade space. I renovated my own loft the year after I graduated.

At this Peet's, the banquette is the first thing you notice. Lining a long solid wall. Outfitted with a dozen or so tables-for-one.

A coffee shop used to be a place for socializing. In Europe, especially eighteenth-century France, it nurtured a café culture where people gathered to share and argue about ideas. But not anymore. I guess, in our tech-savvy culture, we've come to prefer our own company. Or have to be satisfied with it. Now, we no longer need face-to-face contact. We commune with tablets or smartphones, even consume news and novels via electronic newspapers and books.

This café has an area for small groups who drop in. Two larger tables and two couches crammed at a streetside corner. Isolated from the banquette by ample space. There, conversations are a mere murmur to banquette habitués. Blotted out with earphones if even the murmur is bothersome.

Ten minutes into sipping coffee and occasionally scanning the room, I glance at the notebook. Suppress an urge to pick it up. I turn my iPad on instead. It's a crutch—something to turn to when my brain goes on break. Or no stray magazines or newspapers are close enough to grab. You could also say it's a badge. Proves I belong. To this place and this time.

First, my email. Heavy with sales talk and content from building trades and tech companies. Places where I've bought or inquired about something.

Then, my news app. The usual. Some event that riles me or saddens me enough about the state of the world that sometimes I want to wallow in blissful ignorance. But always, a rational voice niggles me from my not-so-distant past. Gramps or Nana. "Be aware. Keep abreast of what's happening. Not only here, but everywhere else."

A few news summaries later—Boston marathon bombing; chemical weapons in Syria; tornados, typhoons and flooding; Edward Snowden leaks; more on the mass shooting in Connecticut and failure of gun control efforts; and so on—I turn off the iPad. Take slow sips of my coffee drink. Staring in front of me but not really seeing.

I gulp down the rest of my drink. Glance once more at the notebook. Why has its owner not come back to claim it? Seems I'll have to hand it to the servers when I leave.

It would take little effort to make a short detour to the counter, but again, I can't help being annoyed. It's careless to leave an item like a notebook at a public place. I'm sure it contains something valuable or private the owner would want to protect from snoopers. An embarrassing habit, maybe? A dangerous secret?

I turn on my iPad again. Scan the Flipboard sections on architecture and art for exciting, mood-lifting articles to distract me from depressing news. But nothing catches my interest.

The black notebook. Could I hand it to the servers, not knowing what it holds? Maybe, it's boring but informative, like lecture notes. Or mildly interesting like a diary, giving the idly curious, like me, an intimate view into some stranger's humdrum life. But what if it does hide secrets? One full of intrigue.

If this were a journal of someone I know, I wouldn't even touch it. But a stranger's? No one in the café would care or even notice if I took a peek. What possible harm can I do if I were to read its contents? Some of it, at least. Wouldn't I need to do so to find its owner?

But do I, really? I could hand it to the café staff and be rid of it once and for all.

My father used to say I was unusually curious, sometimes to the point of miscalculating danger. I see no danger in reading a notebook some stranger forgot. Besides, once I hand it over, this would be just another episode in the course of a day. Mundane enough for it to pass and be forgotten.

The First Pages

I pick up the notebook. To my surprise, it's a Moleskine. Prized by many artists for durability and versatility. Or for its name. Like the iPad, it's a sort of badge: "Look, I'm a serious artist." It's not cheap and is one of the bigger sizes—five by eight inches and nearly an inch thick. My curiosity is piqued.

The Moleskine has a front flyleaf prompting the owner, "In case of loss," for a name and contact information. But this one is blank. A little strange, I think. And careless. The Moleskine is usually a repository for its owner's unique imagination and creative ideas. A record of his exploration. If this were mine, I'd never want to lose it.

Maybe the back pocket will yield the owner's name written on a card or a piece of paper. I flip through the pages to the back pocket. It's empty.

The owner wants to remain anonymous? But why?

I skim through the first page, titled Preface. It's inscribed in ink from top to bottom in a careful hand, although flourishes adorn capital letters like A and W. The writer is, without doubt, female. Compulsive enough to mind grammar and word choice.

Preface

While packing the day before I flew back home from Honolulu, Grandma came to my room, said she had a special birthday gift for me, not the usual gift card I get by clicking on a link she sends me by email.

She handed me a thick notebook bound in black leather. A Moleskine.

Use it as a journal, she says. I'll be living in a new place, and though it's immediate family, they're strangers to me. I'll have to adjust. I can let out frustrations, anger, doubts, and fears by writing about them.

She also says I'll be an adult in a few years, and like everyone else, I'll do things that would trouble me, that I'd regret, or wish I'd done differently. Or worse, that can hurt me or others. Writing a journal may help me understand myself better and find a way to cope, heal, and maybe help others heal as well.

In a wistful voice, she added she wished she had done a journal.

I couldn't think of what to write at that time. What is there to know about me, after all? As young and naïve as I am.

I've been happy, felt loved by my family, done well in school. I haven't had much to complain about. Though moving to California was difficult for a while, my family there helped me adjust. All ordinary and boring stuff.

It also bothers me—the idea that once I write them down, my thoughts, my experiences, my life, will be imprisoned within these pages long after I'm gone. But those words will present a view of me that's not the FULL me. How can it do otherwise? We can only write what we know. And I don't know myself very well.

I am intrigued. By an introspective quality in the young writer. Intrigued enough to quash the residual guilt I have. I am compelled to read on.

Her grandmother meant more to the journal writer than anyone else. This weighty Moleskine proves it. This artifact of her young life inconsequential to everyone else is precious to her. Not only because her grandmother gave her the notebook. Writing a journal might, indeed, have helped her cope. Life does throw curve balls at everyone of us.

Choosing a Moleskine says something about the journal writer's grandmother. Grandma must have been artistic. The Moleskine is a better support for pencils, not ink, which bleeds through. Surely, not the best medium to write on. It's an expensive depository for thoughts and observations. But Grandma wanted to make sure her granddaughter would write her journal. So Grandma gave her something she thought was special. That looked special. A notebook that would compel her granddaughter to start her journal.

Apart from being intrigued by the first entry, I am touched by how attached the journal writer seems to be to her grandmother. I know how she feels. I grew up spending most of my waking hours with my own grandparents while my parents worked.

Gramps and Nana were self-declared hippies. Fun to be with. Not afraid to defy convention so long as they didn't hurt others. Eager to nurture my curiosity. They inspired me to be adventurous and go out into the wide world.

My childhood was joyful, thanks to them. Like this young journal writer, I was closer to them than to my parents. I believe they made me who I am. Partly due to their influence, I switched from information technology to architecture.

September2005

Grandma talked about my keeping a journal two years ago, a month after my parents decided to take me back to their home in California. She wanted to know about my California life and suggested that I take a photo of each of my entries and attach it to the emails I send her.

She said it would be like talking to her or an imaginary friend.

When I was little and lived with Grandma and two aunts, I invented Didi, a girl who lived with us, shared my bedroom, ate with me, and played with me. We talked constantly. She cried when I cried. Being a year older, she knew more things and sometimes bossed me around. She could tease me and challenge me but we had fun together. She had dark curly hair (mine is straight), white skin (mine is light brown) and big brown eyes. We were friends until I was six when she began to disappear for days on end until she left forever.

Before Grandma gave me this Moleskine, I've fabricated excuses to myself to avoid starting a journal—too busy adjusting to my California life, too tedious to write with a ball pen, not enough time to type this journal into my computer so I can send it to Grandma as an email. I owe her that much instead of sending pictures of pages that may not be easy to read.

Then, in August this year, she gave me this Moleskine. Still, it took me a few weeks before I could write my first sentence.

But today is my birthday and I recall what Grandma said about doing a journal. I think it's a good time to start.

So. To begin: I am 15 today, the second birthday I'm celebrating in California. I spent my first 13 years with Grandma and my grown-up aunts, Auntie Celia and Auntie Juanita, in Hawaii so that's where I had my earlier birthdays.

Two weeks ago, after dinner, Mom said, "Wouldn't it be fun to invite your friends to a birthday party?"

This was the first time she'd suggested a party for me and it took me a minute or so to respond. I really didn't want one, couldn't think of anyone I'd like to invite, and I'd always been ill at ease in large groups. But all I said was, "Is it okay to have only the family? I think I'll have more fun celebrating at home with you and Dad and my brothers."

She knitted her brow like she often does when she can't understand or doesn't approve. I could almost hear her thoughts: "What 15-year-old girl does that? Aren't they supposed to love parties?" But she said, "Okay. It's your birthday. You choose."

I think she treats me with kid gloves, maybe because she doesn't really know me. Or she feels guilty because she left me to spend my early growing-up years with Grandma, her mother.

On my first night at my parents' house, Mom came to my room, wanted to make sure I was comfortable. She sat on the bed, asked me to sit next to her, and looking serious, said, "We're your family, you know. This is where you belong."

I'll never forget those words. Somehow, they made me feel kind of guilty. Then she added that they'd all do their best to make me feel at home and with time, things would get better.

As if I didn't know all that. The weird thing was I recognized her as Mom from pictures and her last visit to Honolulu but she still seemed like a stranger to me.

The fact is I miss Grandma everyday and, in my heart, wish I still lived with her. I understand what Mom said that night. I should be with my immediate family. But now, as then, I still think of Grandma and my aunts (the Kamakas of Waipahu) as my immediate family. Maybe that's what I felt guilty about.

My California family picked me up at the Los Angeles International airport the first time I arrived. I guess they wanted to make me feel welcome. Everyone hugged me and said, "Welcome home" but I felt dazed from the plane trip and meeting three brothers who were nearly strangers to me.

I'd only seen my brothers in pictures, and though Grandma said my parents visited us three times in Honolulu, I only remember their last visit the summer I was eleven. They stayed one month. I was shy with them at first, but I think they tried their best to show they cared about me so by the time they left, I was happy to embrace them. Dad, especially. He was so warm and so open.

At the airport, my oldest brother, Jun, stared at me and held me at arm's length before he hugged me tight, kissed me on both cheeks, and said, "Finally, a sister. And such a pretty one, too. I love you already."

(I didn't think I was pretty but it was nice of him to say so.)

Kana and Andy hugged me, too, but they seemed so awkward and forced. I think they had been told what to do.

Jun has been so nice and so helpful that I didn't feel too alien for too long. He's quite a talker, tells me stories about himself and his friends. That's made it much easier for me to share mine with him. Of course, I don't have as much to tell as he does. He was nineteen and in college up north in Davis when I moved here so I see him only on some weekends and on holidays, but he came home the day I arrived. He's graduating from college this year and will be returning to UC Davis to study law.

Kana is seventeen and spends hours on his computer, playing video games or chatting online with his friends. He has no time for me except to say, "Hi sis" before he hunkers down in the room he shares with Andy or "See you, sis" before he leaves the house.

It was Andy, a year younger than me, who I first thought I could make friends with, but he's also wrapped up in his video games. Maybe more so than Kana. He doesn't seem to have as many friends as Jun or Kana and tunes me out when I try to talk to him. He watches me and sometimes he nods his head or shrugs. Then, he smiles and walks away. I guess brothers don't have much they could say to a sister, especially one they've just met. Jun might have wondered what I had been doing all those years I lived in Hawaii, but I doubt Kana and Andy cared.

Jun tells me Andy is a techno-geek who tampers with his computer to make it do exactly what he wants. Jun goes to him when he has a problem with his own computer. Andy's dream is to become a rich game developer. Kana, Jun says, is a bit more of a puzzle to their parents although they're very pleased he wants to go into chemical engineering. But it seems he's only applying to out-of-state schools. He's not a talker like Jun is.

Anyway, we had a delicious dinner this evening. Mom came home from work two hours earlier and went into a frenzy of cooking. Roast chicken, roast pork, rice pilaf and grilled vegetables. After we were all stuffed on her dishes, she produced a birthday cake from a local bakery. It had plenty of raspberries and whipped cream on top. It became a favorite when I had it for the first time last year, on my first California birthday. As an additional treat, Jun promised to take me to the Getty tomorrow. He knows I've been wanting to go.

I think it will be exciting to explore the museum. It's big and modern, like a twenty-first-century palace all by itself on a hill, looking over all of Los Angeles and beyond. It has no turrets, no spires and its roof is flat, but it has acres of gardens and fountains. You also have to ride a tram to the top of the hill. To me, all those make the museum magical, a place where fairy tales can happen. I want to see if it's as beautiful as I imagined it to be based on the pictures I've seen.

I wish Grandma were here, though, but she doesn't like flying. I miss her most on my birthdays and on holidays. I was only a few months old when I went to live with her. And I can't help it that, after two years, I still think of her and my aunts as my immediate family.

My birthday celebration was nice although I didn't talk much. Mostly, Jun entertained us with stories of his college life. My parents responded by reminiscing on theirs. Before we all got up from the table, I thanked Mom, said I appreciated her cooking such tasty dishes. Loved all of them. She smiled. Pleased, I hope, that I liked the dinner she put so much energy into.

Might I have talked more if Grandma had been here? In addition to the Moleskine, she sent me a gift card, like last year, to buy anything I wish, but she knows I'll use it for books. I don't need anything else because my parents buy me everything Mom thinks I need.

In the morning, a flower shop came to deliver a box with a fresh lei of fragrant tropical jasmine from Auntie Celia. They made me feel special, but I also felt self-conscious when Mom asked me to wear it during dinner.

Back in Waipahu this past summer, Grandma had baked me a cake before she handed me the journal. "Early birthday celebration," she said.

It was a pineapple-and-coconut pound cake smothered in mango slices. I love all that tropical fruit, more than cream and raspberries. I'll email her parts of this entry, to tell her about my California birthday.

I'm grateful Mom never asks me why I don't ask any friends from school to the house. Actually, I don't like hanging out with them. All they do is kill time together. They gossip, obsess about clothes and boys, check messages or whatever every few minutes. They're slaves to their cell phones.

I prefer to read books. Maybe, that comes from those days in Grandma's kitchen. My earliest memories are of her kneading and rolling, and filling, shaping, and baking pieces of dough.

Slowly, the long butcher-block table fills with plates of egg rolls and dumplings for steaming or frying, trays of muffins and cupcakes. And in late afternoon, bamboo steamers of hot manapua. The cooked food disappears fast enough, mostly into my aunts' bellies.

When I was about two, Grandma would put me on a high chair with toys and a cookie to munch on. Months later, she liberated me from the high chair to a bar stool with a back. I would sit by the counter, color or draw and when I was older, read a book. The kitchen would smell so good and she would hum along whenever a song from a musical she loved was blasting from a stereo in the living room.

Grandma doesn't mind that I read instead of helping her cook and bake.

Baking with Mom is different. I can never just sit and watch her like I do Grandma. She tells me to measure ingredients and has me go through the step-by-step process of baking a sponge cake, which she often makes because it's a family favorite. It's a difficult cake to learn to bake and Mom often ends up doing it herself while I stand back absorbing the frustration she can't hide at my incompetence. She has tried new recipes that have been much easier for me to follow and for which she always praises my efforts. But we don't do other cakes that often.

Maybe because I have no close girlfriends, Grandma likens me to the character who sang "And I can live inside my head" in Les Misérables, a musical she once saw on TV. She thinks that's what reading does to me.

It worried me at first what that line could mean, but she said, "Nothing wrong with living inside your head, just not all the time. We all need to, and reading helps. It enriches your imagination, takes you to worlds outside your own. Makes you sharper."

Some kids at school call me nerdy because I prefer reading to hanging out. But Grandma says I shouldn't worry what others think.

I don't just read, though, when I'm not studying or attending school. I also draw. Not very well, but I have fun doing it. At first, I drew the flowers, fruits, and plants in Grandma's garden. Now, I draw portraits though I don't get a good likeness.

October 2005

I don't share all that goes on in my head with anyone, even Grandma. Especially not what I've been obsessed with lately—Why am I here? In this time and this place? With the people I live with? Do I have a purpose in the gigantic scheme of things, whatever it is?

Is it weird to think those thoughts, to obsess about them? If so, better weird than stupid obsessing about boys; about wearing the current color craze on my nails, lips, and clothes; about who my friends are, how many, and how much they like me. Seems to me that's all those girls in my class do—waste time on superficial things.

How can anyone not see and be bothered by the fact that we're each of us mere specks in this big, big universe? Like specks of dust that can be blown away. Or what if the universe has a humongous vacuum cleaner, ready to swallow us? I get scared when I think of myself as dust, easily blown away or reduced to nothing inside the universe vacuum cleaner.

I went to catechism classes in Honolulu when I was a child. I think Grandma and my parents wanted to make sure I didn't turn into a Mormon or a Buddhist. Nuns who taught the classes reminded us often that life on earth is temporary, a preparation for everlasting life in paradise.

When I was nine, I asked where paradise was, and they said, "You'll know when you leave this world. But remember: you must be good. Say your prayers and ask for forgiveness if you want to go to paradise."

The nuns also said paradise is God's kingdom and we'll finally see him there. There where "everyone is happy and has no worries."

But I asked, "How do we know all that if no one still alive has ever been to paradise."

"You'll know." They smiled, the beatific smile of a sisterhood privileged, unlike us, to know heavenly secrets.

Mom and Dad don't worry about paradise. They're both more concerned about what's going on in the world: There's much uncertainty. Many countries can't get along and go to war because of religious differences.

That makes the idea of God and paradise even more confusing. Do we believe in a different God if we have a different religion? Do we, then, go to a different paradise?

Now, when I look back to those days, I wonder how much of that nun talk is propaganda to entice us, impressionable kids, into Catholicism.

Grandma says it's easier to focus on my own fears than all those large questions. When I lived with her full time, she held me close when I was afraid. She listened to my fears and was always sympathetic. But when I told her at my last visit about these scary questions about life, she had no answer. She said, "I try not to think about them."

Sigh! Does anyone know? Will I ever stop asking, "Why are we here on earth? Why Life?"

Though I'm not sure what I'm on earth for, I believed—until two days ago—that my life meant something. But this little quote I came across on the internet made me doubt that belief:

Man's life is but a jest,
a dream, a shadow, bubble,
air, a vapor at its best."

I now have it on this poet's authority that I am a Nothing. A joke, a dream at best. I console myself. So is that poet and so is everyone else—all Nothing. But why, then, are we here at all?

I meant to skim through the entries. Pass on the burden to Peet's staff of returning the notebook to its owner.

Fifteen-year-old girls don't interest me. They're usually shallow. Self-absorbed but not self-aware. This young woman seems atypical. I conjure up an image of her. Shy, plump, eyeglasses, raging acne— she's at that age, after all—which may explain why she isn't very social. But I also imagine depth in the eyes behind those glasses. A mind pulsating with life and its mysteries, and in spite of myself, I read her musings with great interest.

I leaf through the pages. Something is written on more than half of the notebook. The rest is empty. Poetry quotations follow a couple of entries.

How many people still read poetry? But I love it. The dreamier, the better. It's one of my guilty indulgences after hours of working with designs and blueprints.

I'm tempted to go on reading but my watch tells me I've gone past my break time. And I have to go back to work for a meeting in fifteen minutes. I'm presenting my research on different metals for construction, particularly Corten. One of our construction projects specified modern materials. Metal came up—inevitably. We argued about what metal to use, how to incorporate it in the design, and the cost of building when using metal.

I close the black notebook. An unexpected twinge of regret in my chest. I would never know how this young woman has been navigating her world. She would be about twenty-three by now. What kind of person has she become? Do all these large questions— existential ones I've also reflected on—continue to concern her?

Picking up coffee cup and Moleskine, I go to the service bar.

"Someone left this," I say to a server wiping the counter who I haven't seen before. Aaron is gone. He usually leaves half an hour after I arrive.

"Okay, thank you." She doesn't bother to glance at me or stop her chore. She takes the notebook. Throws it into what I assume is a bin under the counter.

I raise my hand holding the empty cup to protest the treatment of the Moleskine. But the server is back at the register asking the next customer for his order. I drop my cup into a trash bin at the base of the counter and continue my way to the door. But before I reach it, I pause. Fight an impulse to return to the service bar to take the Moleskine back. I should have kept the notebook. I'm sure I'll find a way to return it to its owner.

But my watch chimes, and I hurry out of Peet's and back to the architectural office. Outside, a cool breeze under a hazy late winter sun hastens my pace.

Lucien

Wednesday, February 2013

"Did anyone come for that notebook I left with you, guys, yesterday?"

The young woman preparing my order glances at me. The same server cleaning the counter the day before. She ignores my question until she hands me my café mocha. "A black notebook, right?"

I nod, surprised that she actually remembers.

She cranes her neck to look under the counter. "No, still here. Want it back?"

"Well … I'm not sure …. Yes, why not?"

"Wait." She takes quick clunking steps. Sounds like clogs with chunky heels. At the end of the service bar, she disappears below the counter. Comes back up. Plops the Moleskine on the counter without so much as a glance at me. She clunks back toward the coffee machines.

I snatch the notebook off the counter. Her indifference to it yesterday bothered me. I've decided to find the owner myself.

Last night, as I drifted off to sleep, my last thoughts were of the journal writer. Though written when she was only fifteen, her first entry told me much about her. Much that resonated with me. I'm now intensely curious what the rest of the journal would reveal.

Morally, anyone would argue it's wrong to read a very private journal. And yet I can't help myself. Anyway, we're strangers. The writer and I. So I tell myself.

Peet's isn't as busy as yesterday and I choose a table by the entrance. I take a few sips of my coffee drink. And open the journal to the second entry.

Moral questions still fester, somewhere in the back of my mind. What if the owner arrives, catches me reading her Moleskine?

Hypothetical scenario, my inner voice says. She hasn't come back for it since yesterday. Take a few more sips of café mocha. Think of it as a tonic to assuage guilt feelings. In any case, we're all voyeurs when we let our PC guard down. And mine has been vanquished by my unusually curious nature.

The second entry comes a year later. Why, I wonder. No deep musings on life and paradise in all that time? Busy being a teenager? Good for her. I've had my share of such musings and, in retrospect, I believe they got me nowhere.

July 2006

It's late afternoon, and I'm home in Southern California for a week before I fly to Honolulu to spend my summer break with Grandma. I'm free. For a

52

couple of months, anyway. No papers, no teachers, no deadlines. I can sleep as long as I need to.

I sit on the grass, fragrant from fresh mowing, the cut leaves cushy and cool underneath me. The wind blows, strong and briny from the ocean a few miles away. The fronds on palm trees lining our street sway with the wind, like in a dance.

Birds have built nests on the eaves of our house. A small flock flew in, only minutes ago, maybe from hunting for food. I can hear their wings flapping.

Coo-coo roo-coo, they sing as they perch on the roof. Have they left little birds in their nests?

Was the earlier part of the day depressing? I can't remember, but the way I've been these last few weeks, it probably was. I didn't have any obvious reason to be sad, but the feeling was there, lurking beneath everything I did. I can't explain it.

Right now, I don't care. Everything around me seems gentle and sweet and my mind is blank. I'm at peace—contented, joyful peace. Like those palms, my body dances with the wind. My arms are light, and I can flutter them like bird wings.

How awesome to be alive, feel one with nature. I am bird, tree, grass, sun, whispering wind.

I hope these coming days will all be like today, though I'd settle for even a few moments of how I feel right now.

October 2006

Since my return from Grandma's house, I've been gearing up from my languid state there in Waipahu, getting back to my regular schedule. I was in Hawaii for summer break—the usual—to recover from the stress of the past school year. I need energy and will power to face up to the life of a student again.

School has started, and everything is now amped up to a frantic pace. I can't be idle anymore. Sigh!

What amazing sensations I felt sitting on the lawn that day. It seems so far away, though it was only a couple of months ago.

For me, life is worth living for such moments alone, but too many people are too busy getting rich, caring only for material things. Make money. Replace that white refrigerator with one of gleaming stainless steel. Make more money. Replace that Toyota with a Mercedes. Make even more money and cruise the Caribbean, which is what my parents did on vacation this summer. Come home with trinkets to display in a glass cabinet. The next day, hurry back to work so you can make more money and boast about your new status symbols to your friends.

Sitting still for hours? Fanciful. Worse, it's a waste of time. They see idle moments as nothing more than a break from making money; or a time to recover from exhausting busy routines.

In the end, will people regret to discover they've missed so much of what life can offer? But it will be too late.

Grandma isn't like any of those people. She will be eighty in three years, but she still delights in the beauty of nature around her. Though not as strong as she used to be, she does what she can to keep her garden vibrant and productive—the fruit trees, vegetables, and flowers she and Grandpa had planted.

Every afternoon, she rests on a wooden bench under her lush mango tree, partially hidden from public view by a hibiscus bush. Her vegetable garden and her roses are in the large yard behind the house, but she has planted fragrant tropical jasmine all over her property. Her boom box plays classical music, occasionally drowned out by cars driving by, or interrupted by neighbors who know her afternoon habit and greet her while they're out on afternoon strolls. She doesn't mind any of that, she says— they're all part of life.

I told her about my moments of sitting in my parents' garden, doing nothing, losing myself in the sounds, the smells, the doings of little creatures and things around me. She understood. I told her I wished I could have shared them with her. But sensations like those are personal, she said. They can't be shared. I might be sitting under the mango tree or on the lawn with her or someone else, but what we experience will be different, shaped by who we are and our mood at the moment. And yet, I do feel as if we belong to a tribe, an old tribe. A tribe of worshippers of stillness and nature.

November 2006

I daydream a lot. Dreams are, for me, another excuse to be idle. They fill a need.

Some believe daydreaming is a waste of time. I can understand that. Most people need tangible success. They have aspirations and ambitions. Having definite goals, not dreams, is how you get what you want.

Daydreams are my fairy tales, and fairy tales speak to the child in me, that part of me that I believe to be pure and noble. Best of all, I have complete control over daydreams.

I reconstruct events, recreate people, reshape destinies, and I don't have to tell anybody about them. My dreams are mine, my own stories of how things should be.

Yes, I can build a world of my own, but I'm grown-up enough to know the difference between reality and my dream world. I store that world away when I deal with reality.

How can I be worse for dreaming?

October 2007

Today, I finished a book. It's not required reading for any of my English lit classes, and I'm somewhat ashamed to admit it's a trashy love story. Why do I read books like this? Because they help me get away for a little while from the serious literature we must read and for which we must write essays in order to pass. They appeal to your gut and your heart instead of your mind.

This semester, my first year at Cal, I opted to spend some time on Russian novels, Boris Pasternak's Doctor Zhivago and Dostoevsky's Brothers Karamasov, The Idiot, and Crime and Punishment. Of these, I prefer Brothers Karamasov because I can relate to the youngest, Alyosha. These books are intensely emotional. and though I only feel it rather than know it, I think they're profound. So, I need to take breaks from them, get lost in something that doesn't tax my brain too much, like a romance novel.

My mother introduced me to romance novels, before I turned fourteen, my first year back in California. Maybe she really didn't mean to, but she was cleaning up the library shelves and found some books getting musty in the corner of a top shelf. She was going to donate them to the local library, but thought, she said to me, that she wanted to share part of her girlhood with me. They belonged to Grandaunt Keola, her father's spinster sister, who gave them to Mom.

"You don't have to read them. I'm sure they're grossly outdated, but take a look, see what we read in those days," she said. "They're easy enough to read,

wholesome romance novels unlike the erotic ones they publish nowadays. Give them back to me if you don't like them. I'll donate them to the library."

So I took those books to my room. Nine of them by some author named Emily Loring who I never heard of. The books smelled of mildew and the first book I opened had turned yellowish. But the binding and the hard cover looked good. They were frayed at the edges but holding the book together.

What induced me to begin reading that afternoon? Well, I wanted to know more about my mother's past. At least, what her life was like at eighteen when she came to the mainland to go to the university.

I've also been curious about writers I've never heard of before. I also have a compulsive habit of reading at least part of every printed article I get my hands on. Whatever it was, I finished that one book before dinnertime.

Not that I liked it. The story was simple and trite, and the characters were ancient. But the whole thing was sweet, the heroine showed spunk, and I got a sense of what interested Mom as a teenager. I must admit her reading choices surprised me. But maybe these books gave her some pleasure while she took a break from chemical elements and formulas.

I can't imagine Grandma reading a book like it, though. The few books of fiction I've seen in the bookcases at her house were written by Daphne du

Maurier, Thomas Hardy, and someone who had a name like a very famous American actress. Elizabeth Taylor, I think. They were also classic (meaning ancient), and they were more complex.

I never read the other books by Emily Loring. After quickly scanning through two or three more, I could tell they followed some formula, and reading one of them was enough. Mom gave a couple to a friend, and she asked me to drop the rest into a book donation bin outside the local library.

Since then, I've read Jane Austen's Pride and Prejudice. It was included in our reading list. I liked it so much, I bought a cheap collection of her novels and read all of them in a week. Something in Jane Austen speaks to me. She's also a classic, much admired by my teachers, and though her stories are set in early nineteenth century, I could relate to her characters better.

Her books are full of hope and happy endings. That's a bit puzzling because I think society in the early 1800s was demeaning to women although people at that time may not have thought of it that way. How can any girl live in a society that thinks she's only good for being a wife and having babies? But Elizabeth Bennett, Emma Woodhouse, and Anne Elliot are heroines with minds of their own. They go their own way while adapting to the customs of their time. I think that attitude is quite modern.

Jane Austen probably saw the inequity in the society she lived in. Though it took me a second reading, I saw that she's taking subtle potshots at the social customs of the period, from the tone she takes in her narrative and the details she gives about characters and settings. So, her books are actually also a form of social commentary.

If you half believe romance novels, you'll think true love is what everyone aspires to, the most beautiful, satisfying feeling man is capable of. The Ideal, if there ever was one, transcending everything material. Maybe, that's what I picked up from Emily Loring.

The serious novels I read tell a different story about love. It might be something people want—many times desperately—but it's more agony than joy. We make it so. We're weak. We make mistakes. We have stupid scruples. We mess up the good things.

Who do you believe? Like my teachers say, the truth may be somewhere in between.

I know little about love. It's an intense emotion, no question. But it's also lust in one's love for a wife, husband, or sweetheart.

There was a popular girl in senior high who flaunted her sophistication, declaring sex is the best part about love. She attracted boys like flies and changed boyfriends every two to three months. I've never understood her attraction, but she did have big *boobs, which must count for a lot if sex is what people value most. But what did she really know about love?*

Does love of God count or love for family and friends? None of that involves sex.

I believe it's when we give without asking for anything in return that we fulfill our best potential as human beings. Like Mother Teresa, for example. Hers is a love for humanity, the noblest form. It doesn't ask for anything back.

But how many of us can be like Mother Teresa? I love my grandma and my family. I kind of believe in God but aspiring to be noble? How many people have what it takes to give themselves selflessly for a cause?

I know I want something more than sex. Something deeper—love that gets into my flesh and bones; love that makes me see life as I've never seen it before. Am I reaching for the moon?

I hope to fall in that deeper kind of love. But if that doesn't happen, I'd prefer to dedicate myself to mankind. I'm not aiming to be Mother Teresa, but I won't settle for anything less than a love that is both consuming and beautiful.

I look at my watch. I've gone past the time I usually return to work. Although no one clocks break time at the office, I am swamped with work. I get up, swipe empty coffee cup, journal, and iPad off the table.

Well, so far, no secrets. The entries I just read are like essays one would write for an English class. And yet they give me a better sense of who she is: an idealist, a dreamer. Like myself years before. And a loner. Like myself. Now.

I think I wasn't a loner when I was her age in the entries I just skimmed through. My grandparents saw to that. They told me stories. Stories which painted a vast world of infinite possibilities. Inspiring me to travel, to connect with people I meet. Stories which nurtured my dreams, but also helped me put things into perspective.

They're both gone now, but everything they taught me is woven into the legacy of the creative life they've left me. A life I've found most satisfying. And consuming. I wish they were still here, though. I need them sometimes.

I'll keep this journal until I find some way of sending it back to the young woman who owns it. I have this premonition—or is it hope—that someday, she and I will meet.

Lucien

Thursday, February 2013

The couches in the corner across the banquette at Peet's are free. On impulse, I make my way to one facing the glass window and mark it with a stray newspaper. Minutes later, coffee drink in hand, I settle down to read the journal with a little more privacy and comfort.

By now, I have quashed my guilt and anxiety about reading the journal. Intrigue is mostly what remains. It's like I'm reading an engaging novel, I tell myself.

The next entry comes two years later. The first couple of years of college are often tough. My young writer might not have found time to journal.

After a few sips of café mocha, I lean back, cross my legs, and begin reading.

September 2009

It's my birthday. I'm nineteen today. Once again, I feel I owe it to myself to look inward. I can't spend as much time soul-searching as I used to. I'm getting drawn deeper and deeper into the world of adults by college and part-time work.

Officially, you're an adult when you turn eighteen, but last year, I didn't feel much change in me. Today, I do feel different, like I have crossed some critical point.

Is something wrong with me? I seem to be always one or two years behind my peers.

Anyway, I'm taking time for reflection today. It's my gift to myself. What do I care about? What do I really want and how can I get it?

I'll begin with an idea Jun will laugh at and say it sounds corny. I love him after Grandma and Auntie Celia, but I think he's not very imaginative. Maybe that's well and good for his future life as a lawyer.

My metaphor for life is flowing water. Flowing water is better than a mere bubble, as one poet once said.

When we're born, we're like a spring. Fresh and pure. Then we gather stuff both good and bad—like debris that spring water gathers when it streams down to a river. Rivers gather more debris as they make their way into the ocean. The ocean is the final destination for flowing water, a fitting metaphor for our lives as adults. The ocean is deep, unfathomable, dangerous. Once there, there's no turning back.

Today, I feel like I'm at the brink of that vast expanse of blue. I see it end where it meets the horizon. But what is beyond that horizon?

I find the ocean threatening. Maybe I shouldn't. I've swum in the Pacific Ocean when I lived in Hawaii.

I've been in a boat looking down its dense blue depth. A denseness that makes me shudder every time. Sometimes the water is so clear you can see starfish and sea cucumbers at the bottom. But you can't assume the water is shallow because you can see through it.

I envy those who can dive into the unknown without fear. I don't know if I can do that. Still— though I'm scared, I'm also eager to see what life has to offer me.

But what happens if you get lost? Would you be lost forever? I have to believe you can rise from wherever you've fallen or sunk into. You can find your way again. You may have to struggle, fight to get to where you want to go.

I take comfort from reading poetry and Emily Dickinson, one of my favorite poets, has wise words for this passage through life. Her words describe life better than those that compare it to a "bubble, a vapor at its best." I also feel music in her words so I like them much more.

The heart asks pleasure first
And then, excuse from pain
And then, those little anodynes
That deaden suffering;
And then, to go to sleep
And then, if it should be
The will of its Inquisitor
The liberty to die.

March, 2010

I guess I'll never be free from moments when I'm anxious and confused about the future, about life.

People close to me tell me I shouldn't worry. I'm well on my way. I think they mean that, so far, I have met their expectations.

True, my future has been designed for me by my parents and my teachers. I have nothing against it, and I see myself fitting into it comfortably. By usual standards, I'm on the track for success. Many will envy me.

I'm a year away from a college degree but with no job prospects yet. That's okay, though. I've applied to a few graduate schools. What's not to be happy about?

The thing is I am faced, for the first time, with the fact that I'm a Woman. It took falling in love for me to see that.

I met Scott in school six months ago, when a friend dragged me to watch a debate he participated in. It might have been love at first sight. I'm not sure. All I know is we felt at ease with each other right away and when our little group went to Café Roma, we talked mostly to each other. I agreed to see a movie with him the following weekend.

He said he loved me a month later. It's really quite amazing how easily you could fall in love when you meet the right person. In loving each other, Scott has awakened me to the fact that everything I do is tied into being a woman. I'm not quite sure yet what that means.

The thing is, though I'm happy, I'm also beginning to have this uneasy feeling I'm being boxed in. I used to think of myself as a person. Just a Person—a young one, yes, but essentially genderless. To me, that's always been true, even when I was younger and my brothers refused to take me on their adventures. Because I am a Girl.

The first time they refused, I was so mad that I shouted, "I'm a person too!"

Jun, who organized those boys' outings on weekends, stared at me for a minute. Then he smiled. "Okay, Person, you can come, but try to keep up. Okay?"

So I became "Person." It grew to be as familiar as my name and took on a new meaning for me. I wasn't just a Girl anymore.

Later, though, they found excuses to exclude me. "Person, you can't run as fast as we do. You're knock-kneed." Or "Person, you can't jump into the river in your dress." (My mother bought me dresses I felt obligated to wear.)

I never listened to my brothers' attempts to turn me off, at least, not until I became aware my body was changing, which only took a few months after I began living in California. My periods came. Even so, to myself, I was still "Person," who happened to have this little problem once a month. On those days when I

*couldn't go on my brothers' little adventures. I
returned to my books.*

*Now, I don't need my brothers. I have a
boyfriend, though he poses new problems for me.
Jun—and sometimes even Kana—is very protective.
He doesn't want to see me hurt. And my mother, for
all her education, is old-fashioned. If she had her way,
she'd prevent me from getting intimate with my
boyfriend until we're married.*

*I don't think she believes being intimate is
wrong so her attitude confounds me. It couldn't be
because of how she was brought up. Grandma is too
loving and forgiving to impose impossible rules on her
children.*

*Anyway, I could do whatever I want if I didn't
always agonize over my actions so much. It's not that I
worry a lot about the right thing to do, but I'm not
sure what I truly want out of life.*

*What do I want, way down deep, in that place
only I can reach?*

*I worry all the time. Will I make good choices,
those that would serve my needs best? Are my choices
going to be restricted because I'm a woman?*

*Yes, I want it all. I'm as much a Person as
anybody else. Though asserting that sounds juvenile
to me now, it does mean a lot to me. I'm as much a
person as Jun is. He's focused on his ambitions to
become a lawyer, but he also plays around. We've
stopped our weekend outings because Jun prefers to*

go kayaking with his buddies and having fun with his girlfriends—so many that I can't keep track of their names.

I don't think I'll feel as free as Jun does, though. He's outgoing, prefers to hang out with friends, and thinks reading fiction is a waste of time. I'm not exactly a loner, but I get lost in solitary pursuits. In reading and inhabiting the worlds of characters in books. In sketching portraits of people around me.

Jun likes law for the money, the "fight," and the challenge it takes to win. In the future, he might go into politics, and a law degree, he thinks, would be an asset. All these things make him a favorite with my parents on top of the fact that he's the first-born.

I told him I want to do something where I can make a difference in the lives of people. Jun said, "Doesn't surprise me. That's altruistic, and it goes with your personality. But how does an English degree figure into that?"

Flippantly, I said, "I'll go teach English in Japan."

Jun: "I still don't see how that can make a difference."

Me: "Increase their job prospects. Maybe expose them to other viewpoints."

He stared at me for a bit. Then, he smiled. "That last one is good. Can help in global understanding."

Compared to Jun, I believe I'm a romantic. His relationships have not lasted beyond a couple of months or so. He tells me he doesn't know if he's ever been in love. He realizes he chooses girlfriends who just want a "good time." But he's sure that he'll get married— "when it's time."

I like being in love, and when the time comes, I'm sure I'll want to become a mother. A mother like Grandma seems to have been. But I won't give up whatever career I end up in.

I can see myself in comparison with my brother and I wonder—Jun seems to know his heart, but do I know mine? And will I be strong enough to follow it? I have pretty much been following a blueprint—what my parents expect, what my teachers and society say I must do. When will Scott feel a need to chime in?

At some point, I know I will want to break away from what others expect of me.

August 2011

Scott has gone off on a solo adventure. For a year, he said.

I saw him a couple of days after I arrived at my parents' home on summer break from Cal Berkeley. The past year, we didn't see each other too often. He had gotten his degree the year before, and had moved back to his parents' home in Gardenia to work in an accounting office in La to fulfill a requirement for his

CPA license. He took the test and is now a certified public accountant.

We drove to a coffeehouse in Belmont Shore, and sat at a lone table on one corner of the service bar after we got coffee drinks and pastries. We chit-chatted about little things. Nothing too important that I can remember. He kept fidgeting in his seat and looking out the glass window. He was restless. Then glancing at me, he said, "Got something to tell you."

But he turned toward the window again and said nothing more for a while. He sipped his coffee drink, picked at his pastry.

I sensed he was avoiding my gaze. I asked what it was he wanted to tell me. He said, "I need a break from numbers."

I said, "Let's go on a vacation together. San Diego, maybe, or Baja California. I could postpone my visit to Honolulu."

He shrugged and didn't answer. I waited. I'd never seen him so uncommunicative. Was he getting bored? We'd been together for more than a year.

Out of the blue, he said, still not looking at me, "I've already made other plans."

"What kind of plans?" I said, surprised and a little hurt that he didn't talk to me about them. I suspected those plans didn't include me. The thought depressed me, but I told myself I should give him space if it's what he needed.

He turned to face me. He looked uncomfortable. "I need time to be alone. Go on an adventure as different as possible from the structured life of an accountant. Free. No one to answer to. No rigid schedules. Getting up late and staying out late when I feel like it. Getting drunk ...you know, things like that."

I must have looked anxious and unhappy by then. He took my hands in his and said, "Baby please, I need to do this."

Was he resentful of the two months I spend in Honolulu every summer?

"Going to Hawaii is escaping," he said. "But that's for you and I don't make a big deal of it. This is my first time going away from all this."

"'All this.' Me included." I guess I sounded sarcastic or accusatory.

"Not fair. I don't complain when you're away in Honolulu."

"I'm sorry. How long? Where is away from all this?"

He looked down at his hands rubbing mine, unaware that if he kept it up, my hand would be raw. He said, "A year. Europe."

I withdrew my hand from his. A year! A lot could happen in a year. I kept silent for a long while. Examining my hands. Thinking.

I told myself I loved him. Love shouldn't shackle. It should be understanding. I should let him

*fly free. And, in any case, his going wasn't up to me.
He had already decided.*

*I was sad. But I said I understood. A few days
later, he left for Europe.*

December 2011

*It's Christmas. We have a big tree in the living
room, decked with red ribbons, sparkly balls of
different colors, jolly little white snowmen, and
adorable little angels with gauzy wings. We've had the
same decorations since I can remember. The only
things that have changed are the lights timed to go on
at five o'clock, and the gift packages. They're gone
from under the tree and are way smaller except for
Mom's perennial gift—her favorite eau de toilette. We
now hang our gifts on the tree.*

*Though packages have been downsized, their
values have not. My father's Home Depot gift card can
be big or small, based on his current gadget craze. We
kids get envelopes fat with checks stuffed inside funny
pop-up cards Mom has chosen. She loves them, and
our Christmas day starts with lots of laughs.*

*The table is set for Christmas Eve dinner.
We're waiting for grandparents—my dad's parents—
to arrive. Jun is already here, back home from law
school at UC Davis. He's busy with the stereo system,
selecting all his favorite Christmas songs from our
digitized music library.*

He's a handsome dude, my brother. No wonder girls go after him. From pictures I've seen of Grandpa, I'd say he's taken after the Portuguese Hawaiian side of the family. Tall, muscular, curly black hair and an easy smile.

He's also a take-charge guy. Tonight, he'll set the right mood for family celebrations. After dinner, he'll turn off the stereo, take out his guitar and we'll sing Christmas carols. He's printed the lyrics for those who've forgotten the words. We always start with "Deck the Halls."

It's a happy time.

But I'm also miserable. As I count my blessings, I can't help counting the things I wish I had.

I immerse myself into the holiday bustle, but I know that tonight, alone in my room, I'll cry myself to sleep. Worse, I'm afraid this won't be the last Christmas that ends in loneliness.

Mom says I'm sentimental, that I take things too hard, but what does she mean? Is sentimental what she calls my "overly emotional reactions"? But all she remembers are incidents from when I was a teenager. When I was adjusting to my newly-acquired family.

That seems so long ago now, even further back in time than the earlier years I spent with Grandma. I don't think Mom will ever know me as well as Grandma does.

These she remembers: I cried while no one else did while watching the news on statistics of innocent

*people getting killed in wars on terror. I had to leave
and go to my room. I squealed and hugged Jun tight
(amid everyone else's quiet smiles) when he got into
UC Davis Law School. I sulked in my room for a day
when Andy made doodles on the drawing I spent
hours on for an art class in junior high. He apologized,
said he didn't know it was for a class project, even
offered to help me recreate it, which was impossible.*

*Mom also says I take trivial things to heart.
Why cry when Andy's puppy chewed my sock? It's
easily replaced.*

*Mom doesn't know how miserable I am. I can't
tell her. But I don't know if I can tell Grandma, either.
She doesn't know about Scott. When I visit her, all I
want is to relive those happy, easy, peaceful days of
my early youth.*

*I haven't heard much from Scott since he left
five months ago. He says traveling is hectic and tiring,
and he doesn't always find time to text or email. He's
sent a few emails. About every three weeks.
Impersonal accounts of places he's visited. Lots of
photos of him in front of sites he's visited. They're
interesting, but somehow, they break my heart. He's
out having fun and I'm not part of it. I know I couldn't
have gone with him. When he left, I had a year yet of
college to go. But it hurts anyway.*

*I tell myself again that I feel freer since we
confessed our love for each other. He's taken me as I
am, put me in touch with a side of myself I hadn't*

previously paid much attention to. He not only freed the woman in me. He also helped expand my concept of who I am. To him, I'm Woman-Person. To Grandma, my family, and myself, I'm Person-Woman.

I feel tied to him not because he wants me to, but because I've realized I'm a one-man woman. In this my mother is right—for me, love is serious business. My attachment is deep and complete.

But it's making me so wretched. Frustrated. I can't have everything I want.

I have control over my actions most of the time, but not much over what others do. What Scott does.

The journal writer is in love. It has changed how she thinks of herself. More than Person. Also Woman. Whatever that means to her. Having lasted more than a year, the relationship could be permanent.

But something is brewing. Scott is on a long "solo adventure." She tries not to resent it; asserts they continue to love each other. But I think she's in denial.

Ah, love. In youthful innocence, we dream of falling in love. And our first love can have a special hold on us, even when it ends in tears and anger. In the early ecstasy and agony of love, we're either not aware of, or we ignore, how complicated it could be. How it could be wrenched away from us. Sometimes so unexpectedly that we reel from the consequences for a long time.

I should know. I've been there.

Luna

August 2012

What a relief to be back at Grandma's. Especially this year. I've just arrived by cab from the airport.

Another phase of my life has passed—I graduated from university last month so I'm officially unemployed, and in need of recouping from the grind of university student life.

She greets me with the usual kisses and a tight embrace at the door. She no longer calls me keiki. I was "my keiki" to her until I was nineteen. In her mind, I passed into adulthood at twenty.

"Why twenty?" I asked two years ago. "The government stamped an official seal of adulthood on me when I turned eighteen."

"Bah, what does the government know about real people? And it isn't always twenty. Your mom became an adult at thirteen. Partly because she's the oldest, eager to boss everyone younger."

"Is something wrong with me?"

"No, not at all. You're too intelligent for anyone to think so. Something has changed about you. I feel it, but I can't put it into words. I'm sure it's a good change. Not in love, are you?" She pauses an instant, throws me a glance. She's not expecting an answer, and I don't give it.

"Up until this year, you were still my keiki. Innocent. But not ignorant. You delighted in learning new things. Trusting, easy to please. Now, you seem restless. I can feel it, though you're calm enough on the surface." She stares at me, wanting me to explain my restlessness.

I stare back. Keep my smile and my silence. But a pang of guilt creeps in. When have I ever kept things from Grandma? At least the important things.

"Well," Grandma says after a while, hooking her arm in mine, "the mango salad is getting soggy as we speak. We'll have all summer for disclosures."

Disclosures? A word I've never heard her use. She expects I'll open up soon enough.

Through our favorite summer lunch of green mango salad, I regale her with a year-full of stories. She's read about them in my weekend emails. But she likes the details I add when we talk.

She asks about my graduation. I've already emailed her about it, described our sumptuous family dinner at a sprawling Chinese restaurant by the bay, which Dad's relatives and Mom and Dad's friends attended.

What I haven't told her is how I was tempted to boycott the graduation ceremony. No matter how symbolic it's supposed to be, I couldn't see the point of going through a ritual, receiving a rolled piece of blank paper, as I sweat in a borrowed black cap and toga. I went for the sake of family.

"You really wanna know, Grandma?"

"Of course. It's a milestone, isn't it?"

"Well, to be frank, I found it kind of mind-numbing. Fidgeting in my chair for speeches to finish. Waiting for a long line of graduates to march before it's our turn. The class of English lit majors proceed slowly, dragging our feet to the stage. I receive a ribboned blank" —I mimic quotes with two fingers in each hand— "'diploma', hear my family, and only my family, applaud. That's it. My two seconds in the spotlight. I went for Mom and Dad. For pictures they could show off to their friends."

Grandma chuckles. "Careful. You're too young to be cynical."

Grandma is no longer as spry as she used to be, but her mind is sharp. For the last two years, she's taken a nap in the afternoon. When she awakes, she joins me on the bench under the mango tree, where I've been reading one of the paperbacks I brought on this visit. We smile at each other, but we don't speak.

Half an hour later, I close my book. "Who's coming to visit you this weekend?"

"Celia."

"Any of my cousins come?"

"Hardly ever. There's always something or other that keeps them busy."

"I don't see any of them much myself. No reason to come to California, I guess."

"No, I guess not."

"Two years ago, Auntie Juanita was there for a conference. Uncle Liam came. No kids."

She smiles again. We lapse back into silence, enjoying the breeze, and watching the few cars going by. Not too many pass this way. This Waipahu neighborhood is on the edge of town, away from the highway to Honolulu.

"Are you staying all summer?"

"What if I stay longer? Got no more school, you know, and the job market looks bad for someone like me. No work experience. Maybe I'll scope out jobs at the hotels in Honolulu."

"I'd like that, and you know you can stay with me for as long as you want."

I was kidding about the hotel jobs. I still don't know what I want to do for the rest of my life, even after years of college. But I'm sure I'd rather set roots in California instead of Hawaii, where I have a lot more options for a career.

We're kindred spirits, Grandma and I. We can read each other's minds: we know when to leave the other person alone, when the other prefers silence while we sit or do things together, when an offer of comfort is welcome, or when the other desires to talk.

I cherish the afternoons we spend together under the mango tree. We stay at least an hour. I read and she listens to music. From time to time, one of us breaks the quiet—she with bits of gossip about her neighbors; and I with little stories about my California friends and family.

That night, while dining on left-over green mango salad and a savory pudding of Hawaiian bread and mushrooms, we talk some more. The mango strips, no longer as rigid as toothpicks, have become a drooping heap in a pool of juice. But I like them this way and drizzle the tart-salty juice on my pudding.

"Don't you get lonely all by yourself here, Grandma?"

She spears mango strips with her fork, and shrugs. "I'm old. With your grandpa gone ..." She's silent for some moments.

She continues. "Anyway, it's everyone's fate to be alone and lonely some time in their lives. Happens a lot to old folks like me. I'm used to it. And I like quiet. Besides, I walk up to Maggie's when I need someone to talk to. She comes here often enough when Keko is out with his friends. Or I bother Juanita and Celia on the cell phone they gifted me a while back. And Marcia comes to clean on Mondays without fail."

I've asked the same question for the last six years, and she has given me some variation on the same answer. My question shows my concern, and when she gives me the same response, she knows it reassures me she is, indeed, okay. But tonight, I ask something I've hesitated to probe into. Maybe I'm afraid to hear her answer. "Nighttime is hard, though, isn't it? All by yourself here."

She knits her brow as she spears more mango strips. She chews her mouthful of mango and meets my gaze. "Not really. I go to bed early. Wake up before Keko's fighting cocks crow in the morning. I like to listen to them crowing. It begins another day of hope. Another day to tend to my plants and the chickens, read a book, listen to music and watch the life on my street go by. At night, I've no trouble falling asleep. If I do, I put on the playlist of my favorite opera arias you put together for me. Set it to play for an hour."

Her practical answer saddens me somehow. Does it reassure me? Not completely. I suspect it's evasive, but I don't probe further.

I've been uneasy about Grandma for the last two years. And yet, I don't want her to worry that I worry about her. She's anxious not to be seen as being too intrusive. She once said she wanted her children to be able to go about their lives without concerning themselves too much about her.

"Maybe, I should make you another playlist. Give you some variety."

"I'd like that. You can do more than one if you have time. Do one playlist of Rachmaninoff piano concertos."

At nine o'clock, an hour after dinner, we say goodnight. Habituated to my college routine, I stay up till midnight. Usually, I read and once in a while, I watch television. Like Grandma, I'm used to being alone. I grew up with aunts and later, with brothers preoccupied with their own interests and responsibilities. I've learned to rely on my own resources to amuse myself.

As in previous summers, my days with Grandma drift by in tranquility, disturbed only when Marcia and my aunts come. Auntie Celia now comes every weekend and I rarely see Auntie Juanita anymore.

I leave my windows open in the jasmine-scented nights. I lie musing in bed, waiting to be lulled to sleep by chirping crickets and croaking frogs. At my parents' California home, I endure the drone of traffic and planes flying overhead.

Grandma's home has been a place of solace. A place to recoup, escape the growing pressures of life, and indulge illusions of a happy, untroubled life. Maybe, that's why I've never said anything about Scott.

*****

In the middle of September, Mom calls me on the old iPhone she gave me after she bought herself a new one.

"Guess what. You have three letters from three different schools. Two thicker than the third. I'm pretty sure those two are acceptance letters. One is from Cal, your old school. Want me to open them?"

"Yes, yes, please." Grad school is not my first choice for the immediate future. It's a fallback. Jobs for English lit graduates—a major my parents think is esoteric—are scarce. Grad school allows me to bide my time until something concrete opens up. Or—honestly—until I'm sure what I want to do for the next few years.

The two letters are acceptances to Cal and another school in San Francisco, but neither offers any kind of financial aid, not even an assistantship to pay for, or reduce, tuition expenses. I can work part-time, for a professor or a department if I'm lucky.

"Do you know which of these two you'll want to go to? You need to tell them soon what you intend to do."

"You think I should go to grad school?"

"Well, what other choices do you have in this economy? If you went into computers or engineering —"

I cut her off. "I know, Mom. Please don't worry."

"—you can support yourself now. And you don't have to rely on Scott when you get married."

"Mom, please. I'll be okay."

She sighs as she often does when she's lamenting my choices. "Well, grad school at least gives you another option now. You can teach college if you go for a doctorate. Dad and I will loan you money, interest-free, if you can't get financial aid or until you find work. I can give you my old car. Its battery is probably dead, but that's easily replaced. We know how hard it is for young graduates if you're not in the sciences or computers."

*****

Later, while weeding her vegetable garden, I tell Grandma about the phone call.

"So you're not done with school yet," she says as we move to the row of pepper plants from the tomato bushes.

"Graduate school is a fallback. Getting a good job in the next few months looks iffy for me. But I wasn't sure I'd get accepted. I didn't get an early offer, like around February."

"You'll be going back to California at the usual time, then."

"I may have to leave earlier to prepare. I need to work to support myself and gain some experience. Right now, studying is what I'm best at." I chuckle, a little embarrassed. "Grad school lets me put off struggling with the bad job market a while longer."

"Whatever happened to starting a family with some young whipper-snapper? I had your mother when I was a year younger than you."

"Times have changed, Grandma. Anyway, I'm sure you're kidding. You taught grade school for years."

"I had to. I stopped after Juanita was born. Grandpa's business had taken off by then."

85

"Well, no whipper-snapper has asked me to play house."

"I'm surprised—as pretty and smart as you are."

"Grandma, you're biased."

Grandma totters to the row of eggplants and crouches over one of them. "I'm not. I want to see you with some deserving young man one day, though I admit I'm happy having you here to myself as long as possible. In fact, I'd be sorry to see you go so soon this summer. But it can't be helped."

I let her remark slide as I watch her trowel the earth around the eggplant.

She points her trowel to the big red peppers in front of me. "Fetch a basket and pick those peppers."

I get up, but before I could go, she says, "You'll be busier. You'll have both school and work." Her voice is a mere murmur. She's talking more to herself than to me. She's sad, and her remark betrays a note of resignation. She knows from experience with her daughters—Mom, in particular—I may no longer be able to come for summer visits.

I squat behind her and put my arms around her. "Come stay with us in California. It's been five years since your last visit. Mom wishes you came more often."

"She should talk. The last time she came was when she took you away, without much warning, without telling me what she intended to do."

"Oh, Grandma, were you unhappy about that?"

She wriggles out of my arms and gets up. I get up, too. "Of course. It was like taking my youngest daughter away. It wasn't in your best interest. I raised you. She didn't know you like I did. She only came three times."

I believe she's right and feel somewhat guilty at having been complicit in moving away from her to live permanently in California. "I'll stay to the end of September. Job hunting can wait a little longer."

Before the week is over, I accept the offer at Cal's comparative literature program. I'm determined to get work, whether it's flipping burgers, cleaning hotel rooms, or serving diners in a restaurant. Maybe I'll convince my practical chemist parents I'm willing to do what it takes to follow my dreams. That I'm not just biding my time, putting off the next phase of my life—although, back of my mind, I suspect it's what I'm doing. I'm still not sure what I want my future to look like.

I'm not without experience. In my senior year, I taught English as a second language in a school serving many immigrant families. My adviser suggested it when I asked how I could use an English degree. It was volunteer work that required twelve hours a week.

Teaching is not what I pursued my degree for— Mom said it's not what you do if you want to make some money. But I enjoyed the assignment and haven't ruled out teaching. This much I know: I need money to live but it isn't what drives the choices I make.

The day before my return flight, Grandma prepares more mango salad. "I asked Maggie for a few mangoes yesterday. I don't ask very often so she couldn't refuse me. They're a little riper than what I prefer so they're sweeter."

"Always good, tart or sweetish."

She serves the salad with a generous number of grilled shrimps doused in melted butter and as much fried garlic as the dish could take without overpowering the shrimp.

"I don't know when I'll see you again after this summer. So I thought I'd treat you to your favorite dinner. You gobbled up these shrimps when you were little."

"I still do. Really *ono*, Grandma. Never this good in California. Perfect with mango salad."

The day of my flight, I repeat my wish for her to visit us. "Stay a few months. I'm pretty sure Mom would like it, too."

"It's harder to travel when you're my age."

"I'll come get you. Not a problem. Then I'll take you back."

"You'll be too busy."

"I'll make time for you, I promise."

At the last hug for this summer, she says, "Well, we'll see."

Standing next to the waiting cab, I look back at Grandma. She looks so forlorn. A wilting flower waving a hand she can barely raise. I wish I don't have to leave. But a voice prods me on—no longer Mom's but mine: *March along... March. On.*

I shiver with cold fear at a thought I've tried for a while to suppress. *I won't see her again*

Lucien

Friday February 2013

It's ten o'clock, and except for the lamp on my night table, the whole loft is dark. I sit on my bed, cozy under my light comforter. I leaf through the journal to the first of the last three entries.

The journal writer is growing out of her naiveté. Her idealism is being tested. But I miss her early musings on life. Has she abandoned her search for meaning, accepted it gets her nowhere?

Or, might she have found meaning in being in love? She has so much to give. So much that Scott is unworthy of. She would have been happier focusing her ability and energy into something creative.

January 2012

The woman in me is getting numb. I cultivate indifference so I can remain attached to one whose absence is making me doubt we'd ever be together again.

I used to think—a mere two years ago—that there's one man destined for every woman. So how can anyone settle for a second fiddle? I'm sure I wouldn't.

*When I met Scott, I thought he was "the One."
But now, I can't shake this feeling off: Loss is
inevitable. We text about once a week, but we're
getting more and more impersonal. He sends me his
last best photos and I tell him about school.*

*I do still love Scott, and in his last long email, he
said he hasn't stopped loving me. He's been away six
months, and I feel we're growing apart more and
more. Is that gulf real, or is it me, unable to bear the
loneliness of separation?*

*I think I'm getting fed up. Like Jun says I would
be. When he came home for Christmas break, he
whispered to me at dinner that I didn't look happy,
and he asked me about Scott. I told him Scott had
gone to Europe for a few months. He shook his head
and said, "T'ain't good, Person. Whoever said it got it
all wrong. Absence doesn't make the heart grow
fonder. It makes the heart forget."*

*Those weren't hopeful words from one whose
judgment I trust.*

*"Where have all the flowers gone?" Mom sings
this song whenever our family celebrations turn into
showing off our performing skills.*

Where have all my dreams gone?

August, 2012

*I have things to be happy about. Scott is back.
But it's not like it used to be. And I regret now that I*

never told Grandma about him. She might have some good advice for me.

For a while, everything seemed right again between us and those doubts I had—and which he may have had, too—all vanished like bubbles bursting.

By then, he'd been home a month and had moved back north for his first big job at a San Francisco accounting firm. We looked forward to spending every waking moment together and intended to see each other as much as we could before I went on my usual summer break in Honolulu.

We're both visiting our parents in the Los Angeles metropolitan area. Now only a month since we've been together, we've had a misunderstanding. He was supposed to come and take me out this evening to a pizza joint. He came thirty minutes late.

As I opened the door, he muttered an excuse, "Sorry, got tied up fixing things around my parents' house."

I said, "It's okay because Tony has been keeping me company."

He looked past me at Tony, who's sitting on the couch in the living room, as if he didn't know him. I reminded Scott that they've met. He's a family friend—well, Jun's mostly.

He said, "So Jun's here?"

"It was a surprise visit," I said. "Tony was in the vicinity and thought he'd come say hello."

Scott frowned. He looked tired and wasn't in the friendliest of moods.

Tony was flipping through a magazine, but he looked up as we approached him. He put the magazine on the coffee table and rose from the couch. With his wide, engaging smile, he extended his hand to Scott.

Well-built and six feet three inches tall to Scott's slim five feet ten frame, Tony had large hands. His right hand enveloped Scott's in a vigorous handshake.

Scott immediately withdrew his hand and murmured, "I couldn't leave my dad alone to finish repairing a fence. I'm sure Luna enjoyed having you here and didn't even notice the time."

Tony glanced at me and winked. "I hope so. She's probably heard all my good stories and must be bored with them by now."

I said, amused, "At least you know."

Tony chuckled, thanked me for being nice and patient. "I'll make sure to have some new stories next time I visit."

Scott turned to me. "Best be going. I'm starved."

It was a cue for Tony to be on his way. He gave me a hug and a quick buzz on the cheek—the usual family farewell.

I asked him to join us for pizza, sure that he hadn't had dinner.

He politely refused, bade us good night, and left.

When Tony was gone, Scott and I also left for the pizza restaurant.

For a while, he drove in silence. Then, he said, "That was an odd time for a surprise visit. He must know your parents wouldn't be home before 7 o'clock, especially on a Friday evening."

I shrugged. "He knows and he would have waited for them, but we had to leave."

He was silent again. Then, he turned to me. "How often does he barge in like that?" He couldn't hide the annoyance in his voice.

"I'm up north most of the time so I can't tell you."

He said, "It's the end of the school year. I'm sure Tony is aware you'd be home. He would have come later this evening if all he intended was to surprise your parents."

I was getting annoyed. "Maybe Tony wanted to see me, too. We don't see each other much."

Scott glanced sideways at me. Scowling, lips compressed.

"Are you jealous?"

"I couldn't care less. But I've never liked him. I think he's full of himself."

"Well, I like him. And I think you're wrong." I protested a little more vehemently than I meant to. It hurt that he said he couldn't care less. I actually thought Tony was aware of his charms, flaunted them, and used them to get his way. But he had been like

Jun to me and was nicer to me than my other two brothers, so I've been happy enough to overlook his shortcomings.

Scott didn't respond to my retort, but he betrayed his anger by his silence and the rigid set of his jaw.

He slowed down and parked at an empty space several blocks from the restaurant. He turned to me and said, "If you like Tony so much, you should go out with him."

I was bewildered and couldn't answer. He was making too big a deal of Tony's visit and it vexed me, particularly after his remark about not caring. He did look even more weary than when he arrived at the house, so in a conciliatory tone, I said, "Tony's like a brother. That's all."

It didn't help. I doubt he believed me. He begged to be excused, couldn't go to dinner, and wouldn't be good company. He was beat and too upset. Might say something he'd regret. He started the car and turned around, away from the restaurant.

"Scott, please," I said. To no avail.

He dropped me off at my parents' house, and after we did a quick cheek kiss, he drove off. I was hungry, but lucky for me, my parents came home with takeout Indian food.

Scott and I saw each other again two days later. He apologized and said he was too stressed out. But I think he's still suspicious of Tony.

I've known Tony for years. He's one of Jun's best and oldest friends, who I saw often and did a lot of things with that he grew to be like a brother.

About seven years ago, Tony came to live with my family when his parents went to Asia where his father had received a diplomatic assignment. It was the middle of the school year and Tony preferred not to go.

Jun said he had space in his bedroom where he could set up a cot for Tony. So at his instigation, my parents, who rarely refused anything Jun asked for, offered to take Tony in until school was over. But I guess Tony liked it here so much and my parents didn't object. He didn't follow his parents to Asia. He stayed until they returned three years later. He had been living with my family a few months when I first arrived in California.

Tony and I grew close. We spent a thousand days together eating the same dinner, watching the same TV shows, playing tennis, and doing our schoolwork at the same table in the library.

Yes, he teases me, hugs me, and kisses me on the cheeks the way my brothers do the rare times he comes for a visit after his parents returned. Maybe I did have a crush on him, but he has always had beautiful girlfriends. Besides, he's five years older, and at thirteen when I first met him, I could tell he saw me only as a child, a lonely one he tried to cheer up. After a few weeks, I began to regard him the way I did Jun—an older wiser brother. I've had crushes, none lasting except for Vic, another of Jun's friends, which went on for years until I met Scott.

We've talked a lot about this new "problem," sometimes until I'm exhausted. Scott doesn't seem to realize I'm not like him. He thrives on talking about things—over and over. I guess that's why he likes debating while I prefer to keep my thoughts to myself and write about them instead. I've gone along with all the talking.

But I worry. The gulf isn't disappearing.

November 2012

Tonight, I cried because I've found how inescapable loneliness is and how much a part of life it will always be.

I used to think all that's needed for one to beat loneliness is to have a loved one with whom you can totally communicate. Any unhappy thing is less so when shared with that person. I think, in my early years, that person was Grandma. Maybe I thought Scott would somehow be the one with whom I can build a similar bond, sharing freely, being understood and accepted no matter what.

Scott and I had a misunderstanding. We got over it after weeks of talking. But maybe I only thought we did.

He's off again on another solitary adventure. He only told me about it a week before he left, when we were out for a Saturday stroll at the waterfront. The second surprise he's sprung on me about going off somewhere. He'll be away for two months at least, somewhere in Mexico for Christmas and New Year.

I was mad. And hurt. "Do you time your trips on holidays to hurt me?"

He said it just happened that their office closed for the holiday season. He'd been working a lot on weekends and it was stressing him out.

"You don't seem to have time for me anymore."

He was sorry, but he was the new guy in his office and he got dumped on. He needed to get away.

"Then, let's go on a trip together."

He said, "I need alone time to destress."

A response to mute any further argument. We were silent for the rest of our walk until we reached his car. How much more do I need to give to rescue whatever is left between Scott and me?

I had romantic notions that to love someone, I had to give completely of myself. But could it be we give only because we expect the other to return the favor? Am I holding back, afraid I might get hurt? And being hurt by someone I love would be unbearable.

I had high hopes when I first fell in love.

It was important to me that the person I loved was a soul mate. And a soul mate to me was someone who could understand my thoughts, my feelings. Someone to reach out to in my brightest and darkest *moments. Someone I would feel free to share all my thoughts and feelings with because I know they would understand. And care. Someone who would always be there, not necessarily in body, but in spirit—a presence I could sense at every moment so I would never have to feel completely alone.*

But a soul mate is a myth. A romantic notion that could never take shape. An illusion borne of impossible dreams.

While it may be the mature thing to let this notion die, I realize that not having a soul mate means I am alone. Everybody is alone. This must be at least part of what one feels at the moment of death: You are by yourself, finally and definitely severed from everyone and everything. It's quite a frightening thought.

I'm learning; oh, I'm learning. You can't rely on another to make you happy. You must look into yourself and yourself alone for that. Life sucks. It really does. It sucks even more when you realize it's you who've caused your own unhappiness.

Is it my destiny to live like this, often lonely and sad? Is this what everyone has to look forward to?

These last paragraphs are like an arrow to my cerebral cortex. Not my heart—contrary to our usual romantic notions. We'd probably heal faster if the heart is where love resides.

"A soul mate is a myth. A romantic notion that could never take shape. An illusion borne of

impossible dreams." Crushing words. Reawakening the ruins of the youthful love of a callow boy of nineteen pumped for adventure. A love buried now in the deepest recess of my mind.

But the ruins remain. I realize that now. Mostly channeled into a blended life of creativity and routine. Among Gramps' many declarations, one stands out: Being creative is being alive. He's been right so far. I get my highs designing beautiful things. Found fulfillment enriching other people's lives. And yet, I wonder. Has it been enough? Is it enough?

Ten years, I've been quite content. Until this passage. Until this journal.

I close the journal. My eyes sting. I shift my gaze to the silhouettes of trees and renovated buildings outside my arched window.

Where are you now, little idealist, lonely woman? What happened to the girl who agonized about why she was alive at all?

I feel guilty having intruded into your soul. As if I've stolen a forbidden secret, a precious part of you only you have the right to share. Yet you've touched me deeply, and for that, I can't be sorry.

Loneliness is inescapable. You've learned that much. Have you found some serene—if not happy—way to live with loneliness? Accept life, such as it is?

I may not know your name, but I know your agonies. I have a premonition we'll meet some day. You can't be that far away. We may have crossed paths before. On the street. At a bookstore. On the university campus for some performance. At the libraries in the area.

Luna

The Meeting: July 2013

I see only two browsers in the bookstore. In a few minutes past 3:00 p.m., more patrons will come. The bookstore is a short walking distance from a shopping complex and from offices of technology and design companies. The owners have stocked the store not only with books of general interest, but also with specialty books employees of those companies use or may be interested in.

This is my third month working at this bookstore and Asha, who has been employed here a few years, will arrive to run the store in the evening hours. She told me the owners hired me because, of the many applicants, I seemed to have read the most books. For the first time, something I love literally paid off.

One browser—a young man no more than thirty, glasses, thick brown hair, lean, tall, tanned— approaches the counter, three books in his arms. He hands me two and cradles the third to his chest. I take the two and ring them up, but my heart skips a beat when I catch a glimpse of the third. It's thick, black, and has no title, no author name on its spine. A journal? A Moleskine maybe?

"Will these be all for you today, sir?"

He's staring at me, and I stare back. Into deep-set blue eyes behind the glasses. A neatly-trimmed mustache I didn't notice before makes me look at his face again. And he's quite likely *akamai* (brainy), judging from the books he's buying. The Pulitzer-prize winning *Behind the Beautiful Forevers* about some slums in India and the formidably-titled *Kant After Duchamp*, an art book. Books I doubt I'll ever read.

"Yes." He pulls a credit card out of his wallet.

I take the card, glancing at the black journal again before I insert the card into the cash register. "I have a journal just like yours."

"Oh, this?" He's surprised. "It's not mine. I found it at a coffee shop. I have to return it to the owner." His voice is deep, warm, and resonant.

I jerk my head up to stare at him again, though all I could say is, "Would you like a bag for your books?"

"No, thank you."

I stare at the journal as I hand him his books.

"Thank you." He waits and doesn't leave.

"Is there anything else I can help you with?"

"My card, please." He seems annoyed, his left eyebrow arching for a moment.

"Oh, I'm sorry." I snatch his card off the register keyboard. "Here you are, sir."

"Thank you. Your first time working here? I
don't believe I've seen you before."

"I've been here a few months. I work part-time."

He places his books on the counter and the
journal on top of the books. As he takes his time to
put his card back in his wallet, he regards me in a lazy
kind of way. A corner of his mouth slightly upturned
toward his dimple, his gaze unwavering but casual. I
suspect he's taking my full measure and I'm flustered,
and yet I can't help wondering if he likes what he sees.
I look away, at the books on the display shelf.

"Glad to see a new face. Asha is nice, but she and
I don't have much we can talk about," he says.

I face him again. He breaks into a spontaneous,
disconcerting smile. He's rather attractive when he's
not looking serious, particularly with the dimple on
his left cheek.

Cheeky, as well, this brainy ectomorph. I smile
back, a little wider than I meant to, disarmed by his
charming smile. "Thank you for shopping at Minerva
Books and please come again."

"For sure." He picks up his books and journal,
and with a last amused glance at me, he walks away.

I watch him, holding my breath as he approaches
the door. Before he disappears from my sight, I can't
help myself. I run after him. "Excuse me, sir."

He stops and turns around. He's nearly a head
taller than me, and I have to look up at him. Without

the counter between us, he seems intimidating. He's not smiling now, but scowling.

"Yes?"

"I lost my journal."

"Oh," he mumbles, no longer scowling.

He stares down at me. If a gaze could penetrate, his would pass through his glasses and burn the skin on my face. I stare back, trying not to flinch.

"Can I look at your journal, to see if it's mine?"

"You may." But he doesn't hand it to me. "But how can I be sure it's yours?"

"Mine is a Moleskine, too. I can tell you what's written on it, but I can't leave the bookstore unattended. Do you mind coming back in? Should only take a minute."

"I'm sorry. I have to go back to work. I'm late for a meeting already. I can meet you at the coffee shop where I found the journal, and if it's yours, I'll give it back to you there."

I'm disappointed. But right now, it's me asking a favor. I lost my journal months ago and had begun to resign myself to its being lost forever. What's a few more days? Besides, his journal might not be mine.

"I guess that sounds reasonable. When?"

"Tomorrow at two?"

"I work tomorrow. Friday?"

He nods and I turn to go back into the store. "Aren't you going to ask me which coffee shop?"

I stop, pivot on my heels to face him. "Well, I assumed I'd go to the coffee shop where I left my journal and if that's where you found yours, I'll see you there."

He lets loose another wide, dimpled, smile. "Of course. See you then."

Back behind the counter, I replay the encounter in my mind. Why couldn't he have given me two minutes to examine the journal? Did he read it?

The thought stirs mixed feelings, makes me curious. What did he find interesting in the journal and why? He seemed reluctant to part with it. Has he become attached to it? A journal I might have written. Who is he? What does he do? Does he have a family?

Trepidation tempers my curiosity—what if he had read it? But I can't deny I'm eagerly looking forward to Friday. Maybe I've finally found my journal.

Lucien

I've decided to wait for the bookseller before getting my coffee. Maybe I'll even buy her one.

She did fascinate me. Not because she's pretty. A little too pretty for me not to take a second, even a third look. She kept staring at the journal. I was amused, at first. Later, I was somewhat rude to her. She told me she lost one like it. Maybe I got angry. Inside, I mean. I did keep it under wraps. Then it hit me: I wasn't ready to part with my Moleskine journal.

The thought elicits a tug of guilt. *It isn't your journal.*

I've brought it to Peet's for the last few months. Placing it on the table so anyone looking for it can spot it at once. But no one has ever inquired about it.

At the bookstore, this young woman told me she lost her journal—a Moleskine, at that. She startled me. But staring at her, I knew the one I've been safeguarding is hers. We humans have this uncanny ability to pick up subtle cues about people. Mine has been honed in my job. Whatever cues I noticed, I'm more than fifty percent sure this young woman and the journal belong to each other.

Before I met the bookseller, I imagined the journal writer. A bookish girl. Neither pretty nor plain. Someone oblivious of her looks. Shy but affectionate. Intelligent and bespectacled—like me.

The attractive young woman confronting me outside the bookstore caught me off-guard. She had run after me, steps quick and sure. Under the midday sun, her lithe figure seemed fragile. I stared at her. Hard and long, wanting to understand. How did I know she was indeed the owner? Dark-brown, almond eyes, under thick black lashes, defied my stare.

"Hi there!" A voice breaks into my reverie.

I look up. And here she is. Fetching in a red sleeveless knit shirt. The red casting a rosy glow on her cheeks. Denim jeans molding her hips and thighs. At the bookstore, she dressed as the proper librarian. Belted shirtdress. Standing collar. Short sleeves. Skirt below her knees.

"Hi!" I reluctantly tear my gaze away and pull out the chair I've been saving for her. "Well, well, odds are increasing in your favor."

"Sometimes, I get lucky."

Seconds after she sits down, I rise from the banquette. I don't know why, but at that moment, I couldn't bear being that close to her. Is it the thought that, at eighteen inches across the table from me, I could reach out to touch her face? "I'm getting a cup of coffee. Can I treat you to one?"

She hesitates a few seconds. "Yes, why not? Thank you. I'll have a decaf."

"Cream? Sugar? I can get you a coffee drink if you prefer."

"Decaf is fine. Cream, no sugar."

Halfway toward the counter, I glance back. The journal lies untouched on the tabletop. She's looking at it, but she doesn't pick it up.

When I come back with the cups of coffee many minutes later, she's looking around the room. I put her coffee on the table in front of her and reclaim my place on the banquette.

We sip our coffee in silence.

A third down my sixteen-ounce cup—a long two minutes—I put my cup down. Extend my hand to her, "I'm Lucien Lester. I think we should at least know each other's name."

She reaches out with her free hand to shake mine. Her mouth twitches in an amused smile. "Lu-shen, not Lu-shan?"

"Lucien. Blame my parents."

She takes another sip of coffee before she answers. "Lucien, I'm Luna Kamaka-Hart. My parents' hyphenated last names. A bit of a mouthful, I know." She puts her cup down.

I tilt my head to one side. Trying to appear casual as I stare at her. "Luna. You must be part Hawaiian."

"I am—maybe one-eighth by blood, but at least fifty percent in my soul. I'm also the only girl, blessed but sometimes cursed with three brothers. 'A moon among stars,' my mom said. Why Lucien?"

"Only child. Conscious choice my parents made when they got married. I am, they claim, the light in their lives. I'm sure there were times while I was growing up when they regretted that name."

She takes a few more sips of coffee. "You won't find my name anywhere in the journal."

"You're right, I didn't. Why is that?"

"I didn't mean for anyone else to read it."

I frown. "Then, why leave it here at a very public place? Surely anyone who finds it would skim through it to see who it belongs to."

She gazes at me. Her narrowed eyes flicker in defiance. "I was careless. Distracted the last time I was here."

"Hmmm. So convince me this is yours."

She delivers a counterattack. "You aren't too trusting, are you? It has to be better than chance it's mine. I'm here now and not at any of the other coffeehouses in the area. Besides, it's black and clearly a Moleskine."

"If you were in my shoes and you found this very personal journal, would you give it to anyone who says it's probably hers?" I'm dismayed. My voice is louder than it normally is. Worse, I described the journal as "very personal," which means I did more than skim through it.

"No, I wouldn't. You're right. I'm sorry. Anyway, the first entry is September 2005, when I was 15." She still looks annoyed.

I pick up the journal and hand it to her. "Thank you for not peeking into it while I was getting coffee."

"I wasn't sure it was mine. I wouldn't want to read someone else's personal journal." A frown flits through her brow and she turns her face away.

Guilt can be insidious. It has resurfaced to mock my dismay. I've justified to myself why I kept reading the journal. Her first entry enticed me. The next ones interested me enough to keep reading. She was comfortable with solitude. Believed in dreams. Communed with the physical world she inhabited. Was bothered by existential questions and what it meant to love. Stuff I have grappled with at one point or another in my life.

I did feel guilty as I read, but I talked myself out of it. The writer and I are strangers, so reading the journal is like reading a novel.

Growing up, I was rewarded for telling the truth. Omissions didn't count. They were seldom detected. Truth, as always, is my only inconvenient choice to manage my guilt. "Does it bother you I read yours? I had to, you know, to get some clue about the owner. It puzzled me that there's no name, no email or home address."

She clasps the journal to her bosom and throws me a quick side glance. Eyes flashing. Mouth pursed. She doesn't answer.

Not the partial truth, Lucien. Full disclosure. "You might as well know. I did read everything. And I can tell you—you have nothing at all to be ashamed of." I don't have to tell her I read a few entries more than once. *Do I?*

She turns to stare at me, eyes still flashing. "I'm not ashamed of what I've written, but you're a stranger, after all, and that bothers me."

She's miffed. Or worse, angry. This girl who wrote those words about soul mates. Passages in her last entry that made me pause and reflect. Disturbed me, in fact, more than I admitted to myself.

I had believed those words. They helped justify my current existence. The irony is, as I read them in her journal, I began to doubt them. Was I really as content with my solitary life as I thought? Why did those words make me feel my life was missing something?

"I'm truly sorry if I crossed a forbidden line," I say, holding her gaze. "I read your first entry and couldn't stop reading. I told myself your journal was no different from a novel or a film. At least, before I met you. And, anyway, I was a stranger who could have no influence on you. You could vanish me from your life forever with a word or two. It should mean nothing to you that I read your journal."

"But it does. There are only two—no, one— person who I wouldn't have minded giving this journal to, to read." She turns away again.

"Again, I'm very sorry. I want to make amends. Would you let me?" She doesn't answer. Keeps her gaze averted. Have I lost a chance for us to become friends? But how else could I have known you if I hadn't read your journal?

"If it makes you feel better, I'll leave, get out of your sight. You can forget I ever existed."

Again, she doesn't answer, but she turns toward me. Regards me with a faraway look in her eyes. That faraway look I imagined on a pensive, idealistic young woman I met in the black Moleskine. Why did I tell her to forget I exist?

Forget I ever existed—the last thing I want her to do. I try to make light of it. "I'd ask you not to come weekdays, though, between two and three"

"What's with weekdays?" A faint knitting of her brow precedes a hesitant smile.

"I'm always here for my afternoon coffee break."

"I see." She grabs her bag and puts the journal in it.

She's leaving. I sit back against the wall. A sense of loss slowly settling in my chest. But an inner voice pulls me back to reality. *Get with it, man. She's not yours to lose.*

But Luna doesn't get up. She picks up her cup of coffee again and sips it slowly. I take her action as a cue. I raise my cup to my lips and sip.

"I think I'm being rude." She puts her cup down. "I do mean to thank you for returning my journal. I thought I'd lost it forever, and I felt bad for weeks. Now I've got it back. Because of you. But like you said, a journal is very personal." She shrugs, her eyes darting sideways and back to me. "But ... it's done and can't be undone. You could have left it at the counter, though. I came back the morning after I lost it. None of the servers said they'd seen it."

"I did hand it to a young woman the day you left it. But she must not be working in the morning. Anyway, I wasn't sure how well they took care of lost things. I think she dumped it into a big dirty bin. It had sweaty sunglasses, coffee-stained books, and smelly socks, among other things. So I took it back the next day. From the first entry, I understood the journal is precious to its owner. I wanted to give it back in person. I guess I was wrong assuming you'd return the same afternoon. Or the next. I've always placed the journal on the table for everyone to see."

A blush creeps up her cheeks. "I didn't mean to sound like I doubted your good intentions. I am deeply grateful, believe me. And I don't ever want to imagine you never existed. But I'm feeling kinda awkward. You've read my musings. That's like peeking into my soul. You'd need my permission to do that. I don't even know who you are."

She forgives me? "Ask me any question you want. Anything you think will even the score. I'll answer everyone of them. Truthfully."

"But that isn't easy for me to do."

"No, I suppose not." I look at my watch. "Let's see. We've been sitting here together more than half an hour. Plus ten minutes talking at the bookstore, where your cash register read my credit card info. I'm no longer a total stranger, am I?"

"Maybe not. Still..."

"Would you believe me if I tell you I may not be a great guy, but I'm honest and I do try to be polite?"

She smiles. "I think you can argue your way to prove a point. So, yeah, you're smart, and you care. You could have trashed my journal but you didn't."

I grin. "I believe those are compliments. I'll take them, thank you. And if you're game, I'd like to proclaim this moment the start of a budding friendship. Would you agree to meet here again for a getting-to-know-me session? How long would you need to ask me questions to build your trust in me? One long meeting? A few shorter ones?"

She smiles again. "You're funny."

I wasn't trying to be funny. All I want is to see her again. I say lamely, "There, you've found another one of my good qualities."

Luna's smile fades and in a more subdued tone, she says, "You seem like you could be a good friend, but I'm afraid I'm not very sociable at the moment. Still getting used to the reality of a breakup."

She presses her hand to her chest. Blows out a long breath through her lips. Is she aware of her action? She seems too distracted to be. She shoots me a quick glance. "I can't believe I told you that."

"Scott?"

She's askance. "Yes... It's so weird you know more about me than my family."

I reach out to hold her hand, reassure her. But I catch myself. *Slow down Lucien.* I draw back, grasping my cup of coffee instead.

"I didn't mean to blurt that out. My family doesn't know I've broken up with Scott."

"Maybe you needed to unburden yourself. A breakup is too devastating to suffer in silence."

She stares at me. A mix of curiosity and suspicion in her eyes. "You know that from experience?"

"Doesn't everyone?" I'm dodging her question. "Anyway, I think you think I'd understand. Because, as you said, I might know you better than your family. Or because I'm a stranger, I'd be a neutral sounding board."

"You're not a psychologist or a psychiatrist, are you?" She regards me with wary eyes.

I shake my head. "No, no. My friends are creative nerds and I'm one myself. In our profession, we need to know people. Deep down—what drives them; what they value so we can design ..." My voice trails off.

Luna's eyes are directed at me but I doubt she heard me. She has drifted into some private realm. A minute passes. Two minutes. Three .... I wait. Uneasy. Fidgety.

I snatch my cup off the table and mumble, "I'm getting another cup. Want another one?"

She glances at me but doesn't answer.

When I return, she says as soon as I sit down, "*C'est la vie, Lucien.*" She laughs. Shrugs her shoulders.

I go along with her attempt at lightness. "So it goes. Yeah, *c'est la vie.*"

I can't laugh. And I'm at a loss for words. She's still dealing with the breakup of her first love affair. Yet she seems unperturbed. A façade I'm familiar with.

The first and only time I had my heart broken, I was nineteen. Younger than Luna is now. Hopeful. Still impressionable. My ego still fragile behind my outward bravado.

I fell apart. But I tried to hide it from my parents. Didn't even tell Gramps and Nana. I succeeded. First, by holing up in my bedroom. My family thought I was recovering from my travels. Then I went off again. This time, to volunteer to build homes in South America. When I returned, I buried my head in books and projects at the university.

I learned heartbreak affects more than your heart. Jumbles up rituals—the big and little habits of your everyday life you rarely give thought to. Worse, it eats at your spirit. Erodes your trust in people. Changes you. Maybe forever.

Have I been living with the consequences of that youthful passion these ten years?

I confess I'm also shocked to realize—instead of feeling sorry for Luna, I feel a flutter of anticipation

in my breast. An eager, hopeful anticipation that a
door, once closed to me, is now ajar. I want more than
a casual connection with Luna. A connection I
wouldn't have had much hope for had she been in a
serious relationship with someone.

I say, "Let life take its course. Go along with what
it offers. I'm offering a getting-to-know-you dinner."

Luna smiles. Then, as if she didn't hear my offer
of dinner, she says, "I took this journal to Peet's to
write about the breakup. I thought it'd help. Get me
used to the fact that I lost a love I thought would last.
That I don't have control over a lot of things. But I
couldn't write. My mind was blank."

"Maybe, blank is good. Sometimes. Things need
to percolate." What else could I have said?

"Is that out of pity or something to make me feel
better?" Has she switched back to my dinner offer? I
thought she hadn't heard me.

I take a slow deep breath, a trick Gramps taught
me when I'm thrown in for a loop. "You mean my
invitation to dinner? Neither. Pity gets you nowhere.
And I can't make things any less painful for you. It's
so you can ask me all the questions you want. Counts
as a distraction, whatever it's worth to you."

"A momentary palliative, then. Maybe it'll do me
good. Scott will see I've moved on. Do you think he'll
be jealous?"

"Yes. Men can be strangely possessive even of women they've broken up with." My enthusiasm has been deflated.

"Good," she says though she doesn't sound enthusiastic. "Maybe, it'll keep me from thinking too much. And you know me enough so I don't have to explain myself. I also like that you're not judgmental."

"I guess I'm racking up the points." I force a smile. But the idea of being a distraction grates at me. I remind myself breakups are hard, even traumatic sometimes. Luna believed Scott was "the one." What they had was forever. She was naïve. Had faith in something transcendent—how could I fault her for that?

I think she can be incisive. And I believe someday she'll see Scott had rudely, cruelly yanked the rug from under her feet.

That grating feeling subsides. My irritation softens into sympathy.

She says, "I believe I'm imposing on you, so if we go out, I'll pay. I'd feel better."

"We'll go Dutch," I answer firmly. "I'm serious about evening the score. We'll focus on you getting to know as much about me as I know about you. Only fair, right?"

"Okay." She leans forward. Stares into my eyes. "Your eyes. What is it about them? Why hide them behind glasses?"

I keep myself from squirming at her scrutiny. I stay on track. "Eight on Saturday night?"

"Can't make it this Saturday. Next week?"

Three days later, Luna sends a message cancelling Saturday's date:

I said yes too quickly. Sorry. I'm not ready for any company at the moment—yours, in particular. You know me too well, but you're a relative stranger. I feel too exposed to you, too vulnerable. It's better this way. For me, at least. Maybe, when I am at a better place in my head, I'll text you.

The Moleskine journal is gone, and my tenuous hold on Luna is slipping away from me. But I cling to some hope. So I reply:

I understand. I'll be here and have no plans to decamp any time soon. Please don't hesitate to call me if you want to talk. I do want us to be friends.

Luna

Weeks Later

It's Friday night. I'm back at my parents' house for a short visit. I called Mom on Wednesday to tell her I'm coming. I had some bit of news to share. She didn't ask what it was about and only said, "Okay. What time do I pick you up?"

I was relieved she didn't ask. I intend to tell them about the breakup with Scott, but I want to do so when I've psyched myself enough to respond calmly to any reaction they might have.

It's been a hectic day, and I'm tired and hungry. From eight this morning until two o'clock, I worked at the bookstore, which had the usually big Friday crowd. From there, I rushed to take a four o'clock flight to Long Beach airport where Mom waited in her car at the passenger pick-up zone.

A light supper that Dad prepared is waiting for us. A steaming bowl of gingery, miso-scented soup of soba noodles, bok choy, mushrooms, and seafood. Though Dad has a limited repertoire of dishes he can prepare, he does them well and aromas from the dish hit the pit of my stomach. I have to restrain myself from picking up the bowl and guzzling the broth. I smile at Dad gratefully after a few forkfuls of noodles.

While we eat, my parents talk about recent incidents of cars being broken into around their neighborhood. The topic is of mild interest to me, and I'm exhausted, but I linger at the table even after I finish my soup.

I expected the soup to revive me. Instead, it made me more aware of my aching limbs, my foggy brain, and my parents' voices floating toward me as if in a dream. Out of habit, I start stacking the dirty dishes to put them in the dishwasher.

"Leave them," Dad says. "I'll clear the table. Go to bed. You look tired."

Startled out of my fog, I raise my drooping head. "Thanks, Dad. I am tired."

After giving Mom, then Dad, a quick peck on the cheek, I retreat to my room, take a shower, and change into pajamas. The shower seems to give me a second wind. I crawl into bed with my iPad, a present from Jun this past Christmas, intending to relax with some light fiction until I feel drowsy. But at half past eleven, I'm still awake. My brain has recharged and my muscles are too twitchy to relax.

Sometime later, I look up from my iPad at a light knock on the door. I bookmark the page I was reading and turn off my iPad. It must be Mom. But how can she still be awake? She's usually in bed by ten even on Friday evenings.

She opens the door and stands at the doorway, staring at me. The night is cool, but she's wearing a flimsy green nightgown and her feet are bare.

"Mom, are you okay? It's a bit late for you to be up isn't?"

She approaches my bed and sits on the edge of it. She doesn't speak for a minute, and something about the way she's staring at the floor troubles me. "Your Auntie Celia called. From Queen's Medical Center."

My breath catches in my throat. I can hear what Mom is going to say before she utters one word. She stares at me, pursing her lips, trying to suppress their quivering. "Grandma had a stroke. She's gone."

I sit up. Mom watches me, waits for me to burst out crying. I'm trembling, but I don't cry. You may sense when someone is about to give you bad news, but until you hear it, you can't tell how you'll react. I heard what mom said, but I can't process it.

Her words seem unreal. I can't imagine Grandma gone forever. I can't imagine I will never set eyes on her again, never hear her voice, never snuggle close to her when I need comforting or want her reassurance. I can't imagine I will never hug her again, feel her solid presence. And most heartbreaking of all, I have trouble accepting I wasn't there at her final hour.

Mom puts her arms around me, pulls me close to her bosom. "She was eighty-four. She lived a good life."

I hug her back, and I feel her body beginning to tremble. She tightens her arms around me, and I hear her subdued sobs. My eyes stay dry.

Moments later, she releases me. I hand her some tissues from the box on my bedside table. She wipes her eyes and cheeks, stained with tears and dark eye make-up. "I've called Jun. He's making arrangements for all of us to fly to Oahu. By tomorrow afternoon, if possible."

She presses my hand before she gets up. "How are you? I can stay with you for a while if you want."

"I'll be all right."

"You sure?"

I nod.

"I'll pack tonight. You should, too, if you find it hard to sleep. That'll help keep your mind off of Grandma and maybe tire you out enough to go to sleep."

"I'm okay. I'll be ready."

She frowns—is she wondering how I'm coping with this unbearable news? She plants a light kiss on my head. "Do you want a sleeping pill? I'll take one myself. I need it. I have to go to work in the morning for a couple of hours."

It's odd she thinks she must go to work the following morning. On a Saturday. How can she if she's so distraught? But I say nothing. Level-headed, decisive, and efficient Mom must have a good reason.

When she closes the door behind her, I get back to my novel. My eyes run across the strings of words on the page, but the strings seem disjointed, the words empty.

I put the iPad down and fumble in my purse for my cell phone. I dictate a reminder to myself to inform the bookstore and ask for two weeks off.

The next day, we fly to Oahu for the funeral. My parents, my three brothers, and I. We had a big breakfast before we left, and my brothers each hugged me tight and said, "Sorry Sis." None of my brothers really knew Grandma who they saw maybe three times in their whole lives.

Jun sits next to me on the plane, watching me with concern in his eyes. Once we're on air and a stewardess announces complimentary drinks and snack, Jun takes my hand in his and holds it most of the way except when we're eating or drinking. I drink the juices, but I can't eat the snacks and lunch we're served.

At the airport in Honolulu, Auntie Celia is waiting for us. Seeing her, eyes red and puffy, wearing a black mourning dress so unlike the colorful Hawaiian prints she loves, I burst into tears, a torrent of grief I must have been reining in. She runs toward me and gathers me in her arms.

These are the first tears I shed for Grandma, and I can't seem to stop them. Auntie Celia is crying, too, but quietly. We're both shaking. I'm still sobbing when she leads us to her family car, her arm around my shoulders.

The big Kamaka family—cousins and uncles and their families from my grandfather's side—are at Grandma's house when we get there. Grandma was an only child, and if she had any relatives left, they would be living either in Spain or the Philippines. Auntie Juanita tells us that except for her and Auntie Celia, everyone will go back to Honolulu in the evening. They will stay in the house with us to sort out whatever needs sorting.

The family lawyer informed my aunts that Grandma wishes to be cremated and her ashes strewn around the mango tree. It seems Grandpa was also cremated, but his ashes were divided into three urns, each of which was given to the three children. I don't know what my mother has done with those ashes. I've never seen an urn among her possessions.

My mom and my aunts accept Grandma's wish to be cremated, but they can't agree on what to do with her ashes. Auntie Celia goes along with her wish, but her older sisters want to keep a piece of Grandma with them. Like Grandpa's ashes, they want those of Grandma divided. That afternoon, the sisters talk, the older two trying to convince the youngest, sometimes in anger they can't disguise. Auntie Celia refuses to back down.

A few of us sit around, listening to them argue. No one dares to interfere. Not even their husbands.

Auntie Juanita, exasperated, finally says, "Celia, we heard you, but you're outnumbered. That's all there is to it."

I've been appalled for some time, listening to them turn Grandma's request into a big deal. Why not respect it and comply with it? I can't help blurting out, "No, she's not. We should do what Grandma wishes. To her, I was her youngest daughter, so I think I have a say in this. As much as you three have."

Mom and Auntie Juanita stare at me, their mouths agape. Auntie Celia seizes her chance. "I agree. She gets her say."

Flabbergasted at my intrusion but too surprised to object, Mom and Auntie Juanita can't summon a quick reply.

I'm emboldened. "Grandma loved that tree. She sits—sat—under it every afternoon. Not one of you knew that, did you? Sometimes even when it rained. It was a source of comfort to her." I turn away to hide the tears that have begun to moisten my eyes.

In a quieter but more vehement voice, I add, "It's where she belongs. Not in some urn you keep somewhere, only to forget about it."

"I need a drink," Mom says, getting up.

By dinnertime, Grandma clearly will have her wish. Mom, the eldest of the three sisters, must have caved in. She announces what she calls the "itinerary" for the next few days, including the scattering of ashes around the mango tree. The word "itinerary" annoys me. It's a word bureaucrats use.

The next day, according to Mom's "itinerary," Auntie Celia and I busy ourselves going through papers in Grandma's writing desk. Auntie Celia finds a box of letters. She hands it to me and says, "I can't go through this. It's too painful. Why can't we wait until after the funeral?"

"I'm not sure. Maybe Mom thinks there's something here that can be used. Like, you know, for a ... eulogy. Or something she'll want to know about before we return to California."

"There's a will. That should say it all."

I shrug. I'm actually quite eager to go through Grandma's letters. Maybe it's my way of continuing to feel her presence.

"I can do this by myself, Auntie Celia."

"Can you? Well, do what you can today. I need at least another day to adjust. I'll take over and finish up later."

At first, I can't help the tears that flow again as I go through the most recent letters at the top of the box, many of them cards for birthdays and Christmases from Mom. The Christmas cards enclosed pieces of printed paper recounting our doings for the year. I could tell Grandma read every enclosure many times. Each piece of paper has several creases on it and a few show traces of stains and thumbprints. I put the cards and their enclosed letters in one pile.

At the bottom of the box is a thick envelope that has yellowed a bit. It's handwritten, not typed like the card enclosures. The postal stamp dates it forty-two years ago. The letter seems to have been crumpled and smoothed out.

The handwriting is unfamiliar, so I look at the last page to see who sent it. I'm surprised to see it was from Grandpa, who passed away years before I was born. The image I have of him—a big and swarthy, wise-cracking, joke-loving *hapa-haole* who was half Hawaiian, half Portuguese—comes from stories Grandma and my aunts have told me and from old-fashioned albums of pictures kept in a bookcase in the library that had been his home office.

Like many locals, Grandma was also *hapa,* but she was half Filipino, half Spanish. Petite, delicate, and pretty. My mother's side of the family is made up of hybrids. "Mongrels," I call us sometimes, which always elicits Mom's disapproving look.

The letter begins:

I love you. You are the love of my life, my reason for being.

The opening makes me smile. How sweet and romantic to start a letter with those words. But a sense of shame seizes me the next instant. Maybe I shouldn't be reading someone else's love letter. But those first lines hooked me. My grandparents must have been married ten years or so when the letter was written, and it warms my heart to know their love endured. But why express it through a letter?

Though the letter brought a smile to my face at first, I go through mixed emotions as I read all of it. It isn't exactly the letter I expected.

*****

That night, after Auntie Celia turns off her bedside lamp in the bedroom we're sharing, I say, "Can we talk?"

"Sure. I can't sleep well these days, anyway. Something bothering you?"

"There's a letter in that box."

"Of course. It's a box of letters."

"It's from Grandpa to Grandma."

"You came across their love letters? I'm not surprised. He was supposed to have written her many. 'Dumbfounded before virtue and beauty,' he used to say."

"It was dated February 1971."

"How sweet! To be writing love letters after years of being married."

"It's more than a love letter."

"Okay. So tell me what it is."

"Well, at first, he tells her many times he loves her, has always loved her. That's so romantic. Made me warm and fuzzy all over. But then ... did you know

Grandpa had an affair? Throughout the letter, he's asking Grandma to forgive him and take him back."

"No way." Aunt Celia sits up and turns her lamp on again. "But what else could he have asked to be forgiven for? I would never have thought it of him, though. Could you tell with whom and for how long?"

"No, no names. Maybe it's someone they both knew. He hid the affair from her. She found out, anyway. From what I can piece together, the affair lasted months, maybe a year."

"Oh my, that sounds serious. You can't hide an affair, not from those who care about you. As dreamy as Mom used to get, she was very much attuned to him. I was born three years after that letter. I was only eight when he died, but all the memories I have of him, the things Mom said about him tell me he'd never hurt her. I felt the love between them. I was sure they had always loved each other."

"He does swear he never loved the other woman and it was all about sex."

"Common excuse. But I can believe it in his case. Anything else that could tell us more what happened? More bombshells?"

"The letter doesn't give details of the affair—not necessary, I guess. They each knew what he was talking about. But there may be another 'bombshell.' He says she doesn't need his forgiveness for whatever she has done, that it was all his fault for straying."

"Wo-ow! I'm not sure I like the sound of that. No details, either?"

"No, that's it. We can only guess. Isn't it shocking to find out Grandpa had an extramarital affair?"

"It sure is. Even at eight, I could see he was devoted to her. Protective, like she was someone fragile. But she wasn't. She was strong and stubborn."

We're both quiet for a few minutes. I have my suspicions about what Grandma might have done to need Grandpa's forgiveness, and I was about to ask Auntie Celia what she thinks. But she turns off the lamp and slides back on the bed.

"Listen, forget about it tonight. Go to sleep. I'll read the letter in the morning and talk to your mom. I'm sure she knows something."

That night, I have trouble falling sleep. With my eyes closed, I can see the letter scrolling through my mind, particular sentences jumping out at me. Then I think about Scott. Wondering where he is and whether his new wife has given birth.

My parents and brothers still have no inkling Scott has gone off to marry someone else. And the events of the past few days blotted out my intention to inform Mom and Dad this past weekend.

By now, my California family is used to Scott's gallivanting abroad. They no longer ask me about him when he doesn't visit for months on end. Jun believes it's only a matter of time before we break up.

The following morning after breakfast, Auntie Celia asks my mother to come to the library.

"Can I come, too?"

"Yes," Auntie Celia says. "I need you."

I follow Mom and Auntie Celia into the library.

Aunt Celia turns to me. "Lock the door behind you."

Mom frowns. "What's with locking the door? Something important you don't want anyone else to know?"

Aunt Celia ignores her remark. "How much did you know about Dad and Mom's relationship?"

"As much as you know, I guess. He loved her. She loved him. They loved us. What else is there to say?"

"No, you must know more. You lived with them so many more years than me."

"Something you really want to tell me?"

Mom waits while Auntie Celia hesitates. "Did you know he had an affair?"

Mom seems taken aback. "How do you know that?"

"Luna found a letter in a box on her desk confessing to it, asking her forgiveness."

Mom frowns in dismay.

Auntie Celia says, "Something in the letter tells me something more was going on."

"Like what?"

"That, maybe, Mom had an affair, too."

I look at Auntie Celia in surprise. I didn't know she was thinking that. It's one of my suspicions.

Mom takes a deep breath and sighs. She's looking unhappier by the minute. "When did Dad write that letter?"

"About forty-two years ago."

Mom stares at her. Sits down on the nearest chair.

"You know!" Auntie Celia says.

Mom looks mournful. "I think I was unfair to Mom."

"What do you mean?"

"I'll tell you something I've kept to myself all these years. Sit down. This isn't easy for me. Luna, can you ask Juanita to join us?"

Auntie Celia pulls a chair next to Mom's and turns it to face her. I go out to call Auntie Juanita.

Minutes later, Auntie Juanita and I sit on the worn-out couch across from Mom and Auntie Celia.

Auntie Juanita says, "What's going on? I'm still exhausted arguing over what to do with Mom's ashes. Don't tell me we have another problem."

Mom answers, "Luna found a letter that you should know about. I think I can explain its content."

"A letter! Something in it for us to fight over? Again?"

Mom scowls at her. "If you will listen and let me talk, you'll understand." She adjusts herself on the chair and clasps her hands on her lap.

"Forty years ago or so, I came home early from school. I forgot to tell Mom we were being sent home at noon, but Mrs. Tanaka came to pick up her kids so she gave me a ride home. The door wasn't locked. I walked in but didn't see Mom. I went looking for her in the kitchen. She wasn't there. I went to their bedroom."

Mom bites her lower lip and looks away, struggling with what she's feeling and thinking. "One of Maggie Tanaka's brothers was in there with her."

A soft "Oh, no!" escapes Auntie Celia's lips.

Auntie Juanita says, "What are you saying? Is that in the letter? Did you write it?"

"No," Auntie Celia says. "The letter was from Dad, asking forgiveness for an affair he had at that time."

Mom ignores her sisters' remarks. "They were in bed with no clothes on. I was twelve, and I knew what it meant."

Auntie Celia says, "Then I'm right. But ... no, not Mom ... I refuse to believe it ... and yet ...."

"I'm telling you what I saw. I locked myself in my room, refusing to listen to whatever she wanted to say. In the evening when I heard Dad's car, then his voice, I came out. Told him what I saw."

Auntie Celia shakes her head. "Oh, Mom!"

Auntie Juanita stares at Mom, frowning, incredulous, and at a loss for words.

Mom says, "I thought he'd be angry, but he wasn't. He just stood there. Mom was sitting on the couch. Then without a word, he took her hand, led her to their bedroom, and closed the door. They made up. I thought he shouldn't have forgiven her. He should have turned her out of the house.

"Everything changed between Mom and me after that. I couldn't forgive her. And for years, I think I was angry at her, not only for myself. For Dad, too."

Auntie Juanita says, "I don't know if I could have forgiven her, if I was you."

"We went on, as if nothing happened. At first, I was also angry with Dad for forgiving her. But I told myself he was a saint. As for Mom ... well, she's Mom, after all, and Dad said we should keep what happened that day to ourselves. But I never forgot that day, and no, in my heart, I guess I never forgave her."

Auntie Celia says, "Poor Mom. I think she knew. Frankly, I've always felt you were cold to her, even when she tried to please you. I never understood it."

"Why shouldn't she be? I would be," Auntie Juanita says.

Auntie Celia glares at her sister. "Juanita, Dad was having an affair that had been going on for a year. Mom had a short fling when she found out."

Mom says, "I didn't know he was having an affair. All those years of being angry with her ... oh, God! Mom, I'm so sorry." She bursts into tears.

We watch her cry in silence.

138

When she's calmer, Mom turns to me. "Can you show me the letter?"

"I put it back in the box after Auntie Celia read it." I go to the desk to get the letter.

"Don't tell anyone else about this, okay? Let's bury their secret with her."

She reads the letter and when she finishes, she passes it on to Auntie Juanita.

Tears stream down Mom's cheeks once more. "I'm so sorry I've resented Mom all these years for what I saw that day. I thought her a monster for cheating on the best, most loving man in the world. But I didn't know."

Auntie Celia says, "Luisa, you were twelve. An impressionable age and you worshipped Dad. Know what I think? She thought it was all she could do to convince him to stop seeing the other woman. And Mom, if she chose to, could hit back as hard. She was also hurting him for hurting her."

Auntie Juanita says, "Maybe she couldn't confront him about it. Mom had a problem being assertive."

Auntie Celia shakes her head. "I think she did confront him, but I bet he denied it and continued seeing that woman."

Mom says, "Yes, I can see him doing that, now that I'm older and know about his affair."

"And Mom was not as passive as you think. She had her way of getting what she wanted, like that bedroom incident you saw that afternoon."

Auntie Juanita frowns. "But why go to that extent?"

Auntie Celia regards Auntie Juanita, then Mom. "Shock value, maybe? Desperate measures? It seems she did get his attention. She got him to stop."

Mom says, "Their marriage survived."

Auntie Celia says, "I think it got stronger."

Auntie Juanita says, "Their affairs are still a shock, though, especially when they come up at a time like this."

After dinner, the three sisters go to the library. They lock the door and talk for a long time. They're still there when I go to bed.

The following morning is the day of the funeral services. The cremation is scheduled for the day after that.

Before we get into Auntie Celia's car to go to church, Mom says to me, "Not a word to anyone about the letter, okay? We burned it last night in the library. I feel so bad about it. I believe Celia is right. Mom was retaliating, thought it was the only way she could get his attention, make him break up with the other woman."

I concur. I've believed Auntie Celia's view from the moment she offered it. At first, I was disconcerted to know my suspicion was right. I've resisted the idea

that Grandma would have an affair to get back at
Grandpa. But alone in bed, going over what Mom and
Auntie Celia have said, I couldn't help admiring
Grandma.

She lived for us, her children. And when he was
alive, for Grandpa as well. She always did what she
thought was right for us, often at the expense of
sacrificing her own needs. She was as selfless a mother
as one could be. But when threatened with the loss of
someone and something precious to her, she fought
for it. And she fought to win. She did what she felt
she had to do. For herself.

Two days later, the Kamakas stand around the
mango tree for the scattering of Grandma's ashes.
The Tanakas are there as well as a handful of others
who came to the funeral services. I can't help
wondering who among Maggie Tanaka's three
brothers—all younger than her—had an affair with
Grandma. I know them by sight, and none of them is
here. I'm sure she chose the second one who, as I
remember, is the best looking of the three. I also
remember Grandma told me the second brother built
the bench under the mango tree.

Starting with Mom, the sisters scatter Grandma's
ashes at the foot of the tree. After Auntie Celia's turn,
she hands me the urn. "I've left you the rest."

I smile gratefully, and pour the remaining ashes
on Grandma's mango tree.

The day ends with what may be the last gathering at Grandma's house for a long time. Maggie Tanaka made a big platter of mango salad, using Grandma's recipe. But maybe the mango was too ripe or Maggie skimped on the fish sauce. Her salad is not as good as Grandma's. Still, I sense Grandma's spirit in it—that complex mélange of tart and sweet and the flowery pungent scent of green mangoes. It will always be with me long after the last lingering taste of mango salad.

That night, in the dark void of Grandma's room, I sleep on the bed I used to share with her when I was a child. I can't imagine that this might be the last night I'll spend in her house, the house where I've spent my best years. What will happen to the things she loved? I didn't see her boom box when we were going through her belongings. Has one of my aunts or cousins claimed it already? What about her garden? Her chickens? All the things that spoke of her? Things which became a part of me while I was growing up.

I have no say whatsoever on what the sisters will decide to do to Grandma's house. I hope they don't sell it. I'm sure they won't sell it—not for a while, anyway. Regardless of what they say now or how they felt about her in the past, they loved her and can't deny Grandma is there somewhere, within each of them, each one of us who she loved.

About the mango tree, I'm not as certain. Grandma is no longer here to protect it. The sisters believe my grandparents planted the mango tree—the last fruit tree she and Grandpa planted together—as the seal to a pact they made after their marital transgressions. A sign to remind them to remain faithful to each other for the rest of their lives. Maybe that explains why Grandma didn't want it cut down. And maybe for that reason, the barren tree will survive.

We fly back to California the next day. I know it will be a long time before I return to Honolulu. If ever I do.

Two days later, I plant a jasmine shrub in my parents' backyard. When it flowers, I want to catch a whiff of tropical jasmine every time I go to the garden. The shrub is my tribute to Grandma, letting her know that I know she's watching over me, wherever she is. That the lessons I learned from her will always be a part of who I am.

Luna

Months Later

How easily we can get blindsided by our emotions. I left Honolulu with my family, sure I had a good handle on my grief. But in the days following our return from Hawaii, I cried every night. Tears of grief for Grandma that I thought would be slowly exhausted, maybe after a couple of weeks.

During the day, I went about my tasks like an efficient machine, not allowing myself to think. But I can't always be busy. Alone toward the end of the day, I feel like a leaf floating on water, drifting to places in myself I've never been.

Grief is treacherous. It sneaks up on you when you least expect it. Grabs you and never lets go. Takes you on a roller coaster ride you can't escape.

I have moments when tears would come, sometimes when I least expect it. But often, when I feel guilty I wasn't with Grandma when she died, and I wasn't able to tell her how much I love her. The only comfort I can turn to is her pillow. No one knows I slipped it in my suitcase shortly after we arrived in Honolulu. I hug it, cry into it until my tears release the faint scent of jasmine and green mangos trapped in it.

It's been two months since Grandma passed away, and my tears are back. For the past few nights, I've gone to bed crying. But my grief has taken on a different color. It has been turning into anger. I'm angry that Grandma was taken away from me when I need her the most. It has been a slow-burning anger and it's eating at my insides.

Tonight, it has assumed a different shape. It's no longer memories of Grandma that have brought on my tears of anger. I see an image of Scott emerging, sitting in his car, the ocean in front of us. Scott showing no regrets, no remorse. Scott shrugging and saying, "Couldn't help it. I'm sorry, but that's life."

The images are quite vivid, though I wonder if that was how Scott really acted when he dumped me. I never knew him to be callous. Or maybe, he was. But I must have been shocked, then terribly hurt, and I blocked the pain of that afternoon. Never let it take root in my memory.

I did not see it coming. Tonight, it's clear to me— Scott lied to me, betrayed me these past two years. How could he after all we had been to each other? We had sworn to love each other for as long as we lived. Such wasted words.

I wipe my eyes and cheeks with the bedsheet. My jaw and my teeth hurt. I've been gnashing my teeth without being conscious of it. A scream, short and bitter, rises out of my chest, filling the room. "You're a jerk, Scott. I hate you."

My heart is beating fast. My breathing is shallow. Only then do I notice that I'm still clutching the sheet with which I wiped tears of anger from my face.

In the months after Scott dumped me, I was aware I went about my days in a kind of stupor, but Grandma's passing has jolted me out of it. As shattering as grief has been for me, it has forced me to face reality.

I'm still panting when I hear a light knock, and Mom pushes the door open. She rushes into my room. "Luna, are you okay, honey?"

She sits on the edge of the bed and reaches out to raise my face. "You've been crying. Are you thinking of Grandma? Is that why you screamed?"

I don't answer. I'm not ready to tell her the scream is anger at Scott's betrayal, at his unfeeling way of disclosing the truth. Anger I've finally allowed myself to feel.

Mom gathers me in her arms. "You're trembling. Oh, my poor darling. I'm sorry I've failed you. I shouldn't have left you with Grandma all those years. I felt so overwhelmed. Building a career. Three kids to take care of, another one on the way. So when Grandma offered to take you ..."

I shake my head. I wanted to tell her: No, you didn't fail me. You entrusted me to someone who gave selflessly of herself. I'll never regret the years I had

Grandma. My tears and trembling are from anger, but not for those years. But words fail me. So complex are my feelings. So intense. So alien to me.

We commiserate in silence. I wallow in grief for Grandma and seethe in anger at Scott. Mom nurses her guilt for having misjudged Grandma and neglected me those early years I lived away from home.

I don't know how long we cling to each other before we let go of the other. Mom says, "I was impressed at how calmly you took the news of my mother's death. I realize now it was shock. Mourning her is inevitable and grief doesn't just go away. So cry as much as you want. Scream, if it helps. Better to let it out. It might do more harm if you keep it in."

"I'm suffering from feelings I can't control. I'm miserable but I'm also angry."

"You loved Grandma best of all—I'm aware of that. You're angry she's gone. That's natural. You'll grieve longer than most of us." She pauses and bows her head. "For me, grief comes with guilt."

Mom closes her eyes and bites her lower lip, as she tries to keep from crying again. When she opens her eyes, she says in a quivering voice, "Forgive me."

I lean over to kiss her. "Mom, there's nothing to forgive. Nothing you have to regret where I'm concerned."

"I'm not as sure as you. And my mother ...I never got the chance to tell her I'm sorry."

"And I wish I had been with her in her last hour."

We sit, silent, leaning against each other. What, after all, can anyone say about regret and forgiveness when the person you should have said it to is gone?

Minutes later, she presses warm lips to my forehead and rises from the bed. "Try to go to sleep. I know it's hard, but tomorrow is work day. When do you fly back to the East Bay?"

"This Sunday."

As soon as Mom closes my door I slip out of bed. After a small trip to the bathroom I take my Moleskine journal from under my clothes in the lingerie drawer. I have not written anything in it since I got it back from Lucien.

I tried to write my thoughts down after Scott and I broke up. But I couldn't. I realize now that I was hurting and didn't want to relive the pain.

Now I feel I'm ready. I think if I write about the breakup, I can begin to purge myself of my anger and lighten my grief. It's my way of closing that chapter of my life.

February 2014: Healing

About a year ago, Scott took me on a leisurely scenic drive on the coast to Bodega Bay. He had recently returned from one of those "solitary" trips he loved to go on. I relaxed in the front passenger seat of his car, happy we're together again, enjoying peaceful unhurried moments. He said he wanted to visit a park in Doran Beach. This park had walking trails along the shore. It was a beautiful sunny day and we'd go for a stroll.

He stopped the car at a beach parking lot overlooking the ocean, but he didn't make a move to get out of the car. I thought he wanted a moment to enjoy the scenery around us—listening to the wind, the squawking and squealing of seagulls. Watching the white caps ride the water to the sandy beach.

I turned to him after a few moments, puzzled to see his knitted brow, a serious look on his face. His mind was some place else. He stayed deep in thought for a few minutes. I wondered: Where's his mind at?

I hesitated to intrude into his thoughts so I opened the door to get out and stretch my legs. He'd come out when he was ready.

But then he spoke. His words all in a rush: "Luna, I'm getting married. I wasn't alone on those trips. I went with someone else." Just those words. Still facing forward to the ocean. No excuses. No attempt to soften the blow.

I pulled the door close again. Inside the claustrophobic confines of the car, the howling wind and the slapping waves on the sand—muffled a moment before—suddenly grew deafening.

Breathing hard and incapable of words, I watched him for a minute or two. I couldn't bear for *him to say more. I gazed out toward the horizon, to the limitless ocean.*

We both kept silent, frozen in place. A few minutes later he said he had gone on his first allegedly solitary trip with the woman and "things just happened." The agitation was gone from his voice and he droned on.

He had met her only a few weeks before they went on a trip together, when a mutual friend had introduced them to each other. She had told him of her dreams of going on a trip to Europe and teased him about joining her. He thought Europe might be fun and he'd always wanted to go. School was over for him and he needed a break before getting a job. A few weeks later, they planned and went on that first trip together.

They were together again on what I had thought was Scott's second solitary trip this past holiday season. A few weeks after the long holiday trip, she told him she was pregnant. She also told him she loved him at first sight and confessed to have done all she could to make him fall in love with her. How could he turn his back on someone who had given him everything she had to give?

He told me all this without so much as a glance at me.

I was barely listening to him by then. I chose to drown out his words with an inner voice that told me I could not change what had already happened.

"Take me home," I said when he stopped talking. I thought I was calm but maybe I only felt numb. I said no more, though I wished I could get out and run as far away as I could from him.

About an hour later, he turned the engine off in front of my parents' house. I said as I opened the car door, "We never had the chance to stroll on the shoreline trail." His head jerked toward me, confusion in his eyes. I was aware my remark was odd, one nobody would have expected after what just passed. But I wanted him to glance at me at least once before we parted forever.

Outside the car, I said as I held the door, "Did you ever love me?" Before he could answer, I banged his car door on him. I was proud of myself for having enough self-control not to shout, curse, or cry.

Even alone in my room, I didn't cry. I sat on my bed, mulling over the last hour. He had been seeing her, this unknown woman he couldn't resist, all the time he was telling me he missed me. When we nearly broke up because he was jealous of Tony, a friend I'd known years before I met him, was he already fishing for a reason to break up?

Did he give me a single thought on those trips? Why couldn't he have told me the truth right from the start? I would have preferred honesty, and maybe it wouldn't have hurt as much. I can accept he fell in love with this girl. They shared so much time, so many experiences together, and it was probably bound to

*happen. But why lie to me about it? For a whole year.
How could he continue to tell me he loved me when he
was already having an affair with his travel
companion?*

*Why couldn't I have said these things to him
that time in Doran Beach? How could I fail to see he
had been drifting away since the very first trip he
took? Maybe I couldn't believe he was leaving me.
How dumb could I get?*

*Grandma's passing away is, for me, a greater
loss than breaking up with Scott. But Grandma's loss
wasn't unexpected. I watched her growing older and
more feeble every year and I was aware the inevitable
day would come when I could no longer hug her, smell
her, hear her voice, enjoy her mango salad.*

*I miss Grandma in a way I couldn't miss Scott. I
sense her presence wherever I am. She's looking after
me even from her grave. It's ironic but lucky for me
that in grieving her loss, I've had to face myself.
Confront my anger against Scott. Confront my anger
at myself for trusting too much, for failing to see what
was going on.*

*I've immersed myself in memories I'll always
treasure growing up with Grandma. Knowing I'll
never see her again, I've grieved. But in grieving, I see
the truth: My stupid attempt to be reasonable. To
think of myself as too civilized to be angry. To deny
that I was betrayed.*

Now I can admit I've been angry at Scott, angry at myself as well. I harbor regrets about what I should have done or not done in our relationship. But I can't let these emotions continue to simmer. So I'm shouting them out: I hate you, Scott.

These past long days of inevitable loss and grief have freed me, made me eager for what lies ahead. I'm determined to emerge from this experience, this chapter of my life, a little wiser.

Thoughts had flowed out of my pen in one long stream and my wrist and thumbs tingle from writing. I read what I wrote and sadness—not anger, but maybe self-pity as well—overcome me once more.

I have said exactly what I think and feel. Nothing more needs to be said. With this entry, I can close the door on Scott and my naïveté. Or can I? Why do I have this nagging feeling that Grandma still has something to teach me?

I recall the letter Grandpa wrote Grandma. It's not that different from my journal. It uncovers a secret—another episode of unfaithfulness. But that episode ended on a more hopeful note.

Was it because Grandma dared to do something out of character to get what she wanted? She took a lover to retaliate, an audacious act that forced Grandpa to face what he could lose if he kept up his affair. He ended it. Grandma—who Mom and Auntie Juanita thought was meek and not assertive enough—did what she could and she won.

But me—what did I do? I shrunk, content to deceive myself into thinking I was reasonable and civilized. Truth is humbling. And exhausting.

I close my journal. Turn off my lamp. Back in bed, I whisper to the darkness, "You're a jerk, Scott. And I was weak, but never again."

The next morning, I wake up and realize I slept through the night. The first night of deep, uninterrupted sleep since Scott dumped me. Incredulous but happy to wake up feeling fresh, not restless like I've done for too many weeks.

I stay in bed a few minutes more. I love how tranquil it is. And the soft bluish light filtering through the blinds is enchanting. Early morning has a gentle murmur to it and I will let it wake up my senses, one by one. Then I'll flex my limbs and my whole body will spring into action.

In the evening, I tell Mom Scott and I are through. We broke up months ago, and he has married someone else.

She cries, "Oh no. Why did you wait this long to tell me?"

"Can't say exactly why, Mom, but I'm over it now."

"It might not have been as hard on you if you talked to us or to Jun about it."

"I should have, but I didn't. I think I grew up, though."

Mom looks into my eyes before she pulls me close and embraces me. "I'm glad you came out of it unscathed. But you know your dad and I will always be here. Please don't wait too long to tell us if you need comforting or someone who'd listen."

"Or give me advice," I say, smiling.

Mom laughs. "That, too."

Lucien

It's been a while since Luna sent me a message cancelling our dinner date. A message which, unexpectedly, disturbed my usual calm. I kept to my cubicle at work and, for a day or two, I couldn't seem to progress on my latest project.

A few days later, another came. I read it eagerly. I thought I'd never hear from her again and I had been sad. Would I never find out what happens to the young woman I came to know through a black Moleskine journal?

This recent message was brief. Her grandma passed away and she was in Honolulu.

I replied, expressing my sympathies for the loss of her grandmother. I understood how much her grandma meant to her. Luna responded with a simple "Thanks."

I didn't tell her I've been through inconsolable grief losing my paternal grandparents. Their influence on me might have been as profound as her grandma's has been on her.

The holidays have come and gone. We haven't texted each other, if only to exchange obligatory holiday greetings. Luna doesn't know I think of her a lot. She might not care if we never meet again. But I can't bear for that to happen. I send her a short message.

If you need shoulders to cry on, someone who can understand your grief, I'm only a phone call away. I've mourned beloved grandparents. Twice.

She answers. Within minutes—which surprises me. I was getting convinced she wants nothing more to do with me. She texts me back: "Thanks."

I choose to believe there's promise in it.

*****

I've been bouncing from one task to another at work. I usually take pressure in stride. Lately, though, I'm stressed out. Nearly missing deadlines. I thought I needed time off. But out of the office, I'm even more restless. Waiting for some big thing to happen, though I can't say what it is.

I've been alone since I came back from volunteering at Habitat in Guatemala ten years ago. Except for occasional times when I seek the softness, the sweet surrender of a woman, I've been unattached. Partly because of the intense study and work architecture exacted of its students and practitioners. But mostly, I'm alone by choice. That's what I tell myself, anyway.

Architecture school was intense. Since I finished school, life has eased up, though not by much. My focus for the last three years has been on work and building a portfolio on which to base a private practice. Then I found and read the Moleskine journal. Now, I wonder: When I busy myself with work and get lost in routine—justifying it as necessary to the unrelenting demands of creative work—am I actually avoiding having to face what's missing in my life?

For the few months I had it, the journal was like a companion to me. I went out less often on dates with different women.

Within the journal resided a friend. One who believed life had meaning worth living for. In her own way. As she searched for herself, probed into her inner heart, struggled to define who she wants to be, Luna opened her soul.

In that soul, I saw a certain hunger. A hunger I once had. Luna's belief in a soul mate who could give her life the fullness she longs for has awakened wishes I had long buried.

I've channeled that hunger into my career. But are all my hopes and dreams invested in it?

In her journal, Luna said she no longer believed in a soul mate after she broke up with Scott. I harbored that belief when the future I dreamed of with Minah, my first love, died. The irony is instead of agreeing with what Luna asserted in her journal, it rekindled my faith in a soul mate.

Now, no matter how fulfilled and satisfied I tell myself I've been, I realize my hunger for all life can offer has lived on. I've merely pushed it somewhere in the depths of my mind.

As long as the Moleskine journal didn't morph into flesh and blood, I was content. I didn't have to confront what I'm missing. But the journal did come alive. It metamorphosed into full living color. Flesh and blood pulsating before me and, later, in my imagination. I thought when I finally found the journal writer, I could continue a fulfilling existence creating for others. Chalk up the Moleskine journal to a pleasant interlude in my relatively young life. One I'd never forget.

Lately, though, I've been spending time reflecting. I'm in the business of making certain dreams come true. And making dreams come true relies on a long, drawn-out social process. Talking frankly to clients. Articulating desires they're unable to tell me. Working with people from different disciplines. The social demands of fulfilling dreams have served me a little too well. Giving me all I thought I could ever want out of a social life.

The trouble is, as I work, I see Luna staring at me. I can't shake her off.

What if I lay my mind and my heart open to her? Only fair, I tell myself. I snooped into her soul. Maybe she'd feel less vulnerable, less uneasy with me if she could look into mine.

Tonight, I'm writing my journal. My first attempt to build a bridge where I hope Luna will meet me.

*****

I've stayed up past midnight. My journal is finished. The send arrow to whisk my message and my journal through the ethernet is waiting. But I hesitate to hit it. The journal is longer than I intended. That's not a problem.

What bothers me is, while I was writing, I felt as if I was cutting my chest. Exposing my soul, my vulnerabilities. I ended up writing about what I believe people should know about me. What would Luna think of the person I'm exposing for her scrutiny? Will it be enough for her?

I thought I no longer cared for what any young woman would think of me, but the little green arrow curving upward is an icon of pointed accusations—she's disturbed you. Muddled your ordered existence. Do you dare send it?

I see her again—flushed, a little breathless as she ran after me. Her dark hair caught in a clasp, swinging like a horse's tail.

Luna

In the fragile calm of the past week, I received an
email from Lucien. Attached to the email is a
document.

*Here's to evening the score between us.
Anyway, I hope this journal does it. I wrote it solely
for your benefit. It's more condensed than yours, but
how many words do I really need to sum up my life?
It's not handwritten like yours. You can call it an
ejournal. Read it? Please?*

I'll read it. As wary as I've become, I'm hesitant to
be drawn into someone else's life. But Lucien pried
into mine without my permission. Now, he's offering
to open his soul to me. That might "even the score,"
like he says. But I'll be the judge of that.

He's smart, funny, and confident—enough to
make me curious. That he seems to be caring and
charming, disconcertingly so when he has the mind to
be, makes him quite attractive. On the surface at
least. But does he harbor demons in his breast that
trouble him? Does he talk about them? Or if he
doesn't, could you read them between the lines?
Inquiring minds want to know. Still, I hesitate to click

on the link to Lucien's journal. I need to be in the right frame of mind.

Several nights later, after a good day selling books and chatting about them with browsers, I find myself ready earlier than I thought. I'm tired but as I'm changing for bed, a text message arrives from Auntie Celia: *The flowers on the mango tree have formed into tiny fruit!* That's all—a short astonishing message of hope and wonder. Possibly, a miracle to cap off my day. The tree has been barren for thirty years.

Instead of a book, I take my laptop to bed. Snuggled under warm covers and propped up on two pillows, I send a short reply to Auntie Celia: *Crossing my fingers.*

I open Lucien's email and click on the attached ejournal.

Lucien's Journal

Like you, my grandparents—on my father's side—shaped my growing-up years. Before I started school, I passed my days with them while my parents went to work. Every time my parents' schedules became hectic, I'd sleep over at my grandparents' house.

I didn't go to kindergarten. Nana and Gramps homeschooled me for a couple of years. When I enrolled in a school—to socialize with my peers my parents said—I went to one in Nana and Gramps's neighborhood so I could walk to their house after school. Those were happy years. My grandparents— former hippies—were fun to be with.

Gramps was full of stories. He said he met Nana at the Woodstock music festival in the Catskill Mountains. Woodstock was both "wild and mellow, fun and mystical, and it set their spirits free" along with the several hundred thousand young people who were there. For years, Gramps talked about all the performers they saw, the people they met, a couple of whom they kept in touch with for years. He sang songs he remembered from the festival. Gramps had a good voice and could carry a tune well.

You might be delighted to know they spent a few Christmas holidays in the early seventies in Honolulu. Why? To "groove" on New Year's Day at the Sunshine Festivals at the Diamond Head crater. That's where they first tuned out on magic mushroom sandwiches.

They "shacked" up, Nana said, when they were twenty, and married six years later when she got pregnant. They blew their meager savings to pronounce their marriage vows in Japan. At the Miyajima shrine, they faced the Torii gate set a few yards away in the sea and swore to love each other as long as they lived. That pledge of love, in fact, was what fueled their life.

Inspired by stories of their adventures, I dropped out after my first semester at the university.

Told my parents I wanted to embark on my own adventure.

I still have vivid memories of that afternoon: Dad is glaring at me, his jaw clenched. Mom is scowling. Dad snatches my math book on the dining table. Bangs it so hard even Mom is startled. He says, emphasizing every word, "You are going to stay in school."

He stormed out of the room and didn't talk to me for a whole day. I was sure my first big passion was dead.

I was depressed.

Then Gramps and Nana got in on the argument. They believed in my quest for adventure—enough, in fact, to talk to their son, my Dad. They were quite persuasive. He relented.

Maybe it helped that my grandparents told him they would give me an allowance to do what I wanted to do for as long as two years. In exchange, I promised to return to the university once I've satisfied my wanderlust.

Nana said, "I never understood why people wait until they die to pass their legacy on to their children. We want to see you enjoy it now to help you discover your own groove."

I was eighteen—innocent and ignorant. Taking Gramps advice to travel light, I stuffed a few underwear and shirts, a couple of jeans, a camera, and my laptop in a backpack to wonder at and wander through the national parks. I'd hop on a Greyhound bus from one destination to the next. At night, I stayed at youth hostels.

Exploring nature was awesome. You'd know what I'm talking about since you grew up in Hawaii. But I got bored after three months gazing at grandeur. I was hungry for social interaction—to stay longer in places I visited and mingle with locals.

Gramps suggested festivals, so I googled "festivals." I started with a few pow wows, thinking that I should get better acquainted with Native American culture. Then I tried gatherings unique to certain states. I had a fun, eye-opening six months. From testing my patience sitting through Shakespeare plays at an Oregon festival to getting sick gorging on scallops in Cape Cod.

I'd strike up conversations whenever I could. Not only at festivals, but also at fast food places where most locals ate. I asked people I met if I could take their pictures, a request they agreed to more often than not and led to exchanging stories and phone numbers.

I listened to a lot of stories and told a lot of my own, met diverse groups of people and witnessed the many different ways Americans celebrate national and local traditions. My experiences were teaching me about life and people in this country, an education no formalized program could ever give me.

My journey awakened my curiosity about the rest of the world. I told Gramps and Nana I wanted to travel outside the US and they said, "Go for it. We wish we could have done more of that. So we'll live vicariously through you. Keep those emails coming."

Excited but apprehensive to explore unfamiliar territory, I set out for England where I would at least understand the language. But it was somewhat of a shock to hear English spoken there. Many times, the British and I seemed to be speaking different languages. They might as well have spoken French—I understood about as much.

I liked London, but I couldn't afford to stay as long as I would have wanted. Everything seemed twice as expensive. Mercifully, general admission to national museums was free.

It's a beautiful world-class city, but I'm sorry to admit, not exotic enough for me. Business districts in the city were full of things American— McDonald's, Burger King, Pizza Hut, Starbucks. In fact, Starbucks seemed to dominate the coffee industry in tea country. You could find it at every corner.

Theater, like tea, to me, is also iconically London. So, of course, I thought I had to go. But the price of entry as well as the theater fare spoiled my plans. Hollywood, California and Broadway, New York invaded theater programs. Most musical productions and even dramas currently showing in London originated in those American cities. I wanted to watch a *Shakespeare play. There was one with Dame Judy Dench, All's Well That Ends Well. Unfortunately, last-minute tickets required paying through the nose. I decided to conserve my resources.*

I also went to Oxford to experience the atmosphere that produces England's intellectual elite. And Bath because everybody else did. But I only stayed a day in each.

From England, I flew to Paris where I hopped on a train on a straight run to Berlin. I had no fixed itinerary. But with a laptop, a downloaded copy of the Lonely Planet, and places I heard about from travelers I met in hostels, I often figured out my next destination one or two days before I boarded a train to anywhere.

Europe was an easy trip. I could get to most cities and towns via efficient train systems. France, in particular, had (and still has) fast trains (the TGV-Trains à Grande Vitesse). They could whizz through the country at more than two hundred mph. It also helped that I wasn't picky about service and accommodations, and I found an association of hostels with a booking site on the internet. Unless some popular event was going on in a town or city, I always found a room or a bed to sleep in.

For three months, I crisscrossed continental Europe from northern France to Poland via Germany and the Netherlands, looping back to southern France through the Czech Republic, Austria, and Italy. From Nice, France, I boarded a train to Spain and Portugal.

I can tell you more about these places next time we meet. This was my first time traveling, and I stuck with the usual tourist sights about which you can read much on the internet. I wanted to stay longer in certain cities. Hungry to explore as much as I could. But I had a limited budget and intended to see Asia as well.

I ended my European journey in Paris where I stayed a month. Paris is a seductive city, and contrary to certain American prejudices, I found Parisians friendlier than the average American. Merchants in bakeries, cheese shops, delicatessens, small corner stores selling all sorts of things, and even strangers I met on a street where nobody else was around, greeted me, "Bonjour monsieur."

True, it was different in the big stores or on a busy street. Everyone went about their business ignoring everyone else. I got bumped on the shoulders many times on Rue de Rivoli and Boulevard Haussmann. Anyway, when you're away from home, you're always somewhat on guard, particularly if you don't know the language. In Paris. Or in Florence. Or Amsterdam. Or London.

Why stay longer in Paris? Because Gramps and Nana visited it once and infected me with their enthusiasm for it. To them, Paris was the center of the cultural world. They both loved art and Nana, an

art history teacher, said they regretted not spending
more time at the museums and walking around the
sites where art revolutions took place. They stayed a
week and wished they stayed months.

The Bohemians in mid-1800s Paris captivated
Gramps and Nana the most. To them, being creative
is at the heart of being human. Being alive. It allows
people to defy conventions. Gramps said a Bohemian
lifestyle no longer existed, but if one were to try to
live it, Paris was the place to be.

By then, I knew that one month was not enough
to absorb the vibes in any place, but maybe with
Gramps's stories, I could visit the places he talked
about and get a deeper sense of the free, artistic life of
Bohemians.

I didn't learn how to live like a Bohemian during
my month in Paris. One could say I got derailed by a
brief, no strings attached, torrid love affair (my first).
I was eighteen, my hormones in full working order.
And chance presented me with a woman who was
banking on those very hormones.

From my grandparents' stories, I believed
whiling away hours in a café on the left bank was
essential to being a Bohemian. So on my first day in
Paris, I went to Le Départ on Place Saint-Michel,
partly for its location by the Seine with a view of the
Notre Dame Cathedral and partly for its past as a
meeting place for writers and artists in the early
twentieth century when it had been Caveau du Soleil

d'Or. (McDonald's and Starbucks have also found their way in Paris). While I was drinking in the whole café scene to store in my memory bank, this lady walked in. She was somewhat plump but shapely and attractive. Long blond hair, fair skin, lively pixie features, and very red lips.

She took a table across from mine. From where she sat, the cathedral on the other side of the river took up more than half her visual field. But she kept glancing at me.

Fifteen minutes or so later, she picked up her cup and bag and approached my table. She sat down and said she could tell I was American.

She turned out to be British, a romance writer who rented a "flat" every summer by Canal St. Martin, a manmade body of water that feeds into the river Seine (which divides Paris into the left and right banks). Daytime, she went to various famous cafés and wrote her stories. At night she had fun. We talked for more than an hour, after which she asked if I wanted to walk her back to her apartment. I couldn't refuse. She invited me in, of course, and I stayed until the following morning. We saw each other every night after that. I had a month's reservation at a hostel, but I never slept there again. Yes, she was older, maybe by about twenty years—a vibrant, fun, lusty lady who taught me a lot.

*I've never read her novels. I rarely read fiction—
no time. But I wonder sometimes if our short affair
ever made it into one of them.*

*At the end of the month, I left for Hong Kong.
A little more worldly, I hoped. On one leg of my flight
from Paris to Hong Kong, I sat next to a couple
taking a brief break from volunteer work at Habitat
for Humanity, a charitable group building housing for
people in less-developed countries. I was curious
about Habitat and asked the couple many questions.
My travels had, by then, sparked a growing
fascination with buildings and monuments.
Fascination that intensified in Paris*

*From Hong Kong, I went to Beijing and
Shanghai, then to Osaka in Japan. I went straight
from Osaka to the magnificent historical cities of
Kyoto and Naga before going to Miyajima where I
wanted to see the Torii gate for myself. Tokyo was my
last stop in Japan and I stayed only a day. A bustling,
crowded and modern city, Tokyo was like too many
other metropolitan cities I'd seen. The Buddhist
temples and Shinto shrines of Naga and Kyoto were
much more interesting and someday, I would like to
return for a more leisurely trip.*

*From Japan, I went to Bali (Indonesia), and
Kuala Lumpur in Malaysia. Asia was, to me, exotic
and strange. Had to be, I suppose. I developed a
special interest in the ancient monuments. I couldn't*

stay too long so I included countries in Southeast Asia in my must-return list.

It had been a somewhat dizzying tour because I wanted to see so much. I learned to eat things new and strange to the Western palate (e.g. sea cucumber, jackfruit, mangosteen, salty fermented anchovies, grasshopper, innards. Drew the line on bull testicles, worms, dog and cat). Saw plants (mostly in Southeast Asia, e.g., carnivorous pitcher plants, flaming red torch ginger, and mimosa pudica, a plant with leaves which fold together when you touch them); and sea creatures (in aquariums) I didn't know existed. Tried to adapt to customs and rituals I found quaint but pleasing.

My travels opened up my world, showed me so many other ways one could live. And think. And love and hate. But they also made me feel small. Traveling to vastly different cultures is exhilarating and transformative. But it's also sobering, and occasionally scary.

I went home, questioning how I wanted to live my life and stayed home to reflect and get my energy back a couple of months. It actually felt strange being home and it took me those months to regain my full American self. But I grew restless. The itch to go somewhere far and exotic hit me again. By then, my allowance had dwindled. I could pay for a round-trip airplane ticket, but not much else.

But the itch was strong and I left again. Not to travel, though. Dad said he'd help fund my trip when I told him I wanted to volunteer for work at Habitat for Humanity's Global Village program in Guatemala. A year later, I spent two weeks relaxing in Kauai and another two weeks hiking on the leeward side of Oahu. Who knows? Maybe you and I crossed paths in the month I was there.

When I returned home, I fulfilled my promise to my father to return to the university. But I switched from computer science to architecture. I mostly aced the course work, finished it in four years (yeah, I'm bragging—don't do that too much), used my year at Habitat toward the requirements for licensure, and passed the exams. Seven years of challenge, hard work, and dealing with doubts and shortcomings for the privilege of creating beautiful, lasting spaces and objects people could take pleasure in while using them.

Lucien

Some minutes past two o'clock. I'm at Peet's devouring a book I've been meaning to read. Someone drags the empty chair across from me away from my table. Chair legs grating at concrete for an annoying few seconds. Destroying my concentration. Clenching my jaw. Scowling, I look up.

Luna. A smidgen of a smile, ill at ease. "Hello, Lucien. I'm not disturbing you, am I?"

My scowl vanishes into a wide smile. "Luna! A wonderful surprise. No, no. I'm glad you're here. I thought I'd never see you again. Please sit down." I close the book, lay it down on the banquette, and move my cup closer to me to give her space on the table.

She's dressed in a black skirt and a yellow T-shirt adorned with the dark gray silhouette of a running bunny. A bunny smiling like a clown. Has she chosen the funny bunny to draw attention away from her eyes? They seem larger and darker. Muted sadness? Lingering pain from her grandma's death? I'm sure it must have hit her hard.

I wave a hand toward the service bar. "Can I get you some coffee?"

"Thank you, no. Been drinking tea all morning. I'll drown if I have another drop."

"How are you, Luna?"

"I'll survive. Still learning, growing up." She smiles. More at ease now, but rueful.

"We all are. I hope to keep growing. Maybe not physically, though." A lame attempt at lightness, but it's all I can think of.

"No, not taller, anyway." A momentary twinkle in her eyes.

"I'm sorry about your grandma."

The smile falters. She blinks a few times. "She lived a good life and, anyway, we all get there, don't we? Sooner or later."

"You've been through a lot lately. I know your grandma meant so much to you." *I wish I could take you in my arms.*

"She did. Still does, wherever she is. She raised me, you know, until I was thirteen." Her eyes glisten from tears held back.

Let me hold you. All I say is, "I know. My grandparents practically raised me, too."

"Yeah, I saw. In your journal. It's why I came. To thank you in person. Must have taken you some time to write it."

"A fraction of the time yours took." Why do we minimize things important to us?

"Yeah, but I wrote mine for several years."

I shrug. Not an issue worth a minute more of our time. "I got to know you well through your journal. So I thought why not introduce myself the same way."

"It took me a few days to be in the right frame of mind to open the file and read it."

"I understand. All that matters is you took the time. Means a lot to me. I'm sorry it's longer than I expected. I hope I'm not such a stranger to you anymore."

A slight shake of her head as she probes into my eyes. "No, not anymore. You had pluck traveling around the world so young. How much freer you've been. Next to yours, my life's been quiet and sheltered. Limited. Constricted even."

"I had good models in my grandparents." Me? Freer? Doesn't feel that way anymore.

"I envy you," she says, her eyes wistful.

"But why? Someone has always been there for you." I'm used to having no one. I seldom visit my divorced parents

"Don't get me wrong. I envy you, but I don't feel sorry for myself. I've been blessed to have a loving family."

"You have and you're young. Time's on your side."

"Yeah. I better not waste it."

"You don't have to do exactly as I did. Follow your own groove as Gramps would say. His advice is still good."

"I'll think about it."

"Well, don't think about it too much. It's an adventure, plunging into something you think is out of character for you. Can be scary. So start small. Do something new. Go some place exotic. Things get easier after that." I'm on a roll, speaking from experience.

Luna nods, but averts her eyes. "I'd like to break out of my shell. Go places like you did. Experience strange unknown cultures. But I confess my stomach turns, thinking of going out there, out of my comfort zone."

"You go to Hawaii every year. Try another Pacific island." I couldn't stop a surge of irritation. "And—at the risk of repeating myself—stop thinking about it too much."

Luna looks away again. She's hurt. And regretting that I hurt her is too late.

"You know, I realize just now," she says, brow knitted, eyes narrowed. "I read about your adventures, but I don't really know you—I mean, not in any depth. Maybe I need details."

My turn to chafe at her remark. "True. Your journal is full of reflections about life. I was busy going places, doing things. Had no time to think. Maybe that's all I am."

What thin skins we have. It's not a beginning to fuel hope.

"Maybe, but I doubt it." She pushes her chair back, picking up the bag she set down on the floor. Her hurt lingers.

"Don't leave. Please. I'm sorry if I offended you. Stay a while longer." I want to reach over, enclose her hand in mine but since Minah in Kuala Lumpur, I've been more cautious.

Luna stares into my eyes. Deciding, saying nothing. I stare back at her, contrite, pleading.

A long, uncertain moment later, a hesitant smile twitches her lips. "How about that dinner? An amicable one. I'd like to hear your philosophy of life."

I grin, relieved, but more than that—surprised. She hasn't ruled me out yet. "You mean you're okay listening to me drone on? Meeting the 'Me' inside this physical shell?"

"You do have secrets, don't you? Or dreams you wish would come true?"

"What good are secrets if you reveal them? I am a WYSYWYG—what you see is what you get." *True for now.*

She purses her lips. "I doubt that. Anyway, how about this Saturday night? Short notice, but I decided two minutes ago to be more open, start doing some things on impulse."

"Really? Just like that?"

"Just like that." She laughs. "Funny how that's all it takes. We're our own worst enemy. But I admit I'm nervous being so forward."

"Can we choose another day, though? I'm seeing someone Saturday."

She lifts a hand toward her face but halts it halfway, dropping it on her lap. "Oh, I'm sorry. I should have known. I don't want to get between you and your girlfriend. Forget it."

I shake my head. "No, no. I'm not in any serious relationship at the moment. Haven't been in one for years. Someone I met a few days ago. First date. She asked me out actually. How about Sunday night?"

She glances at me, eyes twinkling in amusement. "Two dates on one weekend? With two different women?"

I chuckle. "What more could a guy ask for? But ours isn't exactly a date, is it? More like a buddy night out chatting about life, comparing how we see it."

Luna takes her cell phone out and checks something. A calendar, I suppose. "Right. All right. But we go dutch and nothing fancy. I'm a poor graduate student."

"Okay. How about we get some sandwiches. Take a walk around Lake Merritt?"

"How about I make us a little picnic and we go earlier? Sunday's weather forecast seems ideal for a little picnic—mild, sunny and no rain." She shows me the weather forecast on her cell phone.

Luna

We're walking along a path of concrete on the edge of the lake, Lucien carrying my empty picnic basket and a blanket he keeps in his car trunk to spread on the grass, and I, a quarter-full bottle of the wine he brought as his contribution to our picnic.

Bay Area weather is once again asserting its capriciousness. Our perfect afternoon is being swept away by fog and a moist brisk air. Park visitors are drifting back to wherever they came from. Only a few solitary souls remain, lolling under trees on the patch of grass next to the path.

Shivering in our light sweaters, we're among the last couples to leave our comfortable perch on a verdant patch under a large shady tree away from traffic. We're reluctant to surrender our good view of the lake. Neither of us knows nor has suggested where we're going next. But we both sense that we're not yet ready to part for the evening.

It has been a very pleasant afternoon. I've been intensely curious about Lucien's voyage discovering the world and I asked him to tell me more about it. Between mouthfuls of roast chicken, he recounted his adventures in such colorful, lively detail that I was entranced. My desire to see for myself at least some of the places he has seen grew with every new town or city he described.

"Do you live far from here?" I ask as we veer away from the lake and toward the parking lot where we left his car.

"About four miles. My place is a few blocks from work in Emeryville."

Something that suggested itself to me as I listened to his stories has grown into a resolve the moment we left our patch of grass, a resolve that, for me, is daring. Grandma dared, so why can't I? My reason, though, is different.

I've never done anything impulsive, especially one that exposes me to someone I've only known a couple of months and seen less than half a dozen times. But something about Lucien and his stories plucked an inner chord in me that begs to be played out.

As I work up the courage to open my mouth, Lucien says, "What about I treat you to a few tapas and a couple of drinks at that tapas bar on Shattuck? They're open for a few more hours."

"Can we go to your apartment instead?" I say in a voice close to croaking.

He gazes at me under a knitted brow. He thinks I'm old-fashioned and uptight and what I asked is out of character. He's wondering if I'm aware of what my question could imply.

"We can, of course," he says after hesitating a few seconds. "There won't be the usual din of a drunken crowd. We can talk more freely."

The shadow of a frown lingers on his brow. He has agreed, but he's done so with some incredulity.

Minutes later, we're in his loft on the third floor of a renovated building with no elevator. A large, high-ceilinged open space enclosed within two solid-white walls, a back wall with a window, and a wall-to-wall floor-to-ceiling arched window facing the main street. Its dark floor of pockmarked, aged wood planks seems to disappear in shaded areas not hit by afternoon sunshine. There are no interior walls except those of the bathroom.

Furniture and cabinets, mostly white, define living, dining, office, and sleeping areas. A small kitchen is on a corner, with a window to a backyard garden.

I had not imagined how Lucien's apartment would be like, but now that I'm in it, it's not what I expected. Is it the openness of it that surprises me? It's a modern sensibility. How much easier it is to move around in it. And yet I feel ill at ease. Maybe what I'm going to ask him needs the reassuring comfort and privacy of smaller divided rooms with doors.

The loft is in a building that, Lucien says, was once a warehouse. Each of the top two floors has two loft apartments converted into living-work spaces for artists. The first floor houses a couple of offices and a store selling antique furniture and decorations from Asia. There had been plans for a roof garden, but it seemed the building was not engineered to support it. I listen, amused. He's an architect, obsessed with all that information.

Lucien leads me to the living area. "Make yourself comfortable. Can I get you something to drink?"

"A glass of cold water, please."

He returns with two glasses of ice and two bottles of water. "Sparkling or still?"

"Still is okay."

"Great. I get the sparkling." Lucien flashes his dimpled grin, like a boy rewarded with the candy he wanted. He hands me one bottle. He's taken off his sweater and rolled up the sleeves of his shirt up to his elbows. I can't help noticing the hair on his arms.

I laugh. I am a bit nervous. "If you prefer sparkling, why get still water at all?"

"Some of my visitors prefer still. Like you."

He sits next to me on the long couch, an arm's length away. He has put some distance between us. Does he sense my unease? Has he guessed what I'm about to ask? He turns his head toward me. "Do you really want to listen to more of my travel adventures? Aren't you bored yet? I've been regaling you with them for more than two hours."

"You have so many exciting experiences. It's my life that's boring."

"I don't agree. You intrigue me, actually." He adjusts his body to face me, draping an arm on the back of the couch.

"I don't understand why. I've spent my life in only two places. California and Grandma's home in Honolulu and now that she's gone, I may never go back there."

I glance at his draped arm. He watches me, the shadow of a smile on his lips.

"First of all," —he pauses until I focus on his face again— "many people will envy you having lived in Hawaii. Second, you have aunts living there. Why can't you visit again?"

I shrug. "Maybe I'll visit Auntie Celia some day, but the reason I spent every summer there was Grandma."

"Does her passing away still hurt? Can you tell me about her?" His voice is tender with concern, and for an instant, it throws me off what I want to ask him.

"One of these days. I'm not ready yet," I say as I wonder again how to tell him what's on my mind— that daring request I'm determined to go through. If Lucien agrees, I believe it'll release me fully from Scott's hold. I've realized that my belated anger at him means he still has some power over me. I want to be free of that power; to think of him as nothing but a speck in my universe.

But more important than breaking free from Scott, the request is a kind of passage to help me break out of the constricted space into which I've boxed myself. A space so warm and comforting that it's too easy to get complacent in it. So complacent that I'll never want to leave it. But hearing Lucien's stories convinced me it's not where I want to be. I want a life larger than the box I'm now in. I want to experience as much of the world as I can, see how others have fashioned their lives to suit their desires and needs. Anyway, this is how I rationalize what I'm about to do.

We sit quietly for a minute or two. Lucien is waiting for me to speak. I take a deep breath, tell myself now is as good a time as the next to follow through on the dare I made to myself.

I shift my position to face Lucien. I wondered earlier if I should be blunt and forward. This moment, to me, is crucial. A blatant break from my usual style. and I was afraid I might falter.

I stare into his eyes. He's still waiting, his eyes demanding to know what I have to say. Rather than intimidate me, his gaze liberates the words from my mouth, "Would you make love to me?"

"What?" A mix of surprise, amusement, and disbelief is written on his face. And I'm astonished at myself that I found it so easy to ask him. Me, who's always thought sex is something you do only with someone you love.

"I don't mind if you refuse. I know I've asked you for something you never expected. If I'm not your type, that's okay, too."

He stares into my eyes, as if he's trying to see deep into me to read what's really on my mind. I stare back, holding my body rigid to keep myself from retreating and running away.

He withdraws his draped arm, places his hand on his knee. "If I refuse, it isn't because you're not my type. I think you're very pretty, but your request has hit me like ... an eight-by-eight wood beam crashing on my head. Are you sure about what you're asking? And why me?"

"Why you is easier for me to answer. I don't know too many guys. Also, I know you better because of the unusual way we met. I've felt less shy, more relaxed with you quicker than I have with any other guys."

"Is that all?" he asks, a twinkle of mischief in his eyes.

As if on reflex, my gaze drops from his face to his body. His shirt doesn't bulge with muscles, but his square shoulders and flat stomach exude strength. A rush of blood warms my cheeks, but I force myself to meet his gaze again. "Well, I think you're sexy."

Lucien grins. "That's better. But do you understand what you're asking?"

"I'm not that naïve."

"No, you're not. One who agonizes over what she does as much as you do can't be that naïve."

"I know I'm... old-fashioned... kind of shy and it makes me wonder what I'm missing."

"So you want to break out of your shell by having sex with someone who's not your boyfriend?"

"Well, not just anyone. I'm not sure I'll ever be that free. I did think about this. Asked myself if it's forbidden for friends to make love. Then I told myself the answer isn't important if I mean to take a step against my usual cautious self. If I mean to break into relatively unknown territory, so to speak. Unknown to me, anyway."

"A bit too drastic for you, maybe?"

"Maybe, but just having the courage to ask you— for me, it's already a step forward."

He gazes into my eyes again, says nothing. I tense up once more, trying not to flinch. He rises to his feet after what seemed like forever, smiles, and offers me his hands. "Why are we still talking about it?"

This is it, I tell myself, rejoicing inwardly at my audacity. But the next moment, a flutter of nerves hits me, and blood seems to drain from my body. Can I go through with this? Did I actually expect Lucien to agree?

But I can't stop now. That would be a step back into my constricting box. I'd be throwing away an important victory I hadn't expected to win.

I put my freezing hands into his warm hands. He pulls me up and scoops me up in his arms—that surprises me.

In the space that passes for his bedroom, he puts me down on the bed and sits down next to me. I thought he was going to start kissing me but he doesn't. He watches me. Is he reconsidering?

He says, "Are you sure about this? We can stop this game right now, and I can take you home."

A game! How could he call it a game? I agonized over this. I had to summon up courage to ask him.

"No, this isn't a game. If you think it is or you find it distasteful, all you have to do is refuse. You won't hurt my feelings." I bolt off the bed, but before I can get away from him, he grasps my arm.

"The lady can have a temper. Please stay. I didn't mean it the way it might have sounded to you. I wanted to make sure you do want to go through with this. Please sit down."

I comply but keep my face turned away. I'm still peeved, but for some perverse reason, I'm even more resolute to follow this "game" through. Let it play out. It's a defiance of the usual Me. The Me who let Scott off the hook with not even a peep.

"I'm pretty sure you haven't had a one-night stand," Lucien says.

I shake my head. I'm not naïve, but neither would anyone call me experienced.

"One-night stands," he continues, "often happen between relative strangers. An affair for the night. An experience of the moment for the two people involved. Usually over when morning comes.

"You and I are no longer strangers. The morning after we do this, things may change between us. They may be awkward at the very least. Or you may regret what you've done and avoid me later. That, to me, would be tragic. I want us to continue to be friends. For a long time."

"So do I. I like the Lucien I met in your journal."

"That's only one scenario, though. What if we fall in love with each other because of this experience? Are you ready for that? Or what if only one of us does and the other does not?"

"We can talk about this to death. What if we just let it happen? Take the plunge, you said. I've had my heart broken. Grieved and survived it. If that's the worst thing that could happen after tonight, I think I can handle it."

I don't wait for Lucien to answer. I take his face in my hands and kiss his lips. I'm still feeling shaky, but inwardly triumphant again at my newly-found audacity.

Lucien

I've never been in bed at half past eight at night.
Unless I'm sick, which is a fairly rare occurrence. But
that's where I am. With the girl of the Moleskine
journal. She's sleeping. Peacefully, I think.

We had quite a workout. She surprised me.
Responsive to my every touch, though she could learn
more abandon.

She initiated our first kiss. I expected her to be
shy. Pull back when she realized she had aroused me
to a point of no return. I gave her a chance to retreat
at any minute before then, though I was hoping she
wouldn't.

If I confess nothing more beyond the fact that
Luna evoked long-buried memories of Minah, I won't
be totally honest with myself. With Luna, I tingled
again with the excitement of a first love.

But Luna is not Minah. Minah had her first sexual
experience with me, and she lay rigid and passive. It
took her a few encounters before she felt free to enjoy
my caresses. Even then, her responses were subdued.
A low occasional moan. A slight twitching of her legs
or her hips. On looking back, I realize she had never
been there the way Luna was with me tonight.

Luna isn't a virgin like Minah, but I can tell she has little experience. What surprised me—happily— was how willing she was to shed her inhibitions. Taking her cues from me and letting herself go. She clung and she moaned. Quivered and twitched. Even called out my name, "Oh Lucien. Lucien." What a turn-on that was.

Ever since Minah, my amorous encounters have often been shallow. It hasn't seemed to matter much. You get together with someone you find attractive. Lust takes over and for a while, it consumes you. Then you part. You may wonder if you'll see that person again, yet you take neither time nor effort to contact her again.

Tonight, with Luna, was different. I'm sure part of it is because I already knew her—quite intimately, I'd say.

Luna is the first woman I've cared about since Minah. And yet the connection isn't the same. Minah and I were nineteen and naïve. I'm ten years older. Wiser, surer of who I am and what I want. More in control and not as easy to succumb to another person's influence or charm. But when Luna gave herself to me so uninhibitedly that my body literally ached to possess her, I knew I was lost.

Later, as we lay together, still panting, I felt what I did was not to possess her but to surrender myself to her, to the two of us together. It wasn't just my body in union with hers. It was my whole being.

As I watch her sleep, the irony isn't lost on me that if only one of us suffers from love as a result of this encounter, that one would be me. When this evening is over, I'd keep wondering: Will there be a next time?

I watch Luna's tranquil face. My hand reaches out to caress her. But I hold myself back. I mustn't disturb her.

She stirs. Slowly opens her eyes. Pulls the sheet up to her shoulders. Shifts her body to lie on her side to face me. After our lovemaking, she's being unnecessarily modest. But old habits of modesty must take a long time to die.

She caresses my cheek, smiles, and says, "Thank you. You taught me something about myself this evening—a precious thing."

She comes closer and whispers in my ear, "I've learned I love making love, and I can do so without watching myself all the time. That I can do what I feel like doing at the moment."

"You're welcome, and thank you for telling me."

"You were wonderfully patient. When I first asked you, I was testing myself. What was important to me was I could dare to ask. I didn't think of what could happen if you accepted. But to me, tonight has been quite a revelation."

Luna doesn't need an answer. I kiss her forehead. Most men's egos would swell at such a "revelation." But its effect on me goes deeper. She's rendered me speechless with her frankness. I never knew that a woman admitting I pleased her and she appreciates it could affect me so deeply that I had to blink back the moisture in my eyes.

I hold her close for a while. Grateful that she seems content for us to just lie together in silence. I want to ask: *Will you feel the same way with someone else?* I realize that's my male ego talking and tell myself it's a question better left unspoken.

Luna sits up, clutching the sheet around her chest. Looks down on the floor by her side of the bed, searching for her clothes. "I have to go home. I work at the bookstore tomorrow."

I roll over on my side toward the edge of the bed. Pick up her clothes lying in a heap on the floor. I hand them to her.

"How about a little snack before I take you home? I'm starved and I have some good cheese," I say, sitting up to put on my pants. Am I'm trying to keep her with me a while longer?

"All right. I guess I'm hungry. Does making love do that to you?" she says, chuckling.

An hour later, after some crackers and cheese, I drive her home.

I stop at the loading zone by her apartment. We buss each other on the cheeks.

"Thanks again for what you've done for me today. It's an act of kindness." Her eyes shine. Do I see gratitude? Yes. More than that? I'm not sure, but I'd like to believe so.

"Luna," I say, laying my hand on her arm as she opens the car door on her side. "I didn't agree to make love to you to be kind. You must know you're lovely and alluring. If you've not been aware of it, then I'm telling you now. Most guys would have jumped at your invitation."

"Thanks for that vanity booster. But you aren't most guys. You took some convincing." She smiles and gives me a peck on the lips.

What does she mean "you aren't most guys"? She hasn't met many. Before I can ask, she's out the car door. She waves her hand. Bounds up the steps to the second-floor apartment she shares with Asha.

I don't move until the last glimpse I have of her graceful figure disappears behind her door. I'm alone once again. Pondering her remark.

If I was thinking only of myself, I would have asked Luna to stay the night.

Luna

Before the afternoon I dared to ask Lucien to make love to me, I received another text message from Auntie Celia:

The baby mangos are gone, maybe blown away by the wind or eaten by birds. So sad. Anyway, won't you come for a visit soon?

What does it really matter that Grandma's mango tree has remained barren? You can get mangos at most grocery stores nowadays. But I guess that's not the point. Auntie Celia's hope that Grandma's tree would fruit has some deeper meaning for her. Maybe she sees the fruit as a proof of her parents' devotion to each other. Or on a practical level, if the tree fruits, they won't have any reason to cut it down.

I believe that tree has served us in ways that mattered to us more than the fruit it could not bear. Grandma and I spent countless hours under its shade. Quiet hours. Hours when we were together, but absorbed in doing our own thing. Whenever Grandma sat under its shade listening to music, she might have been reminiscing, keeping Grandpa alive in her mind. To me, those hours have become precious memories. Memories I can summon not only when I miss her, but also when I'm alone and needing reassurance and counsel.

I text Auntie Celia back:

Auntie Celia, don't you think the mango tree is there to remind us of Grandma and Grandpa's enduring love? Maybe love is like that mango tree. We plant it expecting it to produce delicious fruit. But it doesn't. It gives great shade and shelter instead. It delights us with its beauty and robust health. We know it will live for generations. Do you really care that it has no fruit?

I'll plan on a visit, but it won't be soon.

No, it won't be. Can't be. Might be a while, in fact. How can I go into Grandma's house and not find her there? I hope, though, that what I said about the tree would keep it alive.

I have another reason for why I won't be returning to Grandma's empty house any time soon. I'm determined to break free from the shelter of my cocoon. Like a butterfly, I need to molt out of the old shell that protected me. I must fly away—leave behind my happy growing-up years in Honolulu; those days when I was just Person running after my brothers, watching my eldest brother, Jun, live life his way; the wonderful awakening of my first love and the pain from the betrayal that followed. I've learned from those experiences, so they've left more than memories.

They've marked me, indelibly. And as Mom likes to say, we keep on moving on.

Still, I remain a vague slate, even to me. All I know is Lucien is in it. And for now, his is the presence that looms large in my hazy world. A world up to me to shape.

The Sunday I spent with Lucien is a turning point. It's as if, on that day, I was anointed, welcomed into new territory. A territory more uncertain, maybe more dangerous, but also more exciting. Ready or not, I've committed to it.

For now, I have to write about the last two days. I want to remember them.

I pull my journal out of my lingerie drawer. It's been a few weeks since my entry about Scott dumping me. As painful as that experience was—along with Grandma's passing—it's the impetus for me to break out of my old sheltered world.

March 2014: Moving On

Change—one that satisfies—requires bold moves. Bold, according to your experience, because there are people like me, full of book knowledge and learned platitudes, who're inexperienced in the ways of the world. My bold move may be lame to the more adventurous among us.

I've never thought myself daring. Especially not when it comes to asking a relative stranger to make love to me. Enticing him with feminine wiles is even harder. I wouldn't know how to begin.

Lucien is different, though. Maybe knowing he's been privy to my innermost thoughts and apprehensions in this journal held back my usual inhibitions. Besides, he seemed so nerdy, caught within himself, and indifferent to his surroundings when I first met him that he didn't intimidate me. At least, not until a counter no longer stood between us and he stood glaring down at me.

Then we met at Peet's and I've since realized he's the most complex man I've known. It impresses me that he's been around the world. I think traveling to places strange to you leaves a permanent imprint in your psyche. I want to follow his example but in my own way. Plunge myself, as he puts it, into new experiences that matter to me.

Anyway, after I read his journal, I felt he was someone I could trust, a potential friend I could keep a long time. Then he showed me I can be passionate. For that, I owe him and I'm grateful. I will always treasure his friendship.

A few days later, I call my parents before their usual dinner hour.Mom, who answered the phone, says, "Wait. I'll turn on the speaker so your dad can hear what you have to say." A moment later, she continues. "Okay, you're on."

"I'm dropping out at the end of the school year," I say in a tone as matter-of-fact as I can manage.

I can picture Mom scowling and shaking her head. "Why would you do that?"

Dad says, "I can understand Mom's concern. It should take you just another year to finish your coursework and write a master's thesis."

"More than a year. I want to do something else. Books have ruled my life."

"And do what?" Mom sounds irritated.

My parents believe that if you're serious about a task, you plan it. "I'm working on a plan. Researching now. Finalizing when I have everything I need. Then I'll call you. Solemn promise."

The line is silent for a minute so I wait. Again, I picture them, their eyes exchanging messages.

Finally, Dad says, "All right."

I wait a while longer to hear what Mom has to say. "Well, it's your decision. But we would feel more at ease when we know in more detail what's going on with you. Would you share with us not only your plans but also what influenced your decision?"

Typical Mom. Still, I detect a change in her tone I find momentarily unsettling. She's gentler, and the pressure I feel when she tells me what she wants to know is subdued.

"Thank you, Mom, Dad. Like I said, solemn promise. I'll call as soon as I'm certain," I say, both bewildered and triumphant.

Dad says, "We appreciate it. You know you can count on us to support whatever you decide to do."

I'm grateful for Dad's accepting attitude. He has always been more open and forgiving than Mom, but it's Mom we first turn to when we have problems.

I'm not yet done, though. "Thank you, Dad. There's one more change ... soon." I pause for a few seconds, letting my words sink in. "Moving out of the cramped apartment I share with three graduate students at the university. I make enough now at the bookstore, and Asha, the girl I work with, has a vacant bedroom. More space and my very own. A short one-mile walk to campus."

"You're full of surprises tonight," Mom says. "So this girl also works at Minerva bookstore?"

"Yes. Longer than I have. Her roommate left. Asha couldn't afford to pay the rent on her own. We'll be helping each other out. You'll like Asha. Responsible, good-natured."

"Uh-huh. I take it she isn't a graduate student."

"No. Mom. Sorry, gotta go. We ordered pizza. It's here. Kisses to you and Dad."

I'm the only one home and eating leftovers. But I'm exhausted. I went to class, worked in the afternoon, and stressed out talking to my parents. Besides, I had nothing more to say of consequence to them or to me.

Lucien

Two weeks ago, Luna and I made love. I haven't seen her since. Nor have I called her or sent her a message. She hasn't called or texted me either. I try to convince myself I'm fine with the way things are between us.

The architectural firm where I work is small, closely knit. My colleagues are all married. They like to give dinners and little parties because that's the only way we could talk about things other than work. I'm the newest and youngest architect in the firm. I always get invited. Maybe because I'm an eligible bachelor they can introduce to their` single-lady friends. Once in a while, one of those lady friends and I spend the night together.

When I want casual company, I go to the many singles bars in the area, especially one I recently came across. An unusual one. They don't serve alcohol. They serve kava. An acquired taste derived from a South Pacific beverage. Makes you mellow, they say. I don't come for the drink, but for the camaraderie the owners cultivate among their customers. Unlike Peet's, we actually talk to each other. About sports, cultural happenings in the area, big news around the world, even subjects associated with our work.

Nothing personal. This kava bar is good for chilling out in the evening.

My life isn't a model for the American dream. But it's good. I don't intend to change any of it soon. At least that's what I tell myself. Until days pass when I don't see or hear from Luna.

By the end of the second month, I send Luna a short text: *Did I frighten you away?*

She texted right back:

I've been busy. I'll catch you at the coffee shop tomorrow or the day after.

True to her word, I see Luna sitting on the banquette when I get there the following day. Sipping coffee. Watching the entrance.

"Right on time," she says. "Are you on some kind of schedule? Please don't answer. Idle curiosity. I got you your café mocha." She pushes a cup toward me. Picks it up to hand it to me as I sit down on a chair.

"I didn't think you'd notice what I drank."

"Has a distinct aroma, that blend of coffee and chocolate. I order latte—milk without sugar. I like the bitter notes."

"Thank you." I raise the cup and sip. "You're looking good. Glowing. What's up?"

"I sent an application to the Peace Corps. I believe I have a good chance of going."

"The Peace Corps! How'd you come up with that?" *Easy, Lucien. Laying yourself bare.*

"Why not? You worked free for Habitat for Humanity. I'm getting living expenses. Not all of us have grandparents who'll bankroll our adventures. I applied to go to Southeast Asia, a place far away from here. Not only by distance but also by culture. That matters to me."

"Habitat is not your typical adventure. For me, it was work and lots of it. I'm sure the Peace Corps would be the same. But why Peace Corps? You're an English major. Why not teach English in some civilized place like Japan?" *I can't stop myself. I hope I don't sound hostile.*

Luna shrugs. "I will be teaching English and I prefer the Peace Corps."

"Are you sure you're prepared for this?"

"Better than you might think." I catch the same defiant note from when we first met at Peet's.

I shake my head. "It'll be a shock. You may have to fetch your water from a well, go for days without a bath, pee and poop in a smelly latrine, eat with your hands food you never thought of before as food, get sucked by mosquitoes already fat with other people's blood, do things you think are good but which people you help will resist. It can be a thankless, shitty job."

"I'll go through training before they send me on an assignment. Why are you trying so hard to discourage me?" She frowns.

I don't answer. But she's right to ask. *Why am I trying to discourage her?*

She says, "I expected you to be supportive. After all, it's you and your adventures that inspired me to want to go somewhere I can make a difference."

"Yeah, the Mother Teresa complex." *I'm in a bad way.*

Luna sips her café latte, clutching her cup. She looks both bewildered and hurt. "I'll leave if you're going to be like this, and I don't want to do that."

"Don't be so sensitive. Someone has to tell you it can be shitty out in the big bad world."

I could have edited out "don't-be-so-sensitive." But—too late. Then a disquieting flutter roils my chest. She's been encroaching into my sacred space. Space I've cultivated, belonging only to me. Space meant for my treasured solitude. And I've let her, maybe enticed her in. I've never allowed anyone in since Minah in Kuala Lumpur. Luna has crossed the boundary. Now she's leaving.

Luna snatches her bag off the banquette. "Thank you for everything. And good luck on whatever you're up to." Her bewilderment has turned into anger, and she's trying to control it. The hurt remains.

She rises. Walks away. I don't stop her.

Luna

Well, that's that. I lost the person I thought was going to be my cheerleader.

I was waiting to tell my parents about Peace Corps until I've consulted Lucien. I thought he could advise me on how to approach them since he had gone through the experience of convincing balky parents.

At six o'clock in the evening, I'm standing on the loading zone at the Long Beach airport, waiting for Mom. I called her from work this morning, said I had done my research, studied my choices, and am now ready to share my plans with them. Plans and decisions too momentous to discuss over the phone, even on Facetime. Face-to-face, you catch fleeting expressions, subtle gestures, meanings only the direct gaze can tell you. Without delay from flying through cyberspace.

Three hours later, Mom, Dad, and I sit at the dinner table. As usual, any important news or discussion has to wait until after dinner when dishes have been stacked in the dishwasher. Unlike previous times, I feel calm. No fluttering in my chest. No acid or bile in my gut. I'm beginning to feel less intimidated defying Mom's wishes.

I sit at the head of the table, the sacrificial throne for the lamb who announces a dream, a desire, a change, a grievance. Mom and Dad flank me on both sides.

Mom says, "So, Luna, what's your news?"

"My future after the end of this school year. Two years of Peace Corps service."

Mom, who has sat in relative calm against the back of her chair, leans forward. Resting her arms on the table, she turns toward me. "Oh?"

I decided being direct is the best way to tell my parents my news. Better to face their skepticism head-on— "You, Luna? What do you know about the world?" Or worse, their disapproval— "We won't stop you. But know that we're strongly against it."

"I've volunteered for the Peace Corps. I think they'll accept me," I say, my gaze darting between Mom and Dad.

They're taken aback, as I expected, and I have prepared arguments in my head to counter reasons they come up with to dissuade me.

Dad speaks first. "I assume you've looked into what it would take for you to do this volunteer work?"

"I have. There's a lot on their website. Mission, services they provide, countries where volunteers can go—stuff like that. Also, stories past volunteers have written of their experiences. People go on volunteer work to countries all over the world. They come back richer for the experience."

"So which part of the world will you go to do your good deeds?"

"I've been assigned to teach school children in Cambodia for two years."

"Cambodia!" Mom is aghast. "Isn't that where they had a genocide?"

"I didn't exactly have a choice on where to go, Mom. Cambodia is one of the areas with greatest need." I did express preference for a Southeast Asian country in my application, but omitting that little detail isn't lying. And Cambodia is where Peace Corps decided I should go.

Dad raises his palm a few inches from the table, a gesture directed at Mom, and says, "That should be interesting. Different than here for sure. Will the Peace Corps give you some training before they send you out?"

"They will. The first ..."

Mom interrupts. "But you don't speak their language."

"The assignment doesn't specify the need for language other than English, although I think all volunteers get language lessons for their assigned country. I'll learn some Khmer during orientation. I'll be teaching English as a second language to children."

Mom says, "Khmer Rouge, that's it. The communist government that murdered millions of civilians starting with their educated professionals. I saw it in the film *The Killing Fields*."

Dad raises his hand again. Mom leans back on her chair, crosses her arms, and stares at the table.

My parents often communicate with each other without speaking. I've noticed it since I came to live with them. A look, a raised hand, a mouth twitch, a subtle movement of the head or the body can substitute for words. Gestures only the two of them share. Mom is more vocal and active in dealing with us, but Dad—Zen-like in his fifty percent Japanese blood—is more in control of their shared decisions.

Dad says, "It's volunteer work, but are you getting a stipend?"

"Yes. For necessities. Plus housing."

Mom leans over the table again and says, "It's not that I object to your going. But you're my only daughter, and I don't want any harm to come to you."

I say, "I know Mom. But please don't worry. I'm determined to survive, and you've all taught me a lot. I'll learn even more from being out there in a world foreign to me. When I return, I can handle whatever life throws at me."

"I think you will. I'm sure you will. But will you be careful? Text us every day, if only to inform us you're alive, okay?"

I stared at her, incredulous. I didn't expect my news would be received with so little argument. Something has changed Mom.

I get up from my chair and give Mom a hug of gratitude. "I promise to text or email you as often as I can, tell you stories about the people I work with so you'll get to know them. Internet connection can get iffy, but I'll try and try till they're delivered."

She hugs me back and says, "I love you."

I know Mom loves me, but tonight is the first time I ever heard her say it to me.

Later, as I'm getting ready for bed, there is a faint knock on my door. I open it to see Dad smiling down at me. "Good you're not in bed yet. Two minutes?"

"Of course."

Dad comes in and closes the door behind him. "Your mom has been grappling with guilt feelings about your grandma since we got back from Honolulu. I think you know what that's about."

"Yes," I say.

Dad continues, "But that's not all, I think. She regrets having left you in your grandma's care all those years."

"There's nothing for her to regret. Grandma took care of me maybe better than she did her own children. And I think it made her happy that I was there with her."

"Yes, your grandma did a great job with you and I could see you were a joy to her the few times we visited. But knowing all that may not be enough to convince your mom what she did was okay."

"She was building a career, taking care of two little boys. I can see how stressful that must have been. Besides as I understand it, Grandma offered to help." What more can I say? No one but herself can fully assuage Mom of her guilt feelings.

"Maybe I'm also feeling guilty. I could have said something, but I didn't. We felt overwhelmed those early years, she much more so than me. She blamed herself for forgetting her pills, getting pregnant with Andy too soon after you were born. She also feels guilty misjudging and resenting her mom. Since the falling-out between them, she'd avoided contact with her. Now I see that's why she resisted taking you back sooner from your grandma."

I can't help wondering, though, why me and not Jun or Kana. Because a baby requires more work? Because Grandma was used to raising girls, and she might have chosen to take me instead of one of the older boys?

"I don't resent either of you for the decisions you made then. Maybe I would if Grandma had turned out cold and cranky, but she was warm and very loving. You couldn't have entrusted me to anyone better."

"We know that, but guilt and regrets don't go away. One of those things you can't easily atone for. You can only learn to live with it." He kisses my forehead and in a jaunty tone, says, "Anyway I believe you'll have a great adventure in Cambodia. When do you leave?"

"This summer. Most likely July."

"That's a few months yet. Come and say good night to your mom. She's already gone up to our bedroom. I think she's in low spirits."

Luna

Lucien Writes a Letter

Back at the apartment the day after, Asha is still up, glued to the television. She raises her hand in greeting as I walk by. Before I reach my bedroom, she yells above the blasting of guns from one of the action dramas she's fond of watching. "Oh, Luna!"

"Yeah? Need anything from the fridge?" I yell back.

"No, thanks. Some dude came looking for you this evening. Did you have a date and forgot about it?"

I retrace my steps back to the living room. "Wait, what? Who? Are you saying he came knocking on our door?"

Asha's gaze remains glued to the television as she answers. "Yeah. Tall. Adrien Brody in a mustache but without the hook nose. Nerdy, with glasses. But cute. Know anyone like that?"

"Lucien," I say, smiling. "Did he leave a message for me?"

Asha chuckles, throwing me a quick glance. "A letter! Imagine. Who writes letters anymore? It's on your desk."

"How do you know it's a letter?"

"Wrote your name longhand. Kinda thick envelope. I mean, if it isn't a letter, what else could it be?"

"Oh, I don't know. Personalized solicitations for money, ads, answers to an exam," I reply blithely. I can't imagine Lucien taking the time to write a letter by hand.

In my room, I close my door and sit in front of my desk, which is often cluttered with books, papers, and a laptop. Asha has raised the computer screen and propped the letter on its long end against it.

I turn the letter over in my hand, not quite convinced it came from Lucien after our recent not-so-friendly parting. Anyway, he would have called or texted me.

A little too eager to find out who left the letter, I accidentally tear thin pieces off the bottom edges of the letter along with the envelope.

The letter has four pages of handwritten sentences. I leaf through to the last page and there it is: *Sincerely, Lucien.*

Amazing! Wonderful. Here's a guy who sent me an abbreviated journal of his travel adventures in electronic form, and now he's written me a letter in a neat, sprawling hand. He has given his words space to breathe.

As I start reading, it hits me that this is only the second handwritten letter I've read in my life. The first wasn't even addressed to me but to Grandma.

Reading it, I felt like I was intruding into secrets only she and Grandpa had the right to know.

This letter from Lucien is addressed to me, the first ever. What could he have to say on all these pages? Will I finally learn some secret he's kept from everyone?

April 10, 2014

My dearest Luna,

> *First of all, I'm sorry.*
> *I hated myself for letting you leave in a huff. For reacting like an ass to something you obviously feel passionate about.*
> *Your news upset me somehow. I can't fully explain why. All I know is you're leaving. Going to a place where I can't reach you. The prospect of not seeing you for I don't know how long—maybe too long—is what I think I got upset about. Its reawakened memories of despair, fear, and confusion I've buried for ten years. I thought I had matured enough and gotten over them.*
> *My reaction puzzled me at first. What happened in the past is so different from the incident between us. At 19, that past episode in my life brought on a sense of profound loss and bewilderment that took a while for me to recover from. I was forced in a violent*

way to forget someone who meant the world to me at the time. Basking in the warmth of my grandparents' love and confidence in me, that incident devastated me, ate away at my trust in a world of promise and wonderful things.

I felt a similar sense of loss at the prospect I might never see you again.

Maybe you'll understand better what I mean if I disclose what happened ten years ago. It's an episode I left out of the journal I sent you. I've never told anyone about it, not even Gramps or Nana. Maybe it hurt too much to talk about it. Or maybe I wanted my family to continue thinking I was their golden boy.

I knew I wanted to erase the incident from my memory. But erasing a terrible memory never works unless you're afflicted by amnesia. Even then, it can come out in other ways.

In any case, you're the first person to hear this story. And maybe, after confessing this to you, I may be totally free, not of the memory, but of the trauma it had caused.

This episode took place in Kuala Lumpur, where I had planned to end my trip to Asia. From there, I would go to Hawaii to relax on the beach, sightsee at leisure, try surfing, and research my next destination. I had several months left on the allowance my grandparents set aside for me.

I survived Asia by gorging on street food so on my first day in Kuala Lumpur, starved and eager to

taste Malaysian street food—I joined the locals
waiting in line at a hawker's stall. An American
woman who I met at the hostel the night before said
the food here was good and filling.

A short, plump woman, about fifty, her brown
face glistening from the steam rising out of a large
pot, was dishing broth from the pot into a bowl and
filling it with two kinds of noodles. She'd hand the
bowl to a man, also short, plump, and fifty, who
garnished the broth and noodles with pork and prawn
slices, half a boiled egg, and some kind of spinach that
was cooked but still quite green. The whole sequence
was executed with the seriousness of a ritual. And the
bowl looked so fresh and scrumptious it made me
more aware of the painful void in my stomach that had
been growing since I got off the plane the night
before.

The line was long, and my stomach would growl
every few minutes, assaulted by aromas mingling in
the air from hawkers' stalls on every corner of the
street. This time, it growled loud enough that the
pretty girl standing in front of me craned her neck to
glance at my face and my stomach. I had seen many
pretty Asian girls but this one was a little friendlier
and her eyes had a flirtatious glint that seemed to
come naturally to her. She smiled. I smiled back.

But smiles didn't satisfy empty, unhappy
stomachs, and mine rumbled again. The girl turned
toward me once more. This time she spoke to me.

Malaysia was once a British colony, and many Malays spoke English, as this girl did. "Your belly can't wait, huh?"

"No," I said, embarrassed. "I haven't had anything to eat since last night."

She smiled in sympathy, dug into her purse, and handed me a small green package. "Here, this candy should keep you going." She scanned the line in front of us. "Only five more including me. You're almost there."

I took the candy and thanked her. I tore the package and popped what turned out to be tea candy into my mouth. I could survive five more customers ahead of me, but how could I have resisted such an offer from a pretty girl?

Before long, she got her bowl of noodles, and I got mine. She had taken a seat on a bench along one of the communal tables, and with her eyes, beckoned me to sit with her. The person sitting to her right moved to give me space.

Diners were too busy slurping their soup and noodles to be bothered to see who sat next to them or listen to their conversations. So this girl and I talked while we ate. She told me she was a student at the university. I said I had toured Asia and would be in Kuala Lumpur for a month. She was impressed that I was traveling alone and asked me a lot of questions. Everyone else at our table ate fast and left soon after. This young woman and I stayed for a good hour.

The next few days, we saw each other again at the street vendor's stand. On the third day, she told me her name was Minah. I asked if I could walk her back to the university because I wanted to see it. "That would be nice," she said. Before we parted, she offered to show me around Kuala Lumpur after her classes. We spent the next few afternoons together. I'll tell you later what that city is like. For now, I'll confess— Minah and I fell deeply, madly in love. All in the span of a week. I was young, impulsive, and maybe I still believed I was entitled to great things and they would come to me just at the right time. I told myself the time to fall in love had come.

Eager to be smitten by an exotic beauty who took more than a fancy to me, I was convinced what we had was true love. After all, she was in my thoughts every waking moment, and the attractions of Kuala Lumpur no longer interested me as much as she did. She was all that mattered.

I made plans for a life in Kuala Lumpur. I could go to the university and later get a job somewhere in the city. I was full of dreams. Beautiful, joyful dreams I was eager to turn into reality. Minah and I would finish our degrees at about the same time, and soon after, we'd get married and start a family. And we'd travel. She had never been anywhere outside of Kuala Lumpur, and I was eager to show her where I had been and for us to discover things and places new to both of us.

But two weeks after weaving dreams and planning a future with Minah, my hopes and plans burst like overfilled helium balloons.

Waiting for Minah to come out of her last class one afternoon, I sat at a café, reading about expatriate life in Malaysia on my laptop. It wasn't too hot that day, and I still felt fresh from my morning shower. I was relishing the idea of Minah and me exploring her strange country.

But my languid afternoon was smashed into smithereens when a long kris (a sharp scalloped knife) landed with a loud whack on the table where I sat, its blade quivering. It toppled my cup and spilled my Malaysian tea.

I nearly jumped out of my chair. I was more surprised than frightened despite that kris. Before I could see who flung it on my table, a middle-aged Malaysian man dropped his heavy body on the chair next to mine. He snatched the knife and, with his hand clutched tightly around it, propped it on the table, its blade up in the air. I was shocked, frightened, less by the sharp, pointed, undulating blade than the menace that oozed out of the man's eyes. I thought he was so close to losing control that at any second, he could plunge that kris into my heart.

He spouted words in a language I didn't understand. Words that distorted his mouth and bared all his teeth. His eyes threw daggers at me. With every other word, he hit the table with his kris. I sat there shaking but unable to move. He turned toward the street and shouted Minah's name.

I hadn't seen her, and I looked in the direction he turned. There she was, standing several feet away, her arms held back by a stocky young man who bore a resemblance to her. He seemed as menacing as the old man. I knew then the man who threatened me was her father. This was the family I had hoped to attach myself to.

Minah and her brother came to stand next to the table where her father and I sat. Her brother raised a fist at me. Minah was crying silently.

In broken English, her father repeated his threat, told me to leave Kuala Lumpur at once. He would never allow Minah to marry a "dirty, lying, American coward." He pushed me hard and I fell on my butt to the floor, dragging the chair down with me.

Minah's father stood over me, raised his kris and swung it above my head. Minah screamed.

He said, "Don't ever come back, if you want to go on living."

He turned, grabbed Minah's arm and stomped away, dragging her along. Her brother glared at me and stomped after his father. Mina staggered on. She didn't look back.

Later, I wondered if he could actually have struck me in that public place. But who knew what he might have done? It was a culture I was unfamiliar with. Maybe killing a man to save family honor was condoned.

He terrified me enough that I called the airlines while I was running back to the hostel. I booked a flight back home for the following day, my last day in Kuala Lumpur. I was there three weeks.

I was shaken to the core. The nastiness I'd witnessed at school were mere schoolboy pranks, harmless compared to the way Minah's father and her brother had threatened me.

That afternoon, I stayed at the hostel. I didn't leave it for the assortment of street food that constituted my usual dinner.

And I grew up. Unnerved by visions of being hacked in two, my throat sliced deep by the swing of a razor-sharp kris. I shuddered many times at the image and of me coming home in a box, my head nearly cut off from my body.

I couldn't sleep that night. I was still trembling when I boarded the plane to Hawaii the next morning.

On the plane, all I could think of was how precarious life could be—here one moment, gone in a split second. I felt in no condition to stay in Hawaii to continue my trip. I wanted to be home, in the comfort and security of my room and in the midst of the daily bustle of my grandparents' home.

My grandparents picked me up at the airport. I ran to them, held them both tight in my arms. Close to breaking point, my eyes grew moist. Nana made a *joke about me being still a baby in spite of all my adventures. All I could think of was how thankful I was to see them again. I was alive.*

At home, brooding alone in my room, Minah, my broken heart, Kuala Lumpur and the dreams I had started to weave there seemed far away. Unreal. Some figment of my imagination. For a couple of months, I hibernated at home and at my grandparents'. My family assumed I was tired and homesick.

In retrospect years later, I regard that infatuation and the dreams that came with it as the product of my youthful ignorance. I was in a foreign country, and I failed to grasp the deeper meanings of its customs. I guess I believed people there or anywhere else were just people. Not so different from us, though they may look different or believe in different gods, or live in a society with values and attitudes that could seem strange to us.

I was probably also near exhaustion in both body and mind without me being aware of it. I had been traveling for almost two years.

I got over the experience somehow. Or at least, I thought so. Not too long after returning home, wanderlust hit me again. This time, I went to Guatemala to take part in building projects for Habitat for Humanity.

Ten years out from Kuala Lumpur, I was sure I got over the trauma I suffered there. But now I realize I continue to live with vestiges of that trauma. And it's my reaction to your news that forced me to face the truth.

When you've forgiven me, you know where to find me. Please don't leave without saying goodbye.

Sincerely,
Lucien

How horrible that must have been, facing a threat of death far away from home. In a strange land where you have no one to rely on for support. I can't imagine what that was like for a young man barely out of his teens, full of verve and hope, out to conquer the world, and trusting his ability to do so.

I'm touched Lucien trusted me enough to tell me this terrible episode in his life. An episode he's never told anyone. But why tell me all this? It was enough to have apologized.

*****

A couple of days later, I leave the bookstore half an hour early to catch Lucien at his weekday two o'clock haunt. I see him standing at the bar by the window. The café must be busy. He sees me before I come in and raises his hand in greeting.

His lips widen into his lopsided dimpled smile as I approach. "You've forgiven me."

"Can we go somewhere more private to talk? Maybe stroll around the block?"

"Of course," he says, picking up his iPad and coffee cup. Outside, he throws the cup into a recycling bin.

The only empty tables we see are at a noisy Italian restaurant nearby, so we stroll to the end of the long market hall block.

I thank him for his handwritten letter. "I'm deeply touched. Sharing that experience with me. Taking the time to write it. I know how busy you are. A simple 'sorry' would have been enough."

He regards me with a thoughtful frown. "I think I did it as much for myself as I did it for you. It's an episode I've kept to myself these past ten years. I wanted you to trust me. I thought telling you about it might help."

It takes me a moment to respond. My eyes have become inexplicably moist. "I do trust you. I did trust you even without knowing what happened in Kuala Lumpur."

"I'm glad," he says, glancing at me long enough for me to catch a wistfulness in his eyes. He drifts into silence.

I'd like to know what he's going through at this moment, but I could only say, "I've learned how touching a letter can be, how the course of a life can change because of a letter."

He glances at me again with mild interest. "Yeah? What was the letter about?"

"Incidents Mom and her sisters never knew until I found the yellowed letter in a box Grandma kept locked in her desk. Grandpa sent it to her forty years ago."

Lucien's face perks up with curiosity. "Secrets that threatened their marriage?"

"Good guess. But how'd you guess?"

"Happens often enough, I think. My parents separated a few months after I came back from Habitat. I never suspected something was brewing until it happened."

"I'm sorry about your parents, but impressed at your insight."

"I'm not nineteen anymore. And my work taught me how to listen, pay attention, especially to subtle cues. I realized my parents were never as happy together as Gramps and Nana were. Those two were soul mates. Maybe it's rare, meeting someone with whom you feel in total sync. You understand each other even when you disagree or words aren't said."

"I thought I met a soul mate. I was wrong." I blush, recalling Scott. "Maybe you have to work at being soul mates."

Lucien shakes his head. "All relationships need work, but there's a difference. We meet many people we become attracted to, but with a potential soul mate, you sense something deeper—maybe it's intuition. Anyway, it goes beyond the physical."

"More than chemistry?"

"A deeper layer. You're also both aware what you have between you is special. And you agree, without words being said, that you must cultivate it, work on it, maybe even fight for it."

"My grandparents fought their demons to preserve what they had. They celebrated their reunion by planting a mango tree."

"A mango tree. Unique. Original. Has it outlived them?"

"It has. Still big, beautiful, and healthy. But it never bore fruit. Grandma and I used to sit in its shade in the afternoon."

"Wonderful moments shared, leaving you happy memories of someone you love. Ah, what could be better?"

When we have gone around the block, Lucien checks his watch. "Luna, I'm sorry I have to go. I'm already late ten minutes."

"Oh! I'm sorry. I hope I haven't gotten you in trouble."

"Not a big deal. My office isn't actually strict. I keep a precise schedule for afternoon breaks to impose discipline on myself. Time flies when I work."

"You love your job. That's good."

"I do, but I'll leave as soon as I can set up my own practice. My hope, anyway. I want to explore ideas that came to me in my travels and when I was working for Habitat."

We rush toward where I parked my car.

Lucien says, "You free this evening? Will you have dinner with me? We can continue our stories then."

I confess that I thought he'd ask me out, but when he does, I find myself unprepared to answer. "Is it ... a date?"

"What if it is?"

I fumble for the car keys in my purse and don't answer.

"Well, will you?" His voice is soft, imploring.

When we reach my car, I say, "Pick me up at my apartment?"

"Seven o'clock?" Lucien closes my door.

I nod and drive away.

Lucien

I watch Luna's car grow smaller and disappear onto the ramp going south on the freeway. She hesitated before accepting my invitation and seemed in a hurry to get away. Was she uncomfortable? Should I not have said our dinner tonight is a date?

But I can no longer deny, to myself at least, that she has broken through the wall I built to keep out anyone expecting something serious. I had been wary of another broken heart. Of broken dreams. Of a broken spirit. I may have matured enough not to fall apart, but before Luna, I thought: *Why take the risk? And it takes too much out of you.*

I believe I was caught the day we made love after the picnic at the lake. But Luna—still searching, waiting for the world to open up for her—is not ready to fall in love again. She's where I was ten years ago.

I hurry back to my office. No need to rush, but my project manager knows my habits. It's not unusual for him to come to my cubbyhole to talk about a project as soon as I return from the coffee shop.

Three hours fly by. I put away the blueprints I've been working on and dash out of the office. An hour to shower, change, and pick up Luna. It has to be enough.

The restaurant I want to take her to is less than five miles from her place. Often fully booked a month or two in advance, a table opened up when I called. They could take us in this evening. An omen of good luck, this coincidence.

I'm a few minutes late when I ring the bell at the apartment Luna shares with Asha.

Asha opens the door and stares at me. She breaks into a wide grin. "Oh, it's you. I know you. The bookstore. Saw you there a few times. Come in. She'll be out in a sec. Don't know why I didn't recognize you the first time you came. When you left that letter, remember?"

"I think you were totally wrapped up in your video game."

She chuckles. "Yeah, you can get addicted to those games. Do you play?"

"Not lately. Too busy."

Coming out of her room, Luna says "I'm sorry to keep you waiting. The back of one of my earrings fell on the floor. Took a few minutes to find it."

"I just got here," I say.

She's wearing a red shirt and a black skirt that ends above her knees. She's left her thick dark hair loose and flowing down below her shoulders. Along with her pearl earrings and the standing collar on her shirt, her hair frames her exotic beauty. This is the first time I've seen her with some makeup on. She's breathtaking. I can't tear my gaze away.

Asha turns to face her and her eyes light up. "Look at you. Luna, you're stunning, and you're not even all dressed up."

"Thank you, Asha. I'll see you later, okay?"

"You mean tomorrow?"

Luna blushes and doesn't answer.

Asha covers her mouth with her hand. "I'm sorry. Always putting my foot in my mouth. Not my business at all. It's just that if I were a guy, I wouldn't be able to keep my hands off you. Oops—did it again. Sorry."

With a reassuring smile, Luna touches Asha's arm. "No big deal, Asha. Let's go Lucien." She barely glances at me and rushes to the door.

I follow Luna, but as I'm about to close the door, she pokes her head in for an instant. "Enjoy your evening, Asha."

We go down to the car without speaking.

In the car, she says, "Asha is quite uninhibited. I can't blurt things out like she does. But I think she's rather refreshing."

"But it can be embarrassing—being so unrestrained."

"Yes, sometimes. It's been an experience sharing an apartment with her. She goes from one extreme to the other. Some nights and weekends, she'd be home for two or three weeks straight, immersed in her military dramas or video games. Hardly talking except to request that I bring her a can of beer or soda from the refrigerator. Other weekends, she'd bring different men home every night or have her steady boyfriend over for a few days."

"Does that bother you?"

"The first two months, yes. I follow some rigid script in my mind for how to live. Asha's free-spirited. But I've gotten used to her. Particularly those nights of loud moaning when she has a guy with her. It's nights when she's alone that make me uneasy. She forgets to eat or goes for days without a bath. Asha is so different from who I am. Such a generous affectionate soul, an open book. Yeah, I like her."

I catch a note of unease in Luna's tone. It makes me curious, but I'm navigating the narrow passage of a crowded parking lot.

The restaurant we're going into is what critics would call intimate. Ten tables for two. Plus, a bar where you can watch the chefs prepare dishes. It strives to make diners feel like they're part of a family.

I've dined here alone, sitting on a stool at the bar. Enough times for the staff to welcome me with a friendly smile instead of the bright, ceremonious one they give diners who come once or rarely.

Luna is the first date I've brought here, and Janelle, hostess and wife of the executive chef, welcomes her with her friendly smile. To me, the smile comes with a quick arching of an eyebrow.

Luna

"This place is wonderful. Unpretentious, cozy. I'd never have guessed they offer such fancy dishes." Lucien and I chose the same first course of seared scallops and we're waiting for it.

The restaurant serves a prix fixe four-course dinner and offers three choices for appetizer, main course and dessert. The other choices are meat or vegetarian.

Lucien seems pleased. "That's what I love about this place. Intimate ambiance. Not much agonizing over what to order. All you do is wait for the great dishes they bring you."

"It's my first time dining in a place like this. So romantic. I can almost hear violins playing a love song. Sweet, poignant longing. And sensuous."

The background music is actually a lively piano piece playing a tad above a whisper.

Lucien regards me thoughtfully. "Quite an imagination you have. Romantic? Never thought so. But I've often dined here alone."

"This place embraces you with warmth, and I get nostalgic from the aromas coming out of the kitchen." I'm remembering the appetizing smells from Grandma's kitchen.

He smiles. "So glad you like it. I wanted to impress you."

"Well, you have." His remark made me self-conscious, and I wish I could think of something brilliant to talk about. Instead, I find myself blabbering. "On my first date with Scott, we went to a pizza joint. Then we watched a movie in his dorm room. We were students—no money for romantic restaurants. One serving high-end dishes? Forget it. Sounds unexciting, doesn't it?"

"When you're in love, does it matter where you go?" He hasn't taken his eyes off me.

"It didn't to me, at the time. But this is so special. Thanks." I focus on sipping my glass of white wine.

"When you're in love, I think it's you who give out that aura of romance. But in the early stages of courting, you need the right ambiance, the right mood."

This time, I blush at his remark. "Is that where we are, Lucien?"

He regards me intently. "I am, anyway."

I catch my breath at his frank answer. I'm feeling warm and uncomfortable. I regret having asked the question. "But I'm leaving for Cambodia."

"I know, and I don't intend to stop you."

"I can't fall in love with you, Lucien. I'm totally over Scott, but how can I love you if I'm going away?" I sound plaintive, pleading instead of protesting with conviction.

238

Lucien shrugs. "I can't help how I feel. I warned you that night you asked me to make love to you."

"I'm so sorry. I guess I was thinking only of myself."

"I'm not yet in a bad way. I can just chalk this up to ... no, not folly. I'll have to decide as we go along."

"There can't be a 'we,' Lucien. I won't be here." I'm aware my protest is sounding weaker by the minute.

He fixes my gaze again. "In my profession, you can't claim something is impossible until you've fully explored possibilities. Anyway, people have engaged in love affairs via letters for a long time. Sometimes, it's your only option. Like legendary poets Elizabeth Barrett and Robert Browning. They exchanged letters and poetry for a year before she eloped with him. Now, it's much easier and faster to connect through cyberspace."

Eager for a change of topic, I say, "An architect who's a romantic. And acquainted with English literature. Lucien, you continue to amaze me."

"I like poetry, so I remember those two from an elective college course. Otherwise, I know little of literature. But I'm surprised you're surprised." He pauses, stares again at me, his mouth curling toward his dimple. "You need to be a romantic at heart to be able to create art, whether it's superbly prepared dishes, a painting, or beautiful buildings and things people use."

I nod to show him I understand. But as I watch him speak, I imagine taking off his eyeglasses, like he did that afternoon we made love. The way he stared into my eyes those few moments, all I could do was melt into his arms.

He amazes me more than I've admitted—so sophisticated and yet so guileless. In the grip of passion, he had shed his façade, exposed his naked self—I don't mean literally, though, of course, he did that, and I wasn't surprised to see he was lean but muscular.

Now, I'm wondering if I'd regret going to Cambodia.

I don't know if he can see it in my eyes, but I can't take my mind off that afternoon. We gaze at each other, bound by raw emotions we're reluctant to express, some tacit understanding passing between us that words are superfluous at moments like these. But I can't endure his unblinking gaze and I look away. A minute later, I feel some relief to see the waiter approach our table, carrying two plates.

He puts a plate of seared scallops on the table in front of me and the other in front of Lucien. "Seared sea scallops, aioli sauce with fresh tarragon."

For the next few minutes, we give the food our full attention. I restrain myself from devouring the scallops in a few big bites and steal a glance at Lucien to see how he's enjoying the dish. He's cutting a piece of scallop.

"Delicious, isn't it?" he says when he catches me watching him slosh the piece in aioli.

"Hmm," I reply, spearing the last bite of scallop on my plate.

For the next hour or so, we savor the dishes the waiter is serving us. The delicious, potent unease between us can't be put into words in this public place. So we talk about food.

"Great food always reminds me of Grandma." I'm wondering what she'd think of the dishes at this restaurant. Hers were never elaborately prepared but she made them all mouth-watering.

"Was she a good cook?"

"She was a great cook, though you'd never call her dishes fancy."

"What un-fancy dish do you remember best that your grandma made?"

"Has to be her green mango salad."

"You mean unripe mango? Never had that before. Green papaya salad, yes. In Thailand. First time I ever tasted fish sauce. Went quite well with lime juice, mint, and Thai basil."

"Green mango is tart. Doesn't need as much lime juice. Once again, you amaze me. How many Americans know papaya salad, much less eat it? Traveling has expanded your palate, not just your thinking."

"I'd go again if I wasn't trying to establish myself as an architect. I do like what I'm doing now. And I think it's another way of making the world a better place."

"Do you hear yourself? You make fun of what you call my Mother Teresa complex, but you also want to make a difference."

Lucien chuckles and ignores what I said. "Any other exotic dish you like and remember from your grandmother?"

Expecting his reaction to my Mother Teresa remark, I press my lips and frown at him in mock disapproval. He has decided to ignore it.

I leave it alone. "Not exotic. But I love her grilled shrimp doused in butter and a lethal amount of fried garlic. Doesn't kill you, but it can turn you into a pariah."

Lucien laughs. "Then you all have to gorge on fried garlic."

"How about mint? Mango salad has mint. Or mint gum."

"Inadequate. I doubt it works. A camouflage, that's all."

Talking about garlic breath eases the tension. Our dinner ends on shared laughter, forgetting for now things we wished we could've said.

My brain tells me some things are better left unsaid, but my heart is not so sure. I only know I'm faltering on my resolve to go to Cambodia. Maybe he's right. I have a Mother Teresa complex, and have no idea what I'm getting myself into.

We take a slow stroll back to his car, pausing now and then as we share stories. It takes a good hour to get back to my apartment.

Lucien turns the car engine off at the entry to my apartment building. "Thank you for a beautiful evening. I had a great time."

"Me, too. Thank you. A real pleasure of an evening." Not empty words. But trite and safe while my hand hesitates to open the car door. *Push it down. Say good night.* I turn toward Lucien and force myself to smile. *Are you going to kiss me?*

Like two smiling zombies, we sit gazing at each other. For how long, I can't tell. All I know is we come to a silent understanding, and without a word, Lucien turns the engine on again and drives in the direction of his loft.

Lucien

Saturday morning. I wake up, conscious of eyes watching me. I crane my neck to my right.

"Good morning." Luna is smiling. She's lying on her side next to me, hands clasped under her cheek. "Want coffee? I made some."

"How long have you been up?"

"An hour at least. You slug, it's past nine. I borrowed your lavalava, found it in your closet."

"My what?" I look her over. Her shoulders are bare, but from the chest down, she's wrapped in a colorful cloth printed with large blue philodendron leaves like Matisse cut-outs. "Oh, that. My gift to Gramps. I kept it after he died."

"I hope you don't mind. I looked into your closet for a robe I might borrow. Found none. This lavalava was draped on a pants hanger, neatly folded. Stands out among your dark outfits and plain pastel shirts."

"I have a robe, somewhere in a chest drawer. What you call a lavalava has been on that hanger, untouched for five years. You're the only one who knows what it is."

"You mean among the women who come for your one-nighters?"

"You make it sound like I do it every night. It's actually rather infrequent, and I haven't had anyone else come over for months. Except you, and you're definitely not a one-nighter."

"I guess not. After last night."

I ignore her teasing for the moment. "The few women who've peeked into my closet think it's odd I have it. I don't tell them what it is, and they think it belongs to an old love or that I'm a secret cross-dresser."

Luna laughs. "Your grandpa is an old love. And you wear a lavalava around your waist. Like a skirt, right? So, yeah, cross-dressing. Did you get one for your grandma?"

"Mom kept it. I forgot to get her one so she took Nana's when she passed away. Hers is covered with red hibiscus flowers."

"Grandma grew hibiscus in her garden. Used to tuck one behind my ear. Took pictures of me when I was a kid."

"I'd give a dime to see those. Were you already a charmer even then?"

"Can a snotty, spoiled eight-year-old be a charmer? Anyway, I don't have the pictures. I'll have to ask Auntie Celia for them."

"Can't she swish them through the ethernet? A few short minutes—and they should be here."

"They were taken with a Polaroid. They'll have to be scanned." Luna sits up and swings her legs off the bed. "How about I bring you coffee? It's Saturday. Nothing to hurry to."

"Breakfast in bed—that'd be a first. Why not? Any muffins or toast with butter?"

"Banana is all I can find in your kitchen."

"That'll do." I'm wondering how I could entice her to come and join me under the sheets once again. The thought is quickly crushed, but the desire persists. Luna is right. Better not be drawn deeper into an entanglement that could only end in pain.

Minutes later, Luna comes with the only tray I own—a wooden piece of acacia I carved in Guatemala and lacquered years later. On it are two cups of coffee, a small bowl of sugar, a carafe of milk, and a brown-spotted banana.

She lays the tray on the bed as I scoot up to sit. She hands me a cup.

"You've been going through my cupboards, too. Haven't seen that tray for ages." I say, chuckling.

"I needed a tray. Why, is this one of those things you've put away and never used?" She waves her hand over it.

"I thought this one was an artwork."

"You made it?"

I incline my head in response.

"I am impressed. Why not show it off? Put it on your coffee table."

"It's the only piece I've ever carved. It's not that impressive, is it?"

"I like the shape. Very organic. You should do more."

"One of these days I'll make time for another one, but I need a good piece of wood."

As I eat my banana, Luna asks me how I made the wooden tray and what other woodworking projects I'd like to do when I find the time. We're avoiding the subject of her departure for Cambodia. She's eager to go, but if I'm honest with myself, I would rather she stayed.

"Can you sculpt wood into a vase or an animal or a figure?"

I ignore her question. I say on impulse, "I wish I could make you stay." Maybe I'm more anxious about her going away than I realize.

"Lucien, don't. Please don't make it harder for me to go."

"Do I?"

She looks away and doesn't answer.

I grasp her hands. "Good. It means I'm getting to you."

She withdraws her hands and clasps them tightly on her lap.

I watch her rigid body. I want to take her in my arms. Tell her I love her. But I mustn't make it harder for her to go on her mission of making a difference in some tiny corner of the world.

She meets my gaze, her eyes moist and mournful. "I can't fall in love with you. I need to be free when I leave. And I don't want you to be unhappy when I go."

We're out of sync, Luna and I. But I understand her hunger to explore.

I press my lips on her hair. "You know I'm the last person who'll stop you from going. Get dressed. I'll take you home. I'll just hop into the shower for five minutes."

Before I can move, Luna flings herself at me. Presses her face against my chest. "I'm fooling myself. How can I deny how I feel? When I read your letter, I felt like you burrowed through my insides, planted yourself where I'm most vulnerable."

I gather her in my arms. If she can't help how she feels, can I suppress the rush of joy her words brought me?

"Oh, Luna, Luna. I've loved you for sometime. Maybe shortly after you met Scott. I realized I was jealous of him. Didn't think him worthy of you."

"How could you? You hadn't even met me?"

"Crazy, isn't it? But maybe we're destined to meet."

She burrows her face on my chest before she looks up at me. "I guess I should confess, too. Remember that first time we met at Peet's? I stared into your eyes, said there's something about them?"

"How could I forget? The way you stared at me. I think blood rushed from my heart to my head."

"I got all fluttery inside. You have beautiful, expressive eyes, Lucien. They spoke to me. In spite of where my mind was at that day, I'm sure I fell in love with you."

For an answer, I kiss her. Her lips, her eyes, all over her face, her neck. And a voice inside me shouts: *Caution be danged.*

When I raise my head, she says, "Oh, Lucien, what are we going to do?"

"Make the most of the time we have together. I may not like it, but I know you have to go to Cambodia."

I hold her closer to my heart, taking in the smell of her hair, the smoky trace of coffee mingling with the fragrance from her shampoo. Tilting her face to mine, I kiss it all over again. I bury my head on her shoulders. I want to remember the smell of her skin when she's gone.

"You have to go. I believe that's as inevitable as finding your journal. Think about it. Why was it me who found it? I want to believe we're meant for each other and you'll come back to me."

"I'm not as sure as you are. All I know is I don't want to lose what we have between us."

"Neither do I."

"But why do I have to go?"

I let her question hang in the air. She neither needs nor wants an answer. It's more like a lament. If choices were always clear-cut, we don't have to agonize over what to do, and maybe we'd all be happy.

Aware moments like this might not come again, I can't let go of Luna. I'm collecting memories. They might be all I'll have of her.

I guess I got old after Kuala Lumpur. What happened there taught me not to hang on to hopes that fate or circumstance can snatch from me without warning.

I don't get up to shower and Luna lets the lavalava slip on the bed. We make love again, stay in bed awhile, and go to lunch hours later.

Luna

I hear loud voices occasionally drowned out by gunfire before I open the door to the apartment I share with Asha.

She's at it again. Days like these bother me—when Asha is oblivious to her surroundings playing her movies and games. I worry about what may be going on in her head. Often, she's livelier and more communicative. But she can swing from one mood to its opposite quickly.

I push the door open. The television is on, but no one is in the room. I go straight to Asha's room and knock on her door. No answer. I knock again, louder. Still no answer. I open Asha's bedroom door gently.

The sight that greets me is one I never imagined I'd ever see except in movies.

"Asha!"

My breath catches in my throat. My heart is thumping.

Asha is lying, still and naked on the bed, so still that I can't be sure she's alive. Her arms and legs are splayed out, her hands and feet tied to the four bedposts.

I'm trembling as I approach her rigid figure, fearing she might be dead.

"Oh no! Oh no, Asha." I see bruises on her thighs and her breasts, dark red and blue blotches on her face, and smears of dried blood coming out of her lips, drops of it visible on the sheets.

I touch her arms. My hand recoils at how cold they are. I touch her cheeks, her forehead, and her neck the way Grandma did when I used to complain about feeling sick. Asha's face is warm.

She remains immobile, so I place my hand below her breasts. Her stomach is rising and falling faintly but at a regular pace. She's breathing. She's alive.

I fumble for my cell phone and dial emergency.

My arms are shaking and I grip my phone tight. A woman answers. My teeth chatter when I speak, but I manage to get the words out. "It's my roommate. She's unconscious, tied to the bedposts. Maybe beaten up."

I'm not sure I'm making sense to the emergency lady and I'm, by now, near tears.

"Ma'am, can you feel her pulse?"

I put my fingers on Asha's wrist. "Yes, yes, but it's weak."

"Okay. I've dispatched an ambulance. Confirm your address for me, please. And tell me your name."

I give her my name and the address.

"The paramedics will be there in a couple of minutes. Can you open up for them?"

"Yes. Yes, I can."

"Good. Tell me more about your roommate. How old is she?"

"She's twenty-two. Short and slim, but strong. She's black and blue all over. I think I should untie her."

Before the emergency woman can ask more questions, my body jerks at a loud knocking on the front door. I almost lose my grip on the cell phone.

"I think they're here." I run to open the door.

Several people walk in, one after another. Young, vigorous paramedics. One is carrying a bag and two others a stretcher between them. I lead them into Asha's room.

The man holding the bag examines Asha while the others cut the ropes that tie her to the bedposts.

"How is she?" I ask.

He answers my question with another. "Do you know what she took?"

I shake my head. "I wasn't here last night."

A couple more paramedics come in and our little apartment seems all at once to be buzzing with people. Attending to Asha. Asking questions. Poking around the room. Opening drawers. Examining objects.

"Are you family?" the examining paramedic asks, as they're putting Asha on the stretcher.

I shake my head.

"We'll need to contact them."

"I haven't met them, but I'm sure you'll find their number on her cell phone."

Another paramedic holds up a cell phone. "I found this. Is this hers?"

"Yes."

"We're taking her to Sutter Emergency. You can follow us, in case you're coming."

"I'll come."

Before long, the paramedics leave, taking Asha with them.

The room, noisy and chaotic a moment before, is eerily, oppressively silent except for my breathing. Still trembling, I dial Lucien.

Lucien

I drive away from Luna's apartment humming along as the speakers connected to my iPhone blast out a Luciano Pavarotti aria, one Gramps loved to sing. "*Libiamo, libiamo, ne' lieti ca... lici*" are the only words I know of the drinking song from the opera *La Traviata,* but it doesn't stop me. The aria reflects my mood. It's festive, exultant. I imagine Luna when she admitted her feelings for me. I sing along "*Libiamo ...* pom pa-ra-ra-rum pa-ra-ra-rum ...*"

The piece ends, and the warm glow it leaves me lingers. Until I remember we will only have a few months together.

She's going, but we both find it hard to say it out loud. So, implicitly, we agree to forget our parting and spend our remaining hours together in blissful denial. We'll do what new lovers do, oblivious of time and place.

Back at my loft, I play *Libiamo* again. I sit at my desk to doodle designs for furniture. I have been meaning to replace a few of the store-bought furniture I now have with ones I will design and which I'm capable of building. I let my imagination run wild. Time passes unnoticed. I love this part of designing—

before I let considerations of functionality and execution narrow down design choices.

Not too long after we part, Luna calls me. A call I didn't expect. I assumed we won't hear from each other until Friday.

But when she says, "Lucien ..." and hesitates, I know right away something bad has happened.

"Luna, my love, what's wrong?"

"I'm in the hospital, in emergency. Asha ..." Her voice is tremulous. She recounts finding Asha and the condition she was in.

"Oh god, Luna, I'm so sorry. How is she now?"

"I don't know yet."

"I'll come. I should be there in fifteen minutes."

"No, don't come. Not now. I just need to hear your voice to reassure me."

"You sure? How are you?"

"I'm better, not as shaken as I was when I first saw her, lying naked and so still I thought she was dead. I'll go back to the apartment as soon as someone here can tell me how she's doing. They're calling her family."

"Are you sure I can't come? I could bring you some dinner. Keep you company a while."

"I need to get through this, learn to deal with the unexpected on my own. Who knows what I'll be facing in Cambodia?"

Her response gives me a slight pause. Admiring, astonished. She's testing herself. Resolving to be independent, taking control. "If that's what you want. I do understand. Call me anytime you need me."

"Thank you. Can you come this evening? Stay with me? The night might be a little too ... spooky. I think I might freak out if I was alone."

"I can pick you up and take you to my place."

"Just come, please."

Asha's tragic experience reawakens the lessons of Kuala Lumpur. The reality that so much about life is ephemeral, fragile. That happiness can shatter with our actions and, many times, with mere words.

Once again, doubts haunt my thoughts. No, not mere doubts. Dread. I dread the prospect of Luna departing on a solo adventure to Cambodia. Is it my macho protectiveness or the realization I refused to face until now of how much I need her and want her in my life? How my life would lose meaning if I were to lose her?

Luna

It's early evening. Dramatic streaks of yellow and red sweep across the fading blue sky. This morning had been hazy, but by noon, it was clear and beautiful.

In the hours since I left the hospital, I've sat in my room, looking out the window to the ten-story apartment building across the street. My gaze wanders past its many windows for occasional glimpses of its inhabitants. They reassure me life goes on behind its walls, as it does in the twenty-five or so apartments in our smaller building.

Yes, life churns on late into the night, to the tune of discordant but muffled street noises several stories below. And despite the tragedies we can't control. Tragedies that leave us reeling.

The doorbell rings, and I spring up from my bed. Lucien has arrived. It dawns on me: in a dark hour, he's the one I called on impulse. Not my parents. As I yank the door open and see him standing there, my knees go weak. Relieved, yes, but excited, as well.

Lucien stands for a moment, speechless, gazing at me. As soon as he steps in, he pushes the door closed and gathers me in his arms. I burst into tears.

From the time I first saw Asha, bruised and unresponsive, I'd been able to hold my tears back. But like the time I didn't cry at Mom's news of Grandma's death, it's as if my self-control is a dam that breaks at seeing Lucien.

He holds me close, his breath like a warm, wispy breeze on my hair and the nape of my neck, his chest a comforting refuge as it rises and falls in a steady rhythm against mine.

Only after my tears are spent do I notice he's been silent. Never once has he uttered those often-empty words of reassurance we unleash on anyone in obvious distress: "It's gonna be all right."

Maybe I'm becoming cynical, but what do we mean by those words, anyway? How can we know—when even doctors can't tell—what lies ahead for Asha who lies comatose in intensive care?

I raise my head and Lucien, despite the deep caring and concern in his eyes, attempts a smile, his lips curling toward his dimple.

"How are you feeling?"

"Better, now that you're here."

He leads me to the couch. We sit down.

"You've had quite a day today. Can I take you somewhere? Get you away from here for a while?"

"I'd rather we stay. I need quiet distraction, but I don't want to run away from this place. I have to get used to being here after this tragedy."

"Okay. Talk or cuddle up?"

"I don't know that there's much more to tell about what happened to Asha."

"But what about you? It's you I'm thinking of."

"Me?" I frown, as the image of Asha's bruised body passes, unbidden, through my mind and I recall details in the room I had ignored before. A half-open closet with a few gadgets on a shelf and books haphazardly piled on another shelf. Clothes strewn on a chair, a piece of rope draped on the clothes. Emergency personnel had taken a few things they might have thought could tell them if drugs were involved.

"I don't understand any of it. She lay there spread-eagled like someone being offered for sacrifice. Was that all part of some sexual ritual?"

"It was, I think."

"But it's so violent. Asha could have died. How could anyone find pleasure in all that? It's torture."

Lucien doesn't answer. He's watching me. There's a glow in his eyes that draws me away from my blue mood. I entwine my hands behind his neck. He puts his arms around me.

I pull his head down to mine. I kiss him long and deep. "I do love you," I murmur against his mouth. "Will you wait for me?"

"I think I have no choice. But you don't need to make me any promises."

"How can you be so open-minded?"

He shrugs.

I lay my head on his shoulder. "I need to go out there. Prove to myself I'm up to whatever it flings at me. Whatever happened to Asha today—it showed me how much more I need to learn."

"You coped with it."

"I did, didn't I?" I raise my head. "It taught me to pay more attention to the little things people do, even the little things they use or own. They can tell you something about the person they won't usually share with you."

"Yeah, we may all have things we want to keep to ourselves. Life can be harsh, unforgiving, not always the wondrous thing we think it is."

"Life is elusive. But if you understand people, I believe you understand life better."

A frown flits across Lucien's brow, but he attempts a smile. "I do believe life offers us moments, hours, even days of wonder along with the usual drudgery and the occasional tragedy. And you're right. We can understand, accept people, if we know what they've lived through."

"A philosopher! You spend time thinking like I do about things. No, you aren't a pessimist. A realist, surely."

"I've seen the pain in living. Most of us prefer to deny it, rather than face it."

"So we build dreams and play little games." I'm aware I'm guilty of dreams, but I'm also remembering Scott's little games with "solitary" trips.

"Nothing wrong with dreams or even little games. Maybe they're the only way some people cope with drudgery and pain. But for me, facing it is the only way I could overcome it. Or at least manage it."

The following day, Asha's parents arrive. They'll take her back to Georgia when she's well enough to fly. That takes place sooner than I anticipated. Nine days after she was hospitalized, she's back in the apartment, packing. She thanks me for saving her life and we hug in parting. Then she's gone.

How fleeting a presence can be. I'll never see Asha again, and maybe I'll forget her quicker than I intend to. "...*a shadow, bubble, air, a vapor* ...." And yet I'm sure she's left some mark on me, too.

I'll have a problem when Asha leaves. I can't pay the apartment rent on my own. I tell Lucien, knowing what he'll say. It is, I admit, what I also want.

"Why not move in with me? We'll have a couple of months together before you go."

But I can't help myself. I equivocate. "A bit drastic for me. What will my parents say? What will Jun think?"

"You seem to value Jun's opinion. Will his opinion—or that of your parents—change what you decide to do?"

"Mom has been less critical since we came back from Honolulu. She won't like it, but it's my decision, isn't it? Dad will say we're adults, we decide. I think Jun will tell me to go for it."

"What are you waiting for then?"

"It's a bold move. For me. What would Grandma have said?"

"She would have approved."

I grin and nod. "I think you're right. But I'd like to pay some rent. What I paid for the apartment, if that's okay."

Lucien takes a moment to answer. "It'll make you feel better, won't it? Okay, though I'm doing this out of self-interest. My chance to do all I can so you can't resist coming back to me. I'll make it hard for you to find what you and I have together with someone else."

Part 2:
Life in Cambodia

Luna

First Days in Phnom Penh

It's my second day in Phnom Penh. Twenty-nine volunteers, including me, are in a bus slogging through traffic to the National Museum. We will have our first glimpse of the artifacts of Khmer civilization, objects that would show us what it was like, this culture more than a thousand years older than our own.

It was raining when I arrived yesterday, and today, it's sweaty weather—sunny and humid.

We've opened the windows to clear the heavy air in the bus, only to be assaulted by the stench of something rotting mixed with fuel exhaust, and the cacophony of noise from motorbike-driven open carriages winding their way between honking vehicles, all in a rush. In British-sounding English, the bus driver, Mr. Pang, informs us they're tuk-tuks, the most common means of going from one place to another in the city. He's a short wiry man in his fifties with a face like those I've seen in Buddha pictures. Round, serene, and a perpetual knowing smile.

A short while later, we pass a commercial district. Mr. Pang points to a large tiered dome, below which radiates long structures like arms. "The central market. Legacy of the French. Nothing else like it in the city." Its round roof does look incongruously modern. Outside the market, shaded, densely packed mobile stalls have set up shop for the day.

Litter dots the streets. Not as ubiquitous as litter but numerous enough to draw remarks from my fellow volunteers is a fruit at hawkers stands on the bustling street. Fruit bigger than Hawaiian papayas covered in spikes the color of old Granny Smith apples. Durian, declares Mr. Pang. He doesn't smell it anymore, though its stink has settled inside the bus. A few people cover their noses with their hands.

Mr. Pang chuckles. "It tastes good. Like custard. You must try it."

Before long, he turns left on a street with two impressive buildings. He points to one resplendent in gold, red, and blue, shielded by a gold-painted solid wall topped by a line of blue-and-white forms shaped like pineapples. No surprise: the royal palace. Across the street, the museum. Both traditional Khmer architecture.

The roofs on the two buildings are intricate. Multi-tiered, steep, and gabled. But it's the gracefully curved finials rising from the ends of every roof tier that intrigue me, each like a snake rearing its head. Beauty and menace in one form.

Mr. Pang turns another corner and lets us off at the entrance to the National Museum, an impressive rust-red structure. The museum, we learn, is a century old, built under French colonial rule. It follows the lines and layout of traditional Khmer architecture, but is designed and funded—including a recent innovation—by the French.

Fourteen thousand objects of Khmer art, archaeological finds, and sculptures, mostly of divinities, are on display in the museum. We walk through its various galleries with Mr. Pang who is also our tour guide. He stops to tell us about a few of the countless figures of Hindu and Buddhist gods, many in bronzes but mostly in sandstone. I only remember Vishnus with four arms (or sometimes eight) cast in bronze or sculpted in sandstone, Shivas with their third eyes, and elephant-headed Ganeshas. Divine worship is important to Cambodians, nearly all of them Buddhists.

I also remember nagas, which are not divinities but mythological figures sporting multiple reptilian heads. Though not objects of worship, they've been imbued with meaning or power. Odd-numbered heads for masculine energy, infinity, and immortality; even ones for feminine energy, finite time, and mortality. The gender-based meanings attributed to number of heads annoy me. But I remind myself these figures have traveled to our time from so many centuries ago. How could I judge what they believed then when I know so little of this ancient culture? That ancient time?

We walk around display cases of objects from the ancient Khmer period, stopping to look a few seconds when something catches our eyes. Weapons and tools; bowls and jars; gold, silver and bronze jewelry. It's a lot to take in for a couple of hours, but they give us a glimpse into an enviably rich culture dating as far back as, maybe, the first century AD.

Mr. Pang leads us to a garden in the inner courtyard, down one of two crisscrossing paths separating four symmetrical lotus pools. We stop at the intersection of the paths in front of a small gazebo-like structure, its roof patterned after that of the museum and topped by a tall ornate tower (a stupa, he says). In it sits a stone statue—the Leper King. So called maybe because of its rough, scaly skin. It could be Jayavarman VII, the most powerful Khmer king who ruled in late twelfth to early thirteenth century and who might have had leprosy. Again, the contrasts strike me. Tranquil beauty and disease. Power and misfortune.

Mr. Pang gives us a few minutes to enjoy the garden. Curious about how he learned English, I walk with him. He laughs at my question, self-consciously it seems. "Long story. Maybe a little like the crazy history of my country."

He tells me he was born in the mid-sixties and learned a little English as a child in Phnom Penh before Pol Pot's communist army defeated the US-backed government of Lon Nol. Pol Pot's mission to return to an agrarian society began the Khmer Rouge purge of its educated classes. His lingering smile gives way to a grim scowl. "I was nine at the beginning of the killing fields and I had to hide my little bit of English."

I think he's alluding to the film. He must assume I've seen it. He thinks he never "unlearned" English but learned more working for an Australian company in his thirties.

His Buddha smile back on, he glances at me. But he seems uneasy, announces it's time to leave and he must get the group together. He walks away without waiting for me to answer.

Is he being evasive? He talks to a group gathered in front of the Leper King, his voice louder and a little too animated. I wonder if talking about the genocide made him uncomfortable. I wonder, too, if he referred to *The Killing Fields* to escape the burden of explaining the genocide to a foreigner. It seemed like a practiced answer to my curiosity. He must have been asked about it often enough by foreign visitors.

It's a tragedy that a culture with such a rich history has been mired in violent conflict and is today among the poorest. I think four years of genocide could inflict so much damage that they annihilated the hopes, the spirit of a whole country. Almost all Cambodian families had lost relatives in that horrific purge. Are they—survivors like Mr. Pang, in particular—reluctant to talk about it?

In the afternoon, I join my host family. I'll live with them during preservice training in Phnom Penh, before I go to my assigned site.

My host parents and their sons speak a smattering of English and—chaa (meaning "yes")—I'm picking up a little conversational Khmer from the three teenage boys. I teach them the "thumbs-up" sign and they teach me to som pas. Put your hands together like you do when praying, raise them to your chest and bow. It's a sign of respect, the appropriate and usual way to greet and say goodbye. Like "aloha" in Hawaii for both hello and farewell.

They eat an awful lot of rice here. But I grew up eating plate lunches with two scoops of rice in Hawaii so it's nothing new to me. My host family offered me French bread for breakfast my first morning with them, while they ate rice porridge with fish. I said I was okay eating what they ate. So, now, I dig into the rice porridge pot like everyone else. It's healthier than a few strips of bacon and two fried eggs.

I have tasted durian as well, on a dare from my host family. It does taste like custard, though it still smells rotten even when you pinch your nose.

Lucien

Luna told her parents she was moving in with me when she gave up the apartment she shared with Asha. They reacted as she had expected, and her mom expressed interest in meeting me. It took six weeks before we were all free to have dinner together, a couple of weeks before Luna left for Cambodia. Her parents flew from Long Beach on a weekend, rented a car, and came straight to my place. I had pre-ordered dinner from a French restaurant in the area. I suspect it was her mom who suggested dinner at my home instead of a restaurant, aware someone's home could say a lot about him. She's a wise woman.

I like Luna's dad. He's both a good talker and a good listener, as approachable and open as Luna says he is. Her mom is more reserved. She knows what she wants and is clearly the rudder steering the family, though her dad can temper her Mom's actions when he chooses to.

Before she left for Cambodia, Luna and I agreed to do Facetime every weekend. Sadly, that hasn't worked out. We learned the first weekend that you can't rely on Cambodia's internet service. Not even in Phnom Penh, the largest, most modern city in Cambodia.

We had no choice but to resort to emails. Luna decided she'd do journals again, this time of her adventure living a way of life very different from her own here in California.

She's not using her Moleskine. She left it with me for safekeeping. I loaded her iPad with apps including a couple she could use to write her journal. She shares her journals via email whenever she can. I've been collecting them in a folder in my computer. It's insurance, in case Luna loses what's stored in her tablet. And I can always read them whenever I miss her.

We've also been texting. I've sent her one at least once a day, although I'm never sure when she gets them. She's tried to text me when she can connect to the internet.

Our texts have been short, private, and intimate. Meaningful only to the two us. A lot, as anyone might expect, has been about how much we miss each other.

The two months Luna and I had together were wonderful. And they've exacted a price. But I can speak only of its toll on me.

I have suffered, especially in the first six months. From loneliness. From missing Luna. From imagining she's having the time of her life exploring an exotic world of which I'm not a part. But I tell myself— someday, we'll do it together.

I'd been alone since Minah. But because it was by choice, I endured it. Including the boredom that sets in when you only have yourself for company. Loving someone changes your life. Especially when you love her as deeply as I love Luna. You do things that might have seemed silly before. Who would have thought I'd sleep with an outfit I haven't washed in months? Luna used Gramps' lavalava a lot the two months we lived together. I can smell her on it.

Luna told me she's kissed my picture on her cell phone every night. She took the bust-size photo to try out the camera on the new iPhone I gave her the day before she left for Cambodia.

The cell phone kiss is part of her little ritual before going to bed. I'm thrilled she misses me enough to do this. I take it to mean there's promise in our relationship.

People will think we're lovesick fools. I suppose we are—foolishly, achingly but oh so gloriously lovesick. I guess I can now claim I've experienced love that's bittersweet.

I miss you so, Luna. I've kept crazily busy so it won't hurt too much.

I could text her these words, but I don't. I want her to be free to choose how to live her life. Not to worry about me while she faces new challenges. There'll be time enough for commitment if she comes back to me. In the months we lived together, I did everything I could to show her how much I love her.

*****

Luna's first long email, sent only to me, came a few days after she arrived in Cambodia. She spoke mostly of how much she missed me. Since then, she's written her journal and attached them to emails addressed to me and her parents.

Luna to Lucien and Her Parents, October 2014

I'm now living with my permanent family in Doun Teav Village on the outskirts of Batambang City, about 150 miles north of Phnom Penh. Like at my first host family, my room is fashioned from curtains.

My parents, Anchaly and Davi Chea are rice farmers. I have three siblings although only Jorani, who's fourteen, lives at home. She's in my morning English class. Her two older brothers work in Phnom Penh. I haven't met them yet.

Our house, smaller than the one I lived in on training, is on stilts. The space within the stilts is like a ground floor without walls, and tamped earth under our feet. It has a platform larger than a king-size bed, made of wide bamboo slats. Great for resting on hot afternoons when winds are blowing. A hammock hangs on ropes tied to beams under the house. Ov (meaning "father") uses it for siestas and on particularly warm nights, he sleeps there, too.

We use mosquito nets at night, and insect repellent wherever we have skin exposed. Peace Corps training staff couldn't stress that often enough.

Mosquitoes are vicious blood-sucking creatures. They leave welts where they feast on your blood, and they can cause malaria or dengue fever.

The rural countryside is beautiful. Bucolic in the best sense of the word. Fruit trees and palm trees scattered here and there. Miles and miles of rice paddies, so green at this time of year. I've never seen such a green landscape.

I've been told the ruins of an eleventh-century Hindu temple are near, about five miles. It's called Ek Phnom Temple. It's not the most famous. That distinction belongs to Angkor Wat.

Batambang has several temple ruins, five of them on Banan Mountain. From Doun Teav Village, we can see the mountain, but not the ruins. Can you believe Cambodia has an ancient civilization? Several centuries older than that of the United States.

I had butterflies in my stomach on my first day of teaching. But it didn't take long before I felt more at ease. First, I met the faculty. Then the principal took me to the classroom to introduce me to the students. There, on my desk, was a vase brimming with flowers. Pupils in my classes picked them from the area. Lavender and pale-pink lotuses and a bunch of fragrant, yellow flowers I've never seen before. They had three fat petals spread like wings and three more clustered in the center. Rumduol, they said. Indigenous to Cambodia, it's the national flower. Its perfumy fragrance was so strong I could smell it before I entered the classroom. They tell me it's used in herbal medicines and lip wax.

It was such a touching gesture, I did the som pas to the class. That elicited smiles. Some pupils even clapped. It was a good first day.

My students come from grades seventh to twelfth. I think it's better to start language learning when they're younger, but we're here to meet the local school's needs.

The students seem eager to learn, though it won't be easy. My Khmer is bad and they find it difficult to pronounce English words. I offered free private lessons, but I didn't sense much enthusiasm for them. Except for Jorani, my kid sister. She wants to be ahead of everyone else and to speak like me by the end of the school year.

Luna to Lucien and Her Parents, November 2014

We start our days early. By six o'clock, we're having breakfast. My parents leave for the rice fields and Jorani and I wash the breakfast dishes and spoons. My first class starts at seven.

We only have dirt roads where I live. They get churned into mud by heavy rains and when water overflows from rice paddies. By the time I arrive at school, my shoes are covered in mud, which I have to scrape off before I go to my classroom. So Mae suggested I get flip-flops and change into a pair of sandals at school.

As I walk to school, I see people already working in the rice paddies. They're rectangular fields flooded with water, shored up on all sides by long and narrow mounds of earth.

Mae (Khmer for "mother") says they're transplanting rice shoots. They take a handful of shoots in one hand, bend to stick them into the flooded ground, and repeat these movements until all shoots are planted—backbreaking work done by machines at home.

Rice is life for Cambodians, in more ways than as a staple of their diet.

We're approaching harvesting season and rice fields have turned golden. I'm writing this on a weekend afternoon, sitting cross-legged on the bamboo platform. Watching golden stalks dance in waves with the breeze. Jorani is doing her homework, Ov is snoozing in the hammock, and Mae is in the kitchen making rice cakes.

I love tranquil afternoons like this. They remind me of Grandma under her mango tree.

Luna to Lucien and Her Parents, June 2015

My Cambodian mother is soft-spoken, doing her chores in silence. I see her at breakfast, at dinner, and while she prepares meals. She doesn't announce mealtimes, but we know when we hear the thud of plates on the low table. We come, sit cross-legged around the table, and serve ourselves.

Jorani practices her English at dinner time. We start with me asking her about school. At our first session, she put her spoon down on her plate, sat up straight, and answered me in both French and English. "Ça va. Good. J'aime apprendre English. I ...like ... to learn."

"Why do you like to learn English?"

"Pour quoi? ... Uhh ...parce que..."

I prompted her. "Because ..."

"Because I like to ... go..." —she paused, glancing at her mother— "to université." She fell back into Khmer, and we finished dinner mostly in silence.

Her English is much improved and she's more relaxed. We carry simple conversations in English. Once in a while, she resorts to Khmer. I don't stop her. I think she does this so her parents could understand. It's only then they show interest. Before I came, I suspect they focused on eating. It's serious business, done efficiently in half an hour.

My family eat what's on their plates to the last grain of rice. I first noticed this when no one stood to leave the table after eating. I still had a few grains bathed in sauce on my plate while theirs looked clean. I didn't know they were waiting for me to eat my plate clean as well. After a few minutes, Mae, my host mother, stood up and collected the plates. By the following dinner, I understood what was going on. Now, I try to eat everything on my plate, but that last grain of rice requires two fingers, not a fork or spoon, to pick up.

I have lived eight months with my Cambodian family, but I still don't know my parents well. Ov's face is blank. Mae's is unfathomable. Except for Jorani, she doesn't look directly at anyone. I've seen her peeking sideways at Ov or glancing surreptitiously at me. It's as if she has secrets she would betray if you look into her eyes. She intrigues me the most.

Another teacher at school told me she's made sure her children continue schooling until at least the ninth grade (secondary education goes to twelfth grade). She wants Jorani, the brightest of her children, to go to college. These bits of information intrigue me, especially because dropout rates are high and only a quarter of pupils finish high school. The two Chea sons, Ang and Sieu, both graduated from high school before going to Phnom Penh to work.

Someday, I want to ask Mae, without sounding intrusive, her future hopes for Jorani.

Luna wanted to write a journal every weekend, but she's been too busy to keep it up. A lot of little things crop up. Local problems no one seems to anticipate. They ask her, and she gets involved. It's in her nature to help.

Her days, though full, have been fairly repetitious, which is reassuring. It means she's safe.

I've been reading about Cambodia since she left.
There's consensus in the Western press that the
country's government is repressive. Local press is
muzzled or sometimes forced to close down for saying
things the country's leaders didn't like. These leaders
have killed, imprisoned, or threatened opposition
leaders with impunity.

How can I not worry? Cambodia is a country that,
not too long ago, has been torn by wars between
factions in its people as well as between Cambodians
and neighboring Vietnamese. Could another war be
far behind? How long can any group of people survive
violent repression?

Luna sent me an email that justifies my
apprehension.

Luna to Lucien, January 2016

*I debated with myself whether to tell you or not
what I'm about to relate. Events I would prefer my
parents not to know. At least until I get home and tell
them in person. I don't want them to worry.*

*Several weeks after the journal I sent you and
my parents June of last year, something happened at
home. Something that has left me depressed and
doubting many decisions I've made in the year and a
half I've lived here. There isn't an easy way to
describe these events without reliving them, but I
need somebody to listen and understand, help me bear
the weight of what these months have shown me. If*

Grandma were alive, I would have sent this to both of you. But there's only you now to turn to.

I've written how I felt Mae has been bottling something inside her, how she seems to have secrets. Well, one night, it exploded out of her at dinner. Mae literally had a breakdown. About something I haven't fully grasped and probably never can.

What triggered it started with Jorani's unusual behavior. She's a cheerful, carefree child, doted on by her family. This kid loves to eat and always comes to dinner ready to devour whatever dishes Mae has prepared.

She smiles at everyone and greets me "Good evening." But this particular evening, she stepped out, lips pressed together, from behind the curtain that separates her sleeping area from the living room. No smiles, no greeting. And she was scowling, which I've never seen her do.

I wondered what was going on and, it seemed, so did her parents. We watched her serve herself. She's often the first to begin and the first to finish.

Instead of scooping a big spoonful of rice and fish into her mouth as she usually does, she sat immobile, her head bowed. I realized then that her parents waited for her first big bite before they began eating and I had adopted the habit from them. (Grandma, I recall, took her cue to eat from me as well).

After she has had a few spoonfuls, I always ask about her school day. Jorani is determined to be ahead of her classmates in learning English and this overused conversation starter is how I went along with it initially. We have since progressed through a series of questions. I vary them according to what's going on at home, at school, and news items I laboriously read in local papers. Her answers have grown more elaborate across the more than one year she's been practicing English. Our chat has become a dinner ritual. She's an enthusiastic learner and I'm proud of her. Proud of myself, too, for getting her to this point. She's my first true success story.

Anyway, this evening, she didn't eat. None of us did. After a few minutes of uneasy silence, she raised her head and glared at her parents. She asked them a question in Khmer. I could understand enough to know that she said, "Is it true what I learned in history class this morning?"

Much of what she said went right through me, although I could see she was growing more upset. When I heard the words "Tuol Sleng", I knew she was talking about the Cambodian genocide.

Watching Jorani, I didn't notice Mae was shaking. Then I heard her scream. Her face was contorted in agony. Head shaking violently. Hands balled into tight knots on the table.

Mae's scream stunned me, frightened me. It sounded like the prolonged wailing of an animal I've

286

heard in the area. Jorani said later it reminded her of the howling of pigs being slaughtered. It was a cry of anguish, of untold torture and unimaginable suffering.

Mae's scream trailed into tears she couldn't control. Ov sat immobile to her left, across the table from me. He was watching her, but his eyes were vacant. And his lips were compressed so hard against his teeth that I was afraid he'd cut his lip.

I started to get up to go to Mae and comfort her, but Jorani gripped my arm, held me back.

I was bewildered, angry she restrained me, but I sat down again. I told myself Cambodians have their ways. My attempt to comfort might be seen as undue intrusion. I only see what they allow a stranger like me to see. Whatever those ways might be, I could never learn them in my short time here. I needed to respect them. So I remained in my seat, staring at my plate. Jorani began to cry, too.

Ov stayed in his seat, his face like a mask. What inhumane treatment did he suffer under the Khmer Rouge? How did he survive?

Mae and Jorani eventually stopped crying. Mae got up, her head bowed. With faltering steps, she disappeared into their room. Ov hobbled downstairs, his back more bent than usual.

Jorani and I sat at the table a couple more minutes. Then, without a word, I picked up the plate of grilled fish to put it away. None of us ate.

Jorani rose to help me clear the table. She told me her history class had watched a film about the mass killing and torture of nearly two million people by the Khmer Rouge. They had heard vague rumors about it and had never believed them. But the film showed people recounting their experience in what most Cambodians speak of as the three-year-eight-month-twenty-day period in their history. Many were surviving victims of the purge, and others were former Khmer Rouge soldiers. Some classmates thought the incidents were so monstrous that the film must be a hoax. Jorani believed it, but she wanted to make sure the survivors told the truth.

Mae's anguish convinced her.

Things were left hanging in the air when I went to bed. Still trembling as I sat on the edge of my bed past bedtime, I replayed the incident in my mind, wondering again what untold cruelties my Cambodian host parents had suffered. I tried to go on the internet to find out more about the genocide, but I couldn't get a good connection.

The next morning, I dragged myself bleary-eyed into the still-dark kitchen. No one was there except for Jorani, who was dishing out last night's dinner onto a plate.

"Want some," she asked and I nodded. We ate in silence and didn't see Ov or Mae. We felt rather than knew Mae was still in the house. I imagined hearing her footsteps as she paced in their room. Ov

probably slept on the hammock and left for the rice fields before Jorani and I woke up.

We walked to school together, reluctant to speak. Jorani feared plunging again into the agony and anger of the night before, and I was determined not to provoke it.

I had a premonition we were in for harder days ahead.

Luna

February 2016: Days after Truth Is Revealed

Jorani is standing a few paces outside the door as pupils from my last class of the day rush out of the room. She waits until everyone has left before she approaches me. I peer into her face. It's only now I notice her eyes are red around the rims and she has bags underneath them. What a rough, sleepless night she must have had.

I heard her crying last night, though she tried to suppress it. I stood by the curtain and, in a low voice, asked her how she was doing. She didn't answer. I waited and she never answered. Minutes later, there was only silence, and I went to bed and fell into troubled sleep.

Jorani glances at me, her eyes pleading and her mouth pressed in an effort to rein in pain and confusion from spilling out of it. She twines her arm around mine. Without a word, she leads me back to the classroom. I lock the door.

She sits on a chair in the first row. I take the one next to hers, turning it to face her. Her head is bowed, and her hands are clasped tight on top of the flat, wide arm of her chair.

I wait a few moments for her to speak, but she remains rigid and resolutely silent. "How are you doing, Jorani?"

No answer.

"Would you like to talk?"

She nods, her head still bowed. "I couldn't sleep last night."

"I didn't sleep much, either." I grasp her hands, and they twitch in a reflexive attempt to withdraw them, a reflex she resists. She keeps her hands in mine.

I prompt her again. "The film upset you very much."

Raising her head, she stares into my eyes. "Why?" Her voice is shrill with anguish. "How ... how could they do it? The Khmer Rouge. To other Khmers. People like them. Like us. So many people tortured. So many lost families. How ...?"

The despair and anger gripping her whole body cuts through to my heart. My voice fails me. She wants an answer she could understand, that would satisfy her enough to quiet her mind, let her questions rest so she could begin to forget. An answer I could not give. How does one explain to a child an unfathomable atrocity? An atrocity that I—or anyone else including those who perpetrated them—could never fully comprehend, much less explain to another. A madness that, to my mind, would be impossible, if not criminal, for the world to forget.

But I realize I must say something somehow. I couldn't leave this question hanging, for her sake as much as mine. I venture to explain, not the genocide, but my ignorance at how it came about. "I honestly don't know. I wish I had read more about the genocide before I came here, but I needed to deal with my own concerns about going out into a world entirely new to me. Maybe whatever reasons they give to the world or to themselves to make sense of what they've done, there is no way such acts by the Khmer Rouge or any other group annihilating another, could ever be justified."

My response is vague and not an answer. I regret and am ashamed of my ignorance, but maybe it could convey how difficult it is to find answers because there isn't one. We do it all the time—plod along from day-to-day, mired in routine and habits, so we don't have to confront difficult questions, painful memories, or tasks that are too boring or too tough.

Jorani's brow is knitted in anguish. "I don't understand."

"I'm so sorry I can't explain the mass killing. I don't understand it either."

"I was okay before I saw the film."

"And now?"

Tears roll down Jorani's cheeks. Her mouth is open and her chest is rapidly heaving. Long minutes of her crying pass before she could speak again, words sputtering between sobs. "I ... I am afraid. More afraid

... after last night. Mae—she suffered very much ... didn't she? Was she tortured? Were her mother and brothers? How did she survive?"

Without her being aware of it, Jorani has shown me a way to help her. If I can steer her away from the larger questions of how and why the genocide happened and limit them to its effects on her family, she (and I, as well) may find a way to make sense of it. Having a terrible act hit so close to home is heartbreaking. But focusing on its personal toll, on her own reaction learning the person closest to her had been one of its surviving victims, may bring her closer to coping with it, if not understanding it. And since she is deeply concerned about Mae, it might also incite in her the desire, if not the power, to help her mother come to terms with her own agonies.

"Would you like to ask her?" I'm encouraging her to ask such questions.

"No. No, I cannot. She is Mae. I don't ask."

I squeeze her hands in sympathy. I know the invisible barrier that can keep mothers and daughters apart. Putting their experiences behind them— unsettling for Jorani and harrowing for Mae—is going to be difficult but, I hope, not impossible.

Most Westerners believe one needs to talk about a traumatic experience before they can understand and accept it, something Cambodians are reluctant to do, according to our preservice training instructor. They keep their feelings and thoughts to themselves.

They tend to accept fate—how they are treated and what they are given—without question. The words of elders and authority are also sacrosanct.

Jorani withdraws her hands from mine and lays her head on her arms. She is crying as quietly as it is possible to cry.

My heart breaks as I watch this once innocent, trusting, happy girl morph, from one day to the next, into a bewildered and broken young woman. Learning about the genocide has changed her forever. But I need to believe that with time, she will come to terms with her current ordeal. She has the resilience of youth, and I can reassure her I will be there whenever she wants to talk.

I reach over and lay my hand gently on Jorani's head. I remember Grandma stroking my hair when I was upset or couldn't sleep. It was so soothing it calmed me down enough to sleep or return to playing. I stroke Jorani's hair in Grandma's slow caressing way. After some time, her crying slows into subdued sobs and she raises her head.

Her face is drenched with tears. I give her a couple of tissues from my purse. She wipes her face and the tablet-arm of her chair, also wet with tears.

She braves a smile. A very brief one. She spreads her hands, studying them. "Mae has a younger brother. My uncle. He has seven fingers. And he drags his right foot."

"An uncle. Where's he now?" I wasn't aware there's an uncle.

"He lives in a small village in Thailand. Doesn't see anyone including us." She stares at me, her mouth agape as the truth dawns on her. Her uncle had also been a victim.

We sit in silence thick with repressed chaotic emotions, the weight of which keeps us rooted in our chairs. Minutes later, she says, frowning, "Mae has a brother, but Ov has no one else but us."

She lapses again into silence and I join her in it. We don't move until the room begins to lose the diffused sunshine that usually illuminates the room. I get up. "Let's go home, Jorani. Ov and Mae will be wondering where we are."

We don't see Mae that night, but we hear her occasionally moving about in their bedroom. Jorani and I make dinner—rice, boiled water spinach, and grilled fish. She asks Ov if she should ask Mae to come to dinner or bring her a plate of food. Ov shakes his head. He goes downstairs to sleep in his hammock again. We don't see Mae the next morning either.

*****

Though I can be a sympathetic ear for Jorani, I doubt I can help her fully cope with her crisis. And I'm not equipped to help Mae. Before my first class, I call the Peace Corps office. I recall hearing at orientation about organizations helping genocide survivors deal with the violence inflicted on them. Before going home, I contact one offering such counseling. They tell me they have social workers in Siem Reap who can come and see victims in their homes for a limited number of sessions. Siem Reap is less than fifty miles away, but the trip takes two hours because no roads directly connect us to Siem Reap. They ask if I want to set up an appointment. I say I need to consult with the victim (Victims? Ov was most likely a victim, too.)

I come home early evening to an unexpected but welcome sight. Mae is stirring a beef curry dish in the family's deep earthenware pot, releasing mouthwatering earthy aromas, tempered by the sweet creamy scent of coconut milk. It's seldom that the pot comes out and she makes this dish. Our standby staple for dinner is grilled river fish Ov caught the same day. Jorani says she came home to find Mae cutting the small slab of fresh beef. Ov bought it at the market.

Jorani sits cross-legged on the mat across the low table from Ov. I sit to her right. I watch Mae try to lift the hot pot but it seems too heavy for her. She's uncertain what to do. In the past, Ov usually helped her. Tonight, she gives me a quick glance. I get up to help her. She seems smaller, and her back is hunched as if she wants to fold her body into itself.

I want to hug her, tell her she needn't carry the burden of her past by herself. She can talk to me or to Ov or even Jorani and share her burden with us. But I

don't have the words. I was also afraid of being
intrusive.

Before I realize what I'm doing, I gently place an
arm around her shoulder and draw closer to her. Her
arm, warmer than normal from her having stood next
to the stove, is pressed against my side. I feel its
warmth through my dress. Mae doesn't move, but
neither does she shake off my arm. Except for a
handshake when I first arrived, we've never touched
each other.

Jorani is watching us. Ov cranes his head when he
sees Jorani staring at what's going on behind him. On
the surface, an observer would see nothing going on.
For some seconds, none of us moves. We keep our
poses like mimes waiting for the next sequence of our
act. And yet I sense something. An energy, warm and
prickly passing from Mae through me and Jorani. It
seems to bypass Ov and that puzzles me.

Mae glances at me. She doesn't smile but there's a
glimmer in her eyes. I don't recall her ever looking at
me directly. She always keeps her eyes cast down. She
inclines her head toward the steaming pot.

I pick up the pot and put it down on the table.
She follows me and sits across the table. She smiles.
The smile brightens her eyes, but it's so
instantaneous, it's easy to miss.

We eat in silence and take our time savoring the
delicious stew. When we finish our meal, Jorani
volunteers to wash dishes. Mae nods her assent. She

touches Jorani's arm and glances at me again before she goes to their bedroom.

I prepare for bed more sanguine about the days to come, the trepidation of the night before laid to rest at least this evening. I fall asleep certain life will go on as it has before.

Back to school the following morning, I contact the genocide survivors counseling office again to ask if they can come on a weekend. They say someone is willing to do so for at least an initial visit.

As soon as I turn my phone off, I have qualms about the call I just made. Am I overstepping boundaries unknown to me? Boundaries taken for granted by Cambodians?

Would it have been better to leave things as they are? Mae and Ov have raised normal children and as far as I can tell, they live like any other rural Cambodian family. They've moved on from an epic tragedy. Why stir things up now?

To me, it's clear Mae is still troubled by her past. Maybe, so is Ov. And what about Jorani? She's proof direct victims aren't the only ones who suffer from a crime. She's young and doesn't deserve a future encumbered by the consequences of that genocide.

I must help her. I think I can persuade her to talk to the social worker. She can be a bridge for the social worker to open up a conversation with Mae and Ov.

Luna

II. Days after Truth Is Revealed

"Would you like to talk to someone who might have some answers to questions you have about the genocide?" I say, breaking the silence between me and Jorani while we're walking on the dusty road to school. Rice fields around us have been harvested and will soon be sown again with shoots.

She takes a few moments to answer. "But how? I think about it, I cry. I can't cry in front of my history teacher."

"Mr. Phan, you mean?"

She nods, her head bowed.

Although I've heard often enough that Cambodians grow up believing they should keep their emotions hidden from others including their family, I can't help wondering why she can't talk to her teacher. Mr. Phan, her history teacher, has a reputation among students of being one of the most approachable teachers. I've also heard the young generation of Cambodians have become more open, less afraid to show their feelings. And Jorani did open up to me. But Mr. Phan is young and attractive, and Jorani is a self-conscious fourteen-year-old becoming more aware of her sexuality. Like any teenager everywhere in the world.

"I was actually thinking of someone else," I say, lightly touching her arm. "A kind lady trained to talk to survivors of the genocide."

She shakes her head. "But I'm not a survivor. I didn't suffer like Mae."

"You are a survivor, if you think about it. Children inevitably carry within them the experience of their parents. And you wouldn't be here if your parents hadn't survived."

Jorani shudders and leans forward as if she's about to crumple to her feet. I have underestimated how deeply affected she has been by learning about the genocide. I immediately regret my last remark. But I can't take it back, and I won't. True to my own Western upbringing, I believe facing the truth head-on may help her heal.

I clasp her arm in case she falters in her steps. We walk on for a while.

I say, "This lady is a social worker at Siem Reap who's willing to come to the house on a weekend. She's in an office whose work is to listen and help victims who survived the genocide."

She says, her voice plaintive, "I don't know if I can."

"Talk to her like you talk to me. She knows much more than I do and she's been helping other survivors. She can help you better than I can."

We're silent again until we reach the school. I've broached the idea of therapeutic help, and for the moment, I believe it's enough. I intend to bring it up again, convinced she'll continue hurting unless she gets professional help. I have to keep trying until she acquiesces.

We stop in front of Jorani's math classroom, but before going in, she surprises me. "Not at the house. She'll upset Mae and I'm not sure Ov will permit it."

I recall Mae's anguished cry and know Jorani is right. We need to meet the social worker somewhere else.

"You're right. My classroom, then. I have a key to it and use it on some weekends to meet pupils who need extra help.

"Can I stop when I want to? I don't know if I will like it. Or maybe it's too hard."

"It's all up to you, Jorani. The lady will be here to help, but she won't force you into anything you don't want to do."

"Will you be there with me?"

"I'll come to open the classroom. We can ask if I can be in the room with you.

*****

After lunch on Saturday, I tell Mae and Ov Jorani and I have work to finish at school. I don't need their permission, but Jorani does. We leave after helping Mae with the dishes.

303

The social worker, Mrs. Lee, is waiting for us. A Cambodian of Chinese descent, she's fair, plump, and motherly, maybe in her late forties. I ask her if she needs to talk to Jorani alone, but she thinks Jorani is more likely to talk more freely if I stay.

In Khmer, she asks Jorani the usual things about school for the first ten minutes or so. Jorani answers her as briefly as she can, her gaze shifting from Mrs. Lee to rest on me. Then Mrs. Lee says, "I've seen the film your history teacher showed in class. It gave me nightmares."

I watch Jorani. She stares at the social worker, then at me. Her eyes are starting to glisten with tears. I reach out to grasp her hand.

Mrs. Lee shifts her gaze from Jorani to me and down to my hand clasping Jorani's. She isn't disapproving. I think she's telling me: *You can stay, but please interfere as little as possible.* I release Jorani's hand.

Mrs. Lee turns her attention back to Jorani and says, "What did you think of it? Did you get nightmares, too?"

Jorani nods her head but stays silent.

"Would you like to tell me what you thought of it?"

Jorani pleads with me. "I can't do this. It's too hard. I want to cry. Shout. Hit someone, something."

"It's okay to cry," Mrs. Lee says. "I've cried so much over what happened. I was a little girl and I don't know how I've survived. I can't stop my memories of it. But I'm still here."

Jorani stares, incredulous, at Mrs. Lee. "You were there?"

"Yes. I was seven years old, the youngest of five children. Except for an older sister, everyone else died. My parents. My two brothers."

"Oh, I'm so sorry. So sorry. Can you tell me what happened to you? I want to hear it."

"I will tell you, but first I would like to hear what you thought, how you felt about the film. I would also like to make notes on what we talk about. Is that okay?"

Jorani nods.

"Thank you, Jorani. Now, can you talk to me about what it was like watching the film?"

Jorani recounts her reactions to Mrs. Lee in a calmer voice than she did to us on the evening after she saw the film in school. When she can't think of anything more to say about them, she says, "Please, I want to know what it was like for you under the Khmer Rouge. My parents went through it, too. But they don't talk about it."

Mrs. Lee says, "It's very hard to talk about it. Most survivors prefer to forget it, as if it never happened."

Jorani insists on knowing as much detail as Mrs. Lee could recall, and the session takes two hours.

As Mrs. Lee leaves, she asks Jorani if Mae might want to join them next time they meet. She's willing to come again instead of Jorani and Mae going to Siem Reap to see her.

Jorani says to me. "You think Mae should come, too?"

"I think it will help."

"But how shall we make her?"

"We'll talk to her. Gently. We won't pressure her. She will come when she's ready, I'm sure of it."

If there is a time when Mae might be ready to confront her past, that time is now. Since that moment at dinner a few nights ago when a silent understanding passed between Mae and me, I've been able to read the subtle expressions on Mae's face, in her posture and in her movements. Though she's back to her daily routine, she's tense. She masks her tension well enough, but it won't surprise me if it erupts again. A remark, another revelation, or some incident related to her past could shatter that mask.

Three weeks later, Mae, Jorani and I meet Mrs. Lee again.

*****

Mae and Jorani have been talking to Mrs. Lee every other Saturday for the last three months. Jorani has regained some of her old cheery disposition, but she's also more withdrawn.

She used to spend all her waking hours in the common area or on the bamboo platform underneath the house where she did her homework on a small table across her lap. Lately, she's been retreating to her sleeping area when she gets home from school and only comes out about a half-hour before dinner. She tells me she finds she's more efficient when she does her homework on her lap table while sitting on her bed.

She's also quieter at dinnertime. Though we have resumed English practice, she gives me shorter answers and isn't quite as effusive when she thinks she's done well.

I can't tell how much the talking sessions are helping Mae. I would like to believe they've lightened her anguish over her past. She continues to go, so she must be getting something out of those meetings.

I'm not sure how much longer Mrs. Lee will come. She says she will continue as long as the sessions, in her judgment, continue to be fruitful.

As far as I know, no one has told Ov the reason we go to the school on some Saturdays. He says nothing and walks away when the three of us begin our biweekly trek toward the school. He knows why we go, I'm sure of it, and with his usual stoicism, has quietly accepted it.

Once in a while, though, I catch a dark look in his eyes. A look gone in seconds. I don't know what to make of it, and it troubles me.

An Unforeseen Ending

Three months later, as I sit at my desk in my classroom reading and correcting pupils' papers, Jorani flings the door open and bursts in.

Shaking and panting, she says in a frantic voice, "You have to come with me. Ov has a gun. He's going to kill himself."

They're shocking words I have trouble processing at first. I guess I find it hard to believe what Jorani is saying. She repeats what she said, and though I'm still bewildered, her distress prods me to shove the papers I've been correcting in the top drawer of my desk. After I lock the drawer, Jorani pulls me by the arm.

She tells me what happened as we run toward the house, stirring up dust on a road between barren rice fields, golden with ripening grains only two months before. She came home from school early to see Ov sitting cross-legged on the bamboo platform, hands resting on his lap. From afar, his eyes seemed closed, as if he was in deep thought.

Only when she was close enough did she see the gun in his hand. He didn't notice her approach and only opened his eyes when she let out a sharp breath. He stared at her with unseeing eyes.

Frightened and uncertain what to do, Jorani stepped back and sprinted back to school.

From a short distance away, we see Ov doubled up, his head on his knees. Jorani utters, "No," in Khmer. She runs faster, ahead of me.

By the time I catch up, she's standing in front of the platform, a couple of feet from where he sits. She's strangling a cry. I bend over slowly toward him. His body is heaving; up, down, up, down. His breathing is fast and labored. I see no blood.

I call out softly, "Ov."

Ov jerks himself upward, points the gun at me and says, "Back. Go back." Frightened and surprised, I retreat a few steps back and put my arms up. "Ov, it's me, Luna."

Jorani cries out, "No," as she falls a few steps back behind me.

He knows English. A few words at least. This incongruous thought distracts me for a moment. It impresses me. Has he been paying more attention than I thought to the practice conversations between me and Jorani?

Ov points the gun to his head.

Jorani shouts in Khmer, "No, Ov, please. No."

I tell myself to keep calm, but I'm aware I'm trembling all over. "Ov, please, put the gun down."

I'm at a loss what to do, but at that moment, I wish I had taken more time and serious effort to learn

Khmer. I glance quickly at Jorani and say, "Translate."

I say the first thing I could think of. "Ov, think of Mae and Jorani. Who will bring them fish and meat for dinner? They need you. Please put the gun down."

Ov's usually expressionless face contorts as he spews out words Jorani translates. "This is not your problem. Stay out."

"Yes, I'm only a visitor here. In a few months, I'll be gone. But I've come to love this family and I know they mean a lot to you. Mae, Jorani, and your sons, they love you. They'll suffer if you kill yourself. So please give me the gun. We won't tell anyone what happened this afternoon."

Grim and pained after Jorani translated what I said, Ov spits out words as if they were burning his mouth. Behind me, I hear Jorani gasp and mutter, "No."

I turn my head toward her. "Jorani, what did he say?"

She draws in another long breath to keep herself from crying. Fear and perplexity are written on her face. "He said, 'Stay out of this, I say. I deserve to die. I killed too many people.'"

Frozen in place hearing those words, I struggle for a moment, refusing to let them sink in, resisting what they imply. As I allow myself to fully grasp what he means, I feel as if a big, heavy cloud has swallowed me. I can't breathe. My head is in a vise grip.

"Luna, what does he mean?" Jorani's voice pierces the chaos in my brain.

It takes me some moments to answer. "I think he's telling us ... he was Khmer Rouge ... a soldier, a Khmer Rouge soldier."

"No, no, not him."

Ov's face contorts in pain watching Jorani's horrified disbelief. He turns to me and says in English, "Yes, me, Khmer Rouge. I die."

I knew before he confirms it that he has confessed the truth, but hearing him articulate it knocks the wind out of me all over again.

"No, no, no. No!" The first nos uttered under Jorani's breath erupt into an ear-splitting and heartbreaking sound that splinters the atmosphere above the green, tranquil rice fields.

I step toward Jorani and put my arm around her shoulders. Her body is racked by violent shaking. She buries her face on my chest and howls.

Both sickened and angry at his revelation, I try to control my trembling. Words tumble out of my mouth. Forced, insincere words. "Ov, please. We don't want you to die. This family needs you. Mae and your children have suffered enough. Don't let them go through more pain and hardship."

I prod Jorani, "Tell him what I said." She does so between sobs.

He says again, "Me, Khmer Rouge. I die."

I shake my head. "No, Ov. Too many people have died already. Who'll bring Mae and Jorani fish and meat? You're the only one who's done it all these years." More words I utter because I have to.

"So many people I kill. Hundreds, maybe. I, monster. I die."

"Does Mae know you killed people?"

"She know. She not love me. She put up with me. I love her."

I don't contradict him. I say again what one is supposed to say, "Your children love you. Jorani, tell him. Tell him you love him."

I'm still holding Jorani, and she shakes her head against my chest.

I'm watching Ov closely. For an instant, he blinks, a flicker of hope in his eyes. He's waiting for Jorani's reassurance.

But Jorani refuses to raise her head. She shakes it vehemently and says to me, "No, no. I don't love him anymore. I hate him."

Did Ov, with his rudimentary English, understand what she said? The shaking of Jorani's head and the vehemence in her voice could not fail to convey how Jorani feels. Hope dies in Ov's eyes. The plains of his face are crunched in despair.

His despair reawakens my alarm, summoning some instinctive compassion for another human being in obvious agony. "Talk to him Jorani, please. I know you don't mean what you said. It's an awful, terrible thing to learn—but he was young when he became Khmer Rouge, maybe still a boy. He wasn't in control of what he was doing. He probably killed under threat to his own life."

I realize as I speak that I'm trying to convince not only Jorani, but myself as well. That somehow, there's some way to explain, to understand what he did. That though he can never be absolved of atrocious crimes of genocide, someone else who knew what they were doing must be blamed, must be punished for it.

"He killed my uncles. I'm sure of it." Jorani lifts her head from my chest. She steps away from me, advances a step toward her father, and in Khmer, says, "Did you kill my uncles and my grandparents?"

Ov doesn't answer, and Jorani stares at him, shaking her head again. "How could you?" To me, she says, her eyes brimming with tears, "How could he?"

Ov assumes that blank face I've often seen on him, but he's grinding his teeth so hard I wondered for an instant if his jaw could crack. Then in a swift move, he raises the gun to his head.

Fires.

A flash. A sharp loud crackle. Ov's head lurching away from the gun.

He slumps forward, one arm slack above the side of his head. His hand dangles down the bamboo platform.

The gun falls to the ground.

Jorani screams, but I'm too stunned, frozen where I stand. Only a soft impotent "No" escapes my lips.

Blood begins to pool by Ov's head, trickles through the bamboo slots and down to the ground underneath him, staining it.

I'm rooted in place, shocked into immobility. An unforeseen few seconds dragging like eternity. A moment that has changed me forever, that will haunt me as long as I live. I will never again be what I was before Ov fired the gun into his head.

Jorani is panting, sobbing. She turns and runs.

I shout, "Jorani, come back!"

She keeps running. Unsure what to do and scared to approach the body or be alone with it, I run after her. "Jorani, please stop. We need to tell someone. You have to come with me. The police, we must go to the police."

Jorani stops to catch her breath, and wait for me. "He's right. He deserved to die. He was a monster. How could I have loved him?"

"Jorani, he was your father. He was maybe fifteen or sixteen when he became Khmer Rouge, too young to understand what he was getting into."

"He should not have been Khmer Rouge."

"But maybe he had no choice."

Jorani doesn't answer. Then she drops her face on her hands.

I gather her close to me. I have to comfort her. But I also need to feel the solidity of her to help still my shaking. I need her warmth to tell me I'm not alone. "Jorani, we have to tell the police."

Then I remember Mae. Where is she? What if she comes home and finds Ov's body? One of us must find Mae before she goes home.

"Jorani, where's Mae?"

"At the market. She was making rice cakes to sell this morning."

"You have to go, find her, tell her what happened. Can you do that?"

"I don't know."

"You have to. I'm going to the police. I can talk to them in French. I'm sure there's someone there who would understand. Please Jorani, we have to do this."

"But what will I say to Mae?"

"I think you'll know what to say when you see her. Maybe you don't have to say anything. She'll know when she sees you that something terrible has happened. Go. You have to find her before she gets home."

Jorani clings to me for a second or two before she runs in the direction of the market. I go to the police station.

*****

By the time I return to the house with the lone policeman from the small village office, I am reasonably calm. I'm not sure how I looked to him when he saw me, a dazed foreigner clearly not from the area, speaking to him in broken French he didn't understand. But he seemed to know who I was and was concerned enough by my distress.

Before I finished explaining, he rose from his chair and gestured to me to show him what I was babbling about.

He seems in no hurry to reach the house, and I have to slow down to adapt my pace to his. He starts to whistle, and his nonchalance helps me rein in my despair and disbelief at the events of the last hour. Maybe I have to be as detached as he is so I don't fall apart.

A few feet from the house, he stops whistling and he recoils at the sight in front of him. He stands still for a minute, gazing at Ov's body on the bamboo platform. I'm standing behind him, and though I can't see his face, I know he's shocked. He's probably never had to investigate violent killings in this tranquil little village.

He pulls a pair of surgical gloves out of a back pocket and puts them on. He hesitates for a moment before he approaches Ov's lifeless body. He examines it from different vantage points, walking along the length of the platform where the body lies, turning the corner, and bending over to look closer at the head wound. He takes pictures.

He sits on his haunches, scanning the area under the bed, his head turning to one side, then slowly toward the other side a couple of times. The blood under the bamboo platform has seeped into the dirt, leaving only a large magenta stain. A salty, fishy, and musky smell assaults my nose as a light breeze blows through. It's the smell of dried blood. I also notice that flies have begun to swarm around the body.

The policeman pokes at the gun lying on the ground below Ov's hand. He hooks his gloved forefinger through the loop around the trigger, and places the gun in a plastic bag he fishes out of another pants pocket.

He gets up, circles the whole bed, and takes more pictures.

Not once has he touched Ov.

Watching him, it suddenly seems the past hour has been nothing but a dream. It's about as surreal. I hear the faint but sharp clicks of the camera when he takes pictures, but I don't hear the usual sounds I've associated with the place—birds chirping, breezes softly humming, tall coconut trees rustling with strong winds.

For an instant, I panic. What's wrong with me? Am I going out of my mind? I can't lose control now. Mae and Jorani need my help. No, it's only my mind playing tricks on me.

Mae and Jorani arrive at that moment. They stop where I stand outside the perimeter of the house. They stare at me.

Jorani touches my arm. "Luna, are you okay?"

I blink and meet her gaze. "Yes. I think I just got disoriented for a moment."

The policeman pauses in his investigation and greets Mae with a slight bow. They seem to know each other. He goes back to looking, poking, and taking pictures.

Mae glances at the body, sucks in her breath, and turns away. Jorani and I lead her to the hammock where she sits down. She doesn't cry and doesn't look at Ov's body again. Jorani sits down next to her.

A few minutes later, the policeman approaches the hammock to ask them questions. Jorani answers. With her first words, her lips begin to quiver. When asked about what she witnessed, her agitation grows as she recounts what happened. As soon as she stops talking, she covers her face with her hands and bursts into tears.

The policeman stands before them, uneasy, unsure what to do about Jorani's distress. A minute or two later, he bows his head again, and returns to where Ov lies, slumped on the bed.

*****

The policeman has been gone a few minutes. Mae, Jorani, and I remain seated on the hammock, silent, our eyes cast down. But my mind seems to have a way of dissociating itself from me. It keeps firing away just when I think I have calmed down. The image of Ov firing the gun flashes through my mind. I gasp. Shiver with cold despite the heat. Jorani and Mae look sideways at me but say nothing. What is going on in their minds?

Most of us never see someone we've lived with kill themselves. I can say it's terrible. Gruesome. Devastating. Even when that someone has a dark, destructive past they kept hidden for a long time. A past that, though they succeeded in hiding it from others, must have tormented them. But none of those words can say it all.

Until you've gone through it, you can't ever imagine what it's like. It's worse than being hit by a speeding train. A speeding train will kill you, and you won't ever have days ahead to relive those horrifying moments. It's the memories, the flashbacks that could be your undoing.

Sometime later, Mae gets up. Without looking at Jorani and me or the corpse, Mae ascends the stairs to the house. She returns a few minutes later, carrying a bucket of water, rags, and a white sheet. She hands Jorani the *krama* she usually wears on her head to shield her from the sun, and tells Jorani to gather guava leaves. I help Jorani.

Mae steps up the bamboo platform and crawls on her hands and knees next to the body. She dips the rags in water and scrubs off the bloodstains.

She's still scrubbing by the time Jorani and I have gathered as many leaves as the scarf would hold. Mae takes the scarf of guava leaves from us and lays it on the platform. She continues scrubbing.

Jorani returns to sit on the hammock, watching her mother.

As the dried blood liquefies again under the wet rags, I feel queasy. I step out from under the house and into waning sunlight, but I can't blot out the squish, squish of rags rubbing against bamboo. I want to shout, cry, *I'm tired, so tired*, and let my body crumple to the ground.

But I can't lose control now. I drag myself to sit back-to-back with Jorani.

Minutes later, the scrubbing stops. I turn to see Mae scattering the guava leaves over Ov's body. She spreads the sheet on top of the leaves. I learn later that guava leaves mask the smell of rotting flesh.

Mae tells Jorani to throw the rags into a trashcan and the bucket of bloody water on a patch of grass. "Call your brothers," she says wearily. "Tell them Ov is dead. I will explain to them what happened when they arrive. They will make arrangements for the funeral."

She motions for me to help her step down from the platform. Her legs wobble. Her face glistens with sweat, and her hands tremble. Washed-out blood stains her dress. Before I help her up the stairs into the house, I hand Jorani my iPhone and she stays behind to make her call.

321

Inside the house, Mae touches my arm in gratitude and glances at me with melancholic eyes. She disappears into her room. I don't see her again until later that night.

Mae's Story

It's past midnight. I can't sleep, and I can't read. My body is restless, but my mind is blank. Jorani parts the curtain between us. I beckon her to sit with me. I scoot up to give her some space on the bed, glad to be with another soul to commiserate with.

She sits, her head bowed. "I should not have told him I didn't love him. Is it my fault he killed himself?"

Should I feel guilty that I didn't try hard enough, sincerely enough to prevent him from killing himself?

If I have any sense of guilt, I suppress it. I say, "No Jorani, no. None of us knew his past haunted him. He hardly ever said anything. He seemed to me no different from other older men in this village. And he was clearly devoted to Mae, to you and your brothers."

She bows her head lower and crosses her arms tight around her chest as if she's comforting herself. I doubt my answer reassures her.

An unusually clear and strong voice says in Khmer, "He was good to us, his family."

I look up to see Mae holding aside the curtain that shields my personal space from the living area. Her pale-yellow dress reflects light on her face. It

323

strikes me how serene she looks. She approaches Jorani.

"But I could not love him. And he knew it."

In a plaintive voice, Jorani says, "Mae, I don't understand. What do you mean?"

"I'll tell you my story, but not tonight. It's only one among many. Maybe if parents like me who survived tell their stories to their children, those terrible years would never be repeated."

Mae is stroking her daughter's hair as she speaks. Her voice is calm. I realize she's not grieving as much as Jorani is.

What agony, what torture did she suffer that she can take Ov's suicide with equanimity? Maybe, even with relief?

But I'm not one to judge. When Ov shot himself after admitting he was a Khmer Rouge, I remember staring at his slumped body and thinking, *Poetic justice.* A tragic atonement. For all the cruelties he inflicted on helpless victims. For the many murders he committed. For willingly participating in the annihilation of innocent people. Maybe it was a callous thought, one I might agonize over in days to come. But at that moment, I couldn't feel sorry for it.

Before I go to bed, I write Lucien and hope the internet sends my email tonight.

Luna to Lucien, March 2016

You know about Mae's breakdown and Jorani's anguish when she learned about the genocide. Well, I have more I must get off of my chest.

These last few weeks have been a nightmare. I would prefer to tell you everything in person, but there's an ocean between us and we need a stroke of luck to do Facetime. Writing this brings back the sorrow, the despair, the disbelief, but I'll burst if I keep it in.

I'll tell you right out: Ov killed himself.

It's the ultimate consequence of Jorani asking questions. Before he shot himself, Ov confessed to being Khmer Rouge and killing many. He must have felt guilty all these years, and it caught up with him, but that's too simple an explanation.

I'll tell you more about the events and my thoughts on it when we meet again. For now, I can pretend you're here to hold me. The memory of that afternoon haunts me. Unbearably.

Hold me please and tell me you'll be there for me when I return.

In the morning, I awake to a notification on my phone. I reach for my cell phone on the small night table by my bed. A message from Lucien. For the first time, I thank Cambodia's internet connection. It came through when it mattered.

I am with you. Close your eyes and you'll feel my arms around you. Rest your head on my chest. Can you hear my heart beating? I can feel yours. Stay for as long as you want. I won't let you go until you're ready. I love you.

I hug my pillow. Read his message a few more times. Tears start to roll down my cheeks. I whisper back, "I love you."

After breakfast an hour later, Mae gets dressed for going out. She dictates what we must do.

"I expect your brothers to be here by noon. Make sure they have something to eat. Ang will know what to do."

She pulls her black *krama* to cover her head and slips on canvas loafers at the entry. "I'll see someone who can make a coffin."

Her transformation fascinates me. She's like a bird released from its cage.

*****

That night, after supper, Mae asks Jorani and me to come to her bedroom. She pats the bed on either side of her and we sit, flanking her. She says she's ready to tell us about her years under the Khmer Rouge.

She takes a sip of water from a glass on her bedside table and begins. "My father was an official in the government of Lon Nol, and we lived in Phnom Penh. He knew there was going to be a Khmer Rouge takeover. All of us, children, already suspected something unusual and dangerous was going on.

"Father said he had sent for a cousin who was a farmer to take us, his children and his wife, to the cousin's village in Batambang province, pass us off as his own and our mother as his sister."

"Father feared for what would happen to us if the Khmer Rouge learned we were related to a Lon Nol official. So my mother, me and my younger brother traveled to a small village. I can't recall the name. My father and two older brothers stayed at home in Phnom Penh.

"Two weeks upon arriving at the village, Mother received news that the Khmer Rouge had captured Phnom Penh and people were being ordered to leave the city. We waited for Father and my brothers to come. But they never did.

"Soon, the Khmer Rouge reached our village. Fathers were separated from families. I remember the fear on the face of our father's cousin as they pushed him forward with the handle of a rifle.

"The Khmer Rouge took the few precious possessions we brought from home, and put Mother, me, and my younger brother in a camp. There were already many women and children in the camp.

"The first thing Mother did was dye the few clothes we were allowed to have. Everyone was told to wear the same clothes of black shirts, black pants, and red checkered *kramas* (scarves). Everyone was put to work in the rice fields.

"My brothers and I had gone to school and unlike Ov, I had learned to read and write, but I couldn't let anyone know that. Mother said that showing off what we know might get us killed.

"We were made to go to meetings where obedience to Angkar was stressed over and over. I wondered who Angkar was and later understood it to be the unseen ruling power. Divisions among classes had been wiped out, Angkar said, and everyone would labor in rice production for the benefit and good of everybody.

"They were lying to us. We worked long and hard, but we never had enough to eat. The bags of rice they gave us did not last as long as the days we were supposed to consume them. People were disappearing, and we saw many beaten up or killed as punishment for reasons that were vague or seemed unjust.

"When after a few months, Father and my older brothers didn't come, I knew we had lost them forever. Mother survived only a few months in the camp. She had always been fragile and weak and died from exhaustion and starvation."

Mae pauses and wipes her eyes. She didn't realize tears have been streaming down her face. "I'm tired," she says in a voice so low I hardly hear it. Jorani and I get up and leave her to rest.

I've never seen the expressions on Mae's face change as much as they did when she was relating her past. Trembling fear, suppressed anger, despairing hopelessness—pain and suffering recalled as if she's reliving them. Despite all that, some inner strength pours out of her, a confidence that seems to surprise her, but which she draws on.

*****

Mae finishes her story the night after the funeral. We sit with Mae on her bed. Ang and Sieu, Jorani's older brothers, sit on a mat on the floor. We listen to Mae's story about being forced to marry.

"One day, three years into Khmer Rouge rule— the year I turned seventeen, several women and I were taken from the field where we were sowing rice shoots and led into a hall. A group of Khmer Rouge soldiers stood on one side of the hall, looking uncomfortable. A few other women prisoners, heads bowed, were on the opposite side.

"The women were informed that a mass marriage ceremony was taking place that afternoon and we were going to be the brides of the soldiers waiting in front of us.

"Every one of the women was silent. We had known of the forced marriages, had heard that women who refused were in danger of being killed. But when I glanced at the man I was supposed to marry, I wanted to run away. I didn't care if they killed me. I recognized him. He was the man who tortured my younger brother. I was also sure he made my father and my older brothers disappear. If I had a knife, I would have struck him then.

"I had watched him cut off my younger brother's fingers after he was caught trying to hide a frog he seized with his hands in a rice paddy. We had been starving. The rationed food was never enough, but taking anything from the rice paddies where we toiled was considered stealing, punishable by torture.

"Ov was not only cruel. He was also ignorant, and I despised him even more for it because I had to hide something I was proud of—that I could read and write.

"I expected to be taken somewhere to be punished for refusing. He took me to a room where I thought he'd force himself on me, and he'd keep on doing it until I could no longer refuse to marry him or until I died. I had heard such stories. But he left me there without doing or saying anything, locking the door behind him. When he came back the next day, he talked to me, promising that by marrying him, he would protect me and my brother, and we would always have enough to eat.

"In the end, I agreed to marry Ov. He had gained stature in the camp and was, by then, an assistant to the head of the camp. I was determined to survive and realized he was the only sure way I and my brother could do so. I still hated him, but it was only later when I heard the rumors of a Vietnamese attack did I know that, in my heart, I still wanted revenge. I was powerless to do it myself, but I believed and hoped spirits would eventually punish him and all the other Khmer Rouge. I wanted to be around to see it."

The retribution came sooner than Mae expected. They had been married only a few months when rumors spread around the camp that the Vietnamese had invaded the country. Fighting had already occurred on the border between Vietnam and Cambodia. The Khmer Rouge were defeated, and camp prisoners in the area escaped or were freed. The Vietnamese were sure to advance deeper into Cambodia.

"One night, a few days after the rumors, Ov woke us up to tell us we were leaving the camp, going somewhere toward Thailand. He said if we all wanted to survive, no one must know he was Khmer Rouge. We obeyed. Years of captivity and fear had robbed me of the person I used to be. I was too exhausted, my spirit too beaten up. We were dependent on him for food and protection.

"We walked through forests at night and hid under thick vegetation during the day. He had packed food for us, stolen from the camp's kitchen. We walked for days and came upon a refugee camp at the Thai border. We could have stayed there but we didn't. We joined lines for food in the daytime and went to the nearby woods to sleep. Ov trusted no one.

"When the war ended, Ov took us to this village. He grew up two villages away, but preferred where we were because, at that time, it was more isolated. He found work and slowly, we built a life as normal as any other in the village.

"Only much later, when Sieu was born, did he tell me he had requested the Khmer Rouge camp supervisor for us to marry. He had been watching me and had fallen in love.

"I buried my hatred after Jorani was born, and later, even forgave him. He had kept his promise. He had devoted his time and energy to making sure his family was safe and always had food and even an occasional feast. I was grateful my children turned out well, especially Jorani, who I'm sure will go to the university. My life with him was peaceful. But I could never love him.

"I told him I never wanted to know how many people he tortured and killed. The atrocities I had witnessed had receded in my memory, but I could never forget them. They would always be there, a stone wall between us he could never break the way he broke my spirit. Only after he died did I realize I held on to the hope that the Khmer Rouge killers must be punished no matter what it takes and how long. I realized that I agreed to marry him because, back of my mind, I will stand as a reminder of the carnage he agreed to participate in.

"All these years, I did what I believed was expected of me as a good wife. But I had dreams that tormented me—my mother's sunken eyes and the sharp feel of her bones under her skin, my brother's hands dripping with blood where Ov had hacked off his fingers, people he dragged by their hair and beaten, or hoisted up on a tree with a noose around their necks until they died.

"Is it wrong to feel that in his dying, my soul is finally at peace?"

The Aftermath

Mae's sons Ang and Sieu arrive midmorning the day after the suicide. Standing shocked and distressed before the body of their dead father, they listen to their mother explain what happened. I can only imagine how much of the truth she tells them.

Ang lifts the white sheet and brushes off the leaves on Ov's face. A faint but unmistakable odor of decaying flesh wafts through the air. Ang covers Ov's face again.

The brothers step onto the bamboo platform. Sitting on one side of the corpse, they press their hands together and bow their heads. Mae, Jorani, and I go up into the house and leave them to pray.

Shortly thereafter, Sieu comes to tell us they're ready to start the preparatory rituals for cremating the body.

Standing in the open air and out of the way, I watch the preparations. I understand from what Jorani told me, only the family can carry these out.

They swathe the body in a fresh white sheet, and surround it with incense. The incense sticks, Jorani says, are for spirits and deities who will guide Ov to his next life. A better sin-free life she hopes.

Soon after the preparations are finished, a Buddhist monk in a flowing orange robe arrives with his assistant, a novice monk. They step up the platform, and sit in front of an altar the family improvised. They start chanting prayers.

The altar has been set up on Jorani's low lap table next to Ov's body. It displays a small picture of Buddha in the same orange robe, sitting cross-legged, his head alight in a golden halo. Several candles and bright-colored flowers in vases cast a warm glow on the picture. The brothers wanted to put a picture of their father on the altar, but Mae says she has no pictures of him.

In the afternoon, villagers trickle in to view the corpse and join the chanting. They sit on the bamboo platform behind the monks, their legs folded back to one side, their hands in the traditional som pas.

I don't recognize many villagers, but I see many more I've met—teachers, pupils, and families I've helped. In the months I've lived with the Cheas, none of these people has visited the family. Jorani doesn't know many of them either. But Cambodian tradition dictates that when someone dies in your village, you offer your presence or support whether you are a good friend of the grieving family or a relative stranger.

Late in the afternoon, when chanting is over and the monks have drunk some milk and left, the family wash the corpse with soap and water, sprinkle it with fragrant potions, dress it, and place it in a simple

home-made wooden coffin two men brought in earlier.
They cover the coffin and leave it on the bamboo
platform for the night.

During three days of rituals, village women bring
dishes or ingredients they would cook over a fire
someone set up outside the house and prepare small
feasts for monks, mourners, and Ov. He needs
nourishment while traveling to the spirit world and,
everyday, a fresh tray of food and drink is placed next
to his coffin. I do what I can to help cook and serve.

Early the next day, the monk returns with two
other monks. After breakfast, they begin morning
prayers. Villagers trickle in once more. Among them,
I see the policeman who investigated the suicide.

After the prayers, we congregate for the walk to
the cremation site.

The brothers, aided by the two men who brought
the coffin, hoist it on their shoulders. Led by the
monks, we walk for nearly an hour to a meadow
surrounded by a thicket of trees. Jorani says the dead
must be carried to a place far away from the living.

Men gather dry wood for the fire. With the coffin
in place on the makeshift pyre, the monks chant more
prayers before Ang lights some twigs in the pyre.

The fire spreads quickly into a hypnotizing blaze.
But as it eats up the wooden coffin and exposes the
blackening corpse, an acidic and bitter fluid rises from
my stomach. Afraid I might throw up, I move away
from the pyre to stand behind the crowd of mourners.

I hear someone gasp but other than that, the crackling fire is the only sound that disturbs the stillness.

It takes a couple of hours for everything to burn and the embers to die down to a flicker. The villagers leave but the family stay to collect the ashes in an earthen jar Mae brought with her. I leave with the villagers.

Back at the house, I find everything but the altar has been put back in the usual place. A few of the village women had stayed and cleaned up.

I stumble up the stairs into the house and lie down on my bed. I doze off, but wake up shortly thereafter to a jumble of voices speaking a language I cannot understand. Disoriented, I look around and remember where I am when I see the curtain by the foot of the bed.

*****

The villagers are gone and the family is at rest. I lie awake in bed, unable to block out the snoring of one of the brothers. They're sleeping on mats in the living area. I toss and turn, reflecting on the events of the past few days.

I can't help but be awed by the people in the village, their compassion, their customs. They shared the family's grief and gave their help and support, as if it's the most natural thing to do. I doubt there are many places back home with such a sense of community. In the wake of sadness or tragedy, it's reassuring to think you're not alone, that you can rely on someone to come when you need help.

Still, I wonder if the family said anything about the suicide. Back home, families are often at pains to hide the suicide of a family member from other people.

A few people might have heard the gunshot or seen the policeman come to the house. Surely, they would have suspected Ov died from something other than natural causes. Mr. Phan—Jorani's history teacher—who attended the cremation rituals told me Cambodians believe death by violent means is a bad death, that it might affect how the ritual ceremonies are conducted and how the villagers react.

And, what would the villagers have done had they discovered Ov was a Khmer Rouge soldier?

*****

A week later, I get a call from the Peace Corps. Phnom Penh newspapers have reported Ov's suicide and they have decided to move me back to Phnom Penh as soon as they find someone to take over. The organization's mission is to respond to the needs of underdeveloped countries, but their first responsibility is to ascertain volunteers are safe and healthy. I was brought here to teach English, not deal with a suicide and its aftereffects. Trained administrative staff will be sent to assess the needs of the Chea family and appropriate help will be provided.

I assured them I was coping well enough, but they believed I suffered a trauma. Did I? How could I have been traumatized more than the family?

Peace Corps calls me a second time to tell me I could stay to the end of the semester. Though I would have preferred to finish the school year, this reprieve gives me two months to do more of what I can for Jorani and Mae. Or so, I tell myself. Deep within, I also realize I can't endure leaving abruptly.

Ang and Sieu stay a few more days. By tradition, they're arranging to provide for Jorani's and Mae's day-to-day necessities, including Jorani's school expenses. The brothers have been sending money to the family since they started working, again following tradition. Some villagers have also contributed enough money for Mae to buy food for the next three months.

Both brothers are unmarried and Ang, the oldest, said he was willing to return to the village and take over the work Ov had been doing. But Mae is adamantly against it. She hasn't actually said why. I suspect it's because she would rather leave the past behind and start a new life. She wants to sell the small land they own, and at the end of the school year, move to Phnom Penh where she grew up. In three years, she says, Jorani will be attending the university there.

It seems Mae and Jorani don't need my help, after all, and I can, in good conscience, return to Phnom Penh for the rest of my assignment. But I am reluctant to leave. I will miss Mae and Jorani and this little village that has welcomed me and taught me so much.

As the day of my departure comes nearer, a sense of being all alone grows inside me. Some days, that sense of aloneness brings tears to my eyes.

You get attached to people you live with and the ties that bind you are deeper when, together, you've shared and coped with a harrowing experience. I need to get used to the idea of leaving, of parting from those who understand my sorrow, my fear, my anger without having to explain myself.

The parting with Jorani has been the most tearful, done over a few nights. She comes to my sleeping area after dinner and cries on my shoulders. I have to reassure her I'll send her emails at least weekly. She wonders if she can come visit me in California.

On my last night with my family, I stay awake for a long while. Jorani has come and gone to bed. Her familiar, gentle snoring as soon as she falls asleep often lulls me to sleep. But tonight, it bothers me.

I am going home, I tell myself. I can leave my memories, my sorrow, and my fear behind. Return to the life I used to have. But can I? I have changed.

For now, I must tell Lucien and my parents I'll soon be home. I reach for my iPad, already packed in my carry-on bag. It's been some time since I composed a joint email to Lucien and my parents.

Luna to Lucien and her parents, May 2016

I'm sorry it's taken me so long to send you my latest news. I'm being moved to Phnom Penh to help prepare for the arrival and orientation of new volunteers.

I know it's been months since my last email. I've been busy. My involvement in this community isn't limited to school and everything associated with it. I'm always asked by someone in the village to help put out fires—mostly little but sometimes big. They seem to think that since I'm a teacher and an American, I have superpowers (just kidding) and can solve most of their problems. It's exhausting. And frustrating. And ego-busting when I fail to help solve or at least alleviate a problem they were initially sure I could solve.

So, I confess I'm relieved to be moving back to Phnom Penh. I'll be there for three months before I return home. I can't wait to see you all again.

Part 3:

Under the Mango Tree

Luna

The Return:

Late in the afternoon, a week before my return to
California, a knock on the door startles me as I pack.
I'm going on a trip to see more of Cambodia, starting
with the famous Angkor Wat. My last and only chance
to see a little more of this country I've lived in for two
years before I leave it, maybe forever.

I'm not expecting anyone, and I vacillate whether
to answer the knock or ignore it. I haven't exactly
been sociable or in the best of moods lately. Let them
think there's no one home.

As far as the Peace Corps is concerned, I have
completed my term of service. For the last three
months, I have assisted in the orientation of new
volunteers, a straightforward process ruled by a
manual. The tasks are clear and specific, discharged
with relative ease. Though boring sometimes, they
kept my mind off the tragic incidents of my last
months at Doun Teav Village.

I'm now free to do as I please. No one I know in
Phnom Penh could have any business with me
anymore. If I don't answer, maybe whoever is at the
door will leave.

Since I've inhabited this two-bedroom apartment, no one has ever come to visit me. Usually, two volunteers share this apartment, but Peace Corps agreed to let me have it to myself. The tragic events of my last couple of months in Doun Teav worked in favor of my request. Besides, I would be here for only three months more.

A second knock, more insistent and repetitive, startles me once more. This time, out of curiosity, I drop the dress I'm folding on the bed and peek through the window adjacent to the door, still with no intention of letting anyone in. But I can't believe my eyes when I see the man standing in front of the door.

Surprised, disconcerted, and excited all at the same time, I open the door and gape at Lucien. Standing as if frozen in place, I can't think of anything to say. I could have said his name, but surprise has struck me dumb. I can't even smile. We look straight into each other's eyes and for a long moment, he stands as still as I am, my chaotic emotions mirrored on his face.

The sight of him is so unexpected. And yet so welcome. My heart skips a beat as he breaks into that appealing dimpled smile that lights up his expressive blue eyes. Seeing his tall, lean frame and clean-cut features, I think: *He's beautiful. Why didn't I see that until now?*

Though tanned and dressed casually in faded blue jeans, a short-sleeved gray shirt, and well-worn leather sneakers, he has a patrician polish that would stand out among the old volunteers. More so since they've adopted the local style of pajama-loose shirt and pants, and rubber thongs or cloth sneakers.

He takes a step toward me and I'm engulfed in his embrace. I pull him into the room, pushing the door closed with my foot.

He kisses me, and I let him. But I feel strange. Off balance. Slow to react. My body has nearly forgotten how to be physically close to a man. Then as much a surprise as forgetting the physicality of love, the reality of Lucien—his characteristic smell, the familiar press of his lips against mine, the fast beating of his heart, his hands firm and possessive on my back—breaks through the haze. And I remember.

My whole body remembers, and I surrender to the feel of his body pressed against mine, so close that I can hardly breathe. To the warmth that suffuses my body as he embraces me and I melt into that first kiss. To the taste of him as we kiss, awakening desire, long suppressed. I wound my arms around his neck and return his kisses.

I don't know how long we were lost in each other's kisses. Kisses of hunger and rekindled love. When we finally part, Lucien caresses my face with such tenderness that tears begin to well in my eyes. Tears of both disbelief and relief that he's right here where I never expected him to be; of wonder that after all I've been through, what we had lives on as intense as ever.

It isn't until he's seated on the lone armchair and me on his lap in the sparse living area that I speak. Lucien hasn't said a word.

Our arms are wrapped around each other, my chin resting on his shoulders. "Are you really here? I feel you. I smell you. I hear you breathe. I tasted you. But I never imagined you and me together here, in this land on the other side of the world."

"Is this real enough for you?" His lips graze my neck and my cheeks, seeking my lips. We kiss again.

"Have you come to take me home?"

"You could say that."

I don't know why but his answer brings tears to my eyes. I bury my face on his shoulder.

"You're crying. What's wrong?"

"Nothing."

"Something must have brought on the tears."

I don't answer for a few seconds. I'm not sad. To the contrary. I'm also aware that apart from suffusing me with joy, Lucien's presence frees me from always being in control. Lightens the burden I've imposed on myself. His coming is a kind of deliverance. I say, "I'm happy you're here. Relieved as well. I can let go, let someone else make decisions."

Lucien is silent for a minute. I don't see his face, so I can only guess what he's thinking and feeling. His arms tighten around me, and when he whispers, "Oh, my love," I know he understands.

For some minutes, we remain quiet. I'm content to rest my head on his shoulder as he relaxes his arms around me.

He shifts his position on the chair. I straighten my body, adjusting to his. I lean my forehead against his. He says, "I'm here, ready to listen anytime you want to tell me more."

"Not yet."

"Yeah, maybe a little too soon?"

I kiss him and say, "All I want right now is to relish your presence."

Minutes later, I remember my obligations as a host. I rise from his lap "I'm not being hospitable. It's a Cambodian custom to offer refreshments to visitors, even strangers."

"I'd like something to drink."

"I have water from freshly-cut coconut. Bought it this morning from a street vendor selling glutinous rice snacks." I take a step toward the pantry for two glasses and the pitcher of coconut water, but I stop and turn to face him again. "Where's your luggage?"

"At Sofitel."

"Oh. Aren't you staying with me?"

"I didn't know what your place was like or if I could stay with you. I read they're pretty conservative about cohabiting unmarried couples and are particularly harsh on women."

"True. I didn't think about that."

"Does that mean I can't entice you into luxuriating with me at the hotel?"

I say archly, "And sully my honor?"

He chuckles. "You've nothing to worry about. Except for staff, I saw no Cambodians at the hotel. A lot of French. They don't care."

"I guess it doesn't really matter. We're foreigners. The world knows most of us have loose morals."

"So you have no qualms going on a trip with me, loose woman?"

"Where to?"

"No fixed itinerary. I took a month off. I was too restless waiting for you to come back to me, more so after the email you sent in March. So here I am at your beck and call. We'll go wherever you want."

I have to pause after taking two glasses from a kitchen shelf, and close my eyes to hold back tears. I'm in danger of turning into a cry-baby, now that Lucien is here.

I look in his direction. He's reading something on his cell phone. I watch his concentration, the ghost of a smile on his lips. I say, "I love you."

He looks up from his cell phone, smiling, beaming, saying, "And I love you."

I realize then that the kisses we shared a few moments ago were not just about our hunger for each other. They were kisses of belonging. Of homecoming.

"Do you want to sight-see in Cambodia?" I say, to give myself time to slow my breathing.

"I'd love to see Angkor Wat with you. It's supposed to be larger than any cathedral in Europe." Grinning, he adds, "With sexy nymphs carved around it."

"I've signed up with a guide to see Angkor Wat day after tomorrow. He'll take a couple or a group for an additional fee."

Lucien's eyes brighten. "Great. We can wing it from there. Like I said, no fixed itinerary. Will that bother you?"

"No. We're together. How can it get bad? But promise we'll go to Paris."

"It's our first trip together. We must go to Paris. What about Japan? I want to take you to places I've visited there. Maybe Vietnam. Or Singapore, which I meant to visit, but didn't because of Kuala Lumpur."

"I'm okay with all of those."

He gives me a thumbs-up. "Okay, then. I'll pace our trip. You need some relaxation time. And I'll book rooms with private bathrooms. That's what I missed the most, staying in hostels. Takes more planning but it's worth the comfort and better water supply."

I return his thumbs-up. "Great. I've become a pro, using an outside latrine at the village. I had to carry a bucket of water every time. But I'd be happy never to go to one again."

I continue what I'm doing, taking the pitcher of coconut water from the small refrigerator under the kitchen counter.

He says, "Packed up and ready to leave tonight? We'll decamp to Sofitel. We have two nights before Angkor Wat."

"Nearly done. I reserved a cheap room for one in Siem Reap to see Angkor Wat."

"I'll try to change your reservation to a double. Lend me your iPad, and I'll work on it. Can I get bus tickets online?

"Don't think so. We'll buy them before boarding."

On the small dining table between the kitchen and the living area, I pour the coconut water into the two glasses. I sense Lucien's eyes on me from across the room. I turn my head sideways, flash him a smile. He rises from the chair, approaches, and picks up the full glass. He guzzles the coconut water until the glass is empty. I swallow mine slowly.

"Good," he says, raising his glass before putting it down. He pours more, filling his glass nearly to the top. He pauses, watches me, takes a sip. I watch him back, wondering if he's adapting the pace of drinking his coconut water to mine. But I get flustered at the intensity of his gaze, and I focus on my glass.

He takes off his glasses, wipes it with the bottom of his T-shirt, and places it on the table. A habit I remember well.

"I'll get my iPad," I say, suddenly feeling a little shy.

He pulls me by the hand and gathers me close. "Later. Not before our reunion is complete," he says as he scoops me up in his arms.

*****

When the guide finishes his canned presentation on Angkor Wat, he tells us we can wander around for as long as we want until visiting hours end.

I've never heard Lucien wax poetic about a structure. And it diverts me that Angkor Wat inspires him into florid prose. About the size of the monument. The two thousand lifelike nymphs. The individuality of each one.

"You know the Khmers started building Angkor Wat in the twelfth century. But did you know," —he says, incredulous— "that's about the time Gothic churches began to be built in France and England? Three hundred years before there was a New World."

It's impossible not to be drawn into his wonder. "It's quite impressive," I say. "Especially the nymphs."

"The Apsaras, the guide calls them. Angkorean angels."

I echo the guide's words. "Pure and supernatural. Famed for their art of dancing, their bodies elegantly poised."

Lucien continues, "Carved for eternity bedecked in jewels and headdresses."

They are, indeed, vibrant and intriguing in their exoticism.

Built as a Hindu temple dedicated to the god Vishnu, Angkor Wat has been gradually transformed into a Buddhist temple.

Three days later, we're in Japan. The sites we visit there aren't as exciting as Angkor Wat. At least, not for me. They are magnificent in their own way but I think the stress of the last few months is catching up with me.

My energy is flagging, and I can't appreciate the iconic architecture Lucien admires. I find places to sit from where I watch and wait while he tours the historical pagodas and temples in Kyoto and Miyajima, and later, in My Son in Vietnam.

I recover some energy as I sit on a narrow wooden porch (an *engawa*, Lucien says), contemplating the Zen rock garden at the Ryoanji temple in Kyoto. I feel at peace and we stay for at least an hour in the same place. We return the next day.

The riverboat cruises on Halong Bay and the Mekong Delta are also relaxing. Maybe gliding across gentle, rhythmic waves, water swishing against the hull, is like being rocked in a cradle. It's so soothing that people are silent or they speak in low voices. Lucien holds my hand on his lap, and I rest my head on his shoulder.

We fly to Paris from Vietnam. I see, riding a cab into the city, that Paris demands to be explored on foot and be lingered over. But by the time we arrive early afternoon, I'm exhausted. We while away that day at a café across the river from the Notre Dame Cathedral.

The next day, we ride to the top of the Eiffel Tower for long views of the city. From there, we walk to the nearby Musée du Quai Branly. It exhibits indigenous art from Asian and African cultures. We're here mainly for the building, designed by a famous French architect Lucien studied in architecture school.

By the time our day ends at the Musée d'Art Moderne de la Ville de Paris, the city museum of modern art across the Seine from the Branly, I'm wiped out.

Lucien, worried and always solicitous, suggests we spend the rest of our trip in cafés or on green benches or chairs at the Jardin du Luxembourg and under the rows of chestnut trees behind the Notre Dame Cathedral. When I protest that we aren't seeing enough of the city, he tells me lolling about in cafés and in the numerous parks is essential to the Parisian experience.

I begin having recurrent nightmares on our second night in Paris. Dreams that wake me up gasping for air. I'm on a muddy road between emerald rice fields. I hear voices and see people preparing a feast. On a table are platters of food. But I smell incense, not the dishes. Strange, I think. One particularly large platter has a dome-shaped cover. Curious, I lift it. There, on the platter, lies Ov's head, a black hole piercing his skull through. Frightened, I run. Ov's head pursues me.

For three nights, I suffer from some variation on this dream. In one, it's not incense I smell but the residual stench of rotting flesh from a skull lying on the white tablecloth. In another, there is neither skull nor platter, but a tablecloth smeared with blood. I always run, terrified, powerless to escape.

After those three nights, I've grown too anxious to sleep and though Lucien is there to embrace me and reassure me, I stay awake. By the end of our first week, I have bags under my eyes, sunken cheeks, little appetite, and trouble concentrating.

When on our sixth day in Pairs, I refuse to get out of bed, Lucien sits next to me and pulls me up in his arms. I rest my head on his shoulders as he strokes my back. He says, his voice soft, "You can't go on like this. I can't stand watching you suffer."

He holds me away from him and fixes pleading eyes on my face. "I'm at a loss how to help you and it breaks my heart. I thought loving you, being there for you, showing you there's much more to the world than what you've seen—a world we could explore together—would be enough to help you heal. But it isn't. You have demons you must face, Luna."

Looking into Lucien's eyes, full of caring mixed with pain, I have to admit to myself I've fallen apart.

My belief that I know myself, that I have control over how I feel, think, and act has been shattered. Ripped inside out by witnessing incidents people don't often encounter: Asha's body bruised black and blue for sexual pleasure. Young Jorani confronting her parents' traumatic past. Mae breaking down and finding resurrection in Ov's death. Ov's suicide.

I coped, or thought I did, through tenacious self-control. I couldn't allow myself to fall apart in the midst of those incidents. But how fragile that self-control was. When Lucien came and I allowed myself to let go, the fact that I'd also been traumatized surfaced in full bloom. I've tried to deny it, suppress it, explain it away. But I failed.

"We should go home," Lucien says. "I think some type of therapy can help you. Paris can wait. We have time enough for all it can offer in years to come."

I gaze at this sensitive, perceptive man, and say, "Let's go to Grandma's home. Let's spend the rest of your vacation time there." My suggestion is a surprise even to me. I don't know exactly what prompted it. But I feel better just saying it.

He pulls me back in his arms and kisses the top of my head, "We shall. Tomorrow, as soon as we can get tickets." He rocks me gently in his arms and adds, "But will you try to eat?"

I smile and nod. "Can we go to Berthilion for an ice cream cone?"

Lucien

Under the Mango Tree

It's late afternoon. Luna and I stand on the sidewalk in front of a stained-wood house in Waipahu—her grandma's house. Waiting for her Auntie Celia to come and give us keys to the house.

"I feel like I'm on a time warp, "Luna says. "I'm older. I've changed. And I'm no longer the same Luna. But everything looks and feels the same around here. Like time stood still for this place. It even smells the same."

She looks up at the mango tree. I follow her gaze. The foliage on the tree is so dense that branches close to the trunk are hardly visible.

Luna says, "It's still here. Thriving." She renders homage to it with the Khmer som pas, pressing her hands together and bowing her head. She smiles. Her face turned up to the sky, she opens her arms.

It takes me a second or two to realize she's embracing the mango tree. Her smile turns into laughter.

I haven't heard Luna laugh for a while. Not in Cambodia. Not on our trip. Her laugh infects me. I laugh, and mimic Luna's gestures. I open up my arms, looking up again at the mango tree. Then, I som pas.

Still smiling, she hooks her arm into mine. We roll our luggage behind us with our free hands. She leads me through a concrete pathway lined with hibiscus shrubs.

We stop by the stairs to an entry porch. Lay our two suitcases and a carry-on bag at the foot of it. Luna has sent her other suitcase full of silk and batik fabrics and other souvenirs to her parents' house. She sits on the top step.

I stand on the porch. Scan the street of stucco houses. Grandma's property stands apart from all of them. Wood house. A towering mango tree on the corner. No one else like it on the block.

Not long after, a small white car stops on the street next to the walkway. A middle-aged woman gets off. Auntie Celia. She fits Luna's description. She's carrying a plastic bag.

She looks up, stares at me. Her lips break into a smile. She waves.

"Auntie Celia." Luna descends from her perch. I follow her back to the sidewalk.

Auntie Celia hands me the plastic bag. Aunt and niece embrace, alternately laughing and crying.

"Let me look at you," her aunt says, wiping her eyes with the back of her hand. She holds Luna at arm's length. Looks her over. Touches her face. Her eyes cloud with concern.

She embraces her again. Doesn't let go until Luna says, "Auntie Celia, I'd like you to meet Lucien."

She turns to me, concern still written on her face. She hugs me. In a voice still shaky with emotion, she says "Thank you for bringing her home."

Inside the house minutes later, we sit around a long butcher block table. Auntie Celia's bag has five boxes of prepared dishes. She unpacks each one and shows us the contents. "I knew you'd be tired and hungry from the flight."

Luna says, "They served us food on the plane."

"Not your favorites, I bet. These are closer to Mom's dishes than Hawaiian Airlines could ever serve you. No mango salad, though."

Auntie Celia says to me, "Luna tells me you've traveled and have been to Hawaii. You must know these dishes."

"I think I do, though I ate mostly plate lunches out of food trucks." I point to each of the dishes. "Manapua, lomilomi salmon, grilled shrimps, long rice, and kalua pig."

"You hit everyone except for long rice. This one is actually Korean. Jap chae. Made with bean thread noodles." Turning to Luna, she says, "You still remember where everything is kept? Can you get plates and utensils for the two of you?

Luna says, "Aren't you going to eat with us, Auntie?"

Auntie Celia shakes her head. "I'm good. I'll just watch you eat. Besides, my stomach isn't on the same schedule as yours. Anyway, I'm too excited. To see you after so many years. And, of course, to meet Lucien."

She smiles at me, holding my gaze. "I wish Mom had known you. She would have approved."

Except for "thank you, this is delicious," Luna doesn't say much while we eat. Relieved to see her devour a plateful of food, I gladly answer her aunt's inquiries about our trip.

Before we finish eating, her aunt says, "I'm tired. Busy day at the clinic. And the kids will be coming home from school soon." She puts two sets of keys on the table and rises from her stool.

We see her to the front door and after aunt and niece embrace again, I walk with Auntie Celia to her car. Luna stands on the porch, watching us.

Before Auntie Celia gets into her car, she says, "Did something happen in Cambodia? Luna looks depressed."

I hesitate. Not sure how much to tell her. And I don't know the whole story, anyway. I say, "Luna hasn't talked about it much. I only know the broad outlines of what happened. Her host parents lived through the Cambodian genocide. Just a few months before Luna finished her stint with the Peace Corps, the father took his life."

"Oh, no. How tragic," Auntie Celia says. "Luna must be taking it very hard. She's such a sensitive child."

"She has occasional nightmares about it."

"Maybe she should go into therapy."

I say, "I suggested it, but she asked to come here. I think she needs the solace and tranquility this place used to give her. If only for a few days. She's come to this home to recover."

"How long will you stay?"

"A week, maybe more. I can call my office to ask for more time off. But I may have to go before she's ready to leave this place."

"She can stay for as long as she needs to." She lays a gentle hand on my arm. "She's written me about you—good things. She's never been effusive about her feelings, but I can tell she loves you very much. Will you call me if you think I can help in any way?"

*****

Luna and I don't leave the house in the next week. The refrigerator has been stocked with groceries and frozen food. The house, to Luna's relief, has signs it's been used, or at least visited from time to time. To her, they mean the house will stay in the family.

The morning after our arrival, she takes me to the mango tree to see if her Grandma's bench is still

363

there. She's almost in tears when she sees it where it has always been. The bench is dusty. She tears leaves from an overgrown hibiscus hedge and uses them to wipe the bench. We sit side by side on it.

She clasps my hand and leans on my shoulder. "Grandma and I sat here every afternoon when I came for summer visits." Her voice is soft, pensive, but it ends with a break as she strangles a sob.

I squeeze her hand gently. She's quiet, though her chest is heaving. I put my arm around her.

We sit in silence and after a while, her breathing becomes even. For half an hour, we hardly move.

I look down to see if Luna has fallen asleep, but she raises her face and smiles. "Grandma is here. I smell her."

I don't feel her Grandma's presence. But the scent of jasmine, though faint, has perfumed the air since we've been sitting on the bench.

She gets up, pulling my hand, and leads me to the backyard. Though the chicken coop she remembers is gone, a garden of herbs, zucchini, tomatoes and bell peppers is thriving. She thinks Auntie Celia planted the vegetables and has tended them. We pick what we can to eat them raw for lunch.

A couple of days later, at breakfast, I watch Luna devour two manapuas and two pineapple slices. Her sallow cheeks are regaining flesh and color, and the bags under her eyes are gone after only three nights of peaceful sleep. Luna has begun to thrive again.

We keep the same routine everyday—Zen-sitting under the mango tree, watering and weeding the vegetable garden, harvesting vegetables, and napping and reading the afternoon away. On the sixth night, we make love, the first time since Luna's nightmares in Paris.

Later, still naked and aglow, we lie face-to-face. She tells me she wants to write a memoir about her experience in Doun Teav village.

"Great idea," I say. "Could be cathartic. Like journal writing has been for you."

"It might not help me understand the genocide— that was too horrendous, too cruel to comprehend— but writing helps me gather my chaotic and unwelcome thoughts together."

I kiss her, happy she's moving on. "Might be the therapy you need. I think writing helps you look at your experiences from the perspective of a third person. Someone outside looking in."

"Actually, there's another reason I want to write about my life in Cambodia," she says, her face becoming more animated. "I want people to know about the Cambodian genocide. I doubt many people are aware of it. Like the Holocaust, it should never be forgotten. Maybe in some small way, I can help keep that part of history alive."

She caresses my cheeks and I grasp her hand, kissing her palm. The lines of her face relax and what I see in her eyes reaches straight into my heart.

Quickens it. Envelops it in warmth that flows through my whole body.

Luna says, "When you arrived in Phnom Penh and you kissed me, I remember thinking *I'm home*. There, in the middle of a strange country I was about to leave. You are my home, Lucien, wherever we are. And whatever the future holds."

I think of the past ten years when I've been alone by choice. Of the trauma in Kuala Lumpur, now locked in a tiny, compartment in my mind. Of how I would still be living all alone, content but not happy. Then I found Luna's journal.

I kiss her again. Not a kiss of passion, but one of tenderness and gratitude. And I reassess my own past. Maybe, Kuala Lumpur was bound to happen, and deciding to devote my life to architecture in the ten years that followed hasn't been a mistake. I was biding my time until I met Luna.

Maybe Fate isn't just a construct. It's real.

Author's Notes

Luna decides to write about her terrible experience in an old country, partly to help herself heal. Can writing help you heal?

Yes, it can. See: *Write to Save Your Life* on my website https://evyjourney.net.

Growing up, I read and drew to let out steam. Then, I wrote. These days, I pour my heart into fiction—my characters assuming my thoughts, hurts,, and joys. Something in all my characters reflect a little part of me. I think it's inevitable even when you write fantasy or sci fi.

I pay homage to grandparents. When both parents work, they get asked to help look after children. My grandmother raised me and was there as I grew up. Her influence has endured.

Love is at the core of all my stories. Aren't they in everyone's if you allow yourself to be vulnerable enough to another? Love strips you bare, opens you up to both happiness and pain. Still, my novels won't fit neatly into the romance genre. Because, ultimately, they're about life, about our messy, complicated, wonderful lives.

My characters are multicultural because I am and we represent the majority in the area we live in. In this book, the heroine travels to a world much older than our own in the US and, yet, its deadly history has sadly caused it to regress.

Dear Reader,

Thank you so much for spending some time with Luna, Lucien, Jorani, and Grandma.

If you like their story, please consider doing a review.

About the Author

Evy Journey writes. Stories and blog posts. Novels that tend to cross genres. She's also a wannabe artist and a flâneuse.

Evy studied psychology (Ph.D. University of Illinois) so she spins tales about nuanced characters dealing with the problems and issues of contemporary life. She believes in love and its many faces.

Her one ungranted wish: To live in Paris where art is everywhere and people have honed aimless roaming to an art form. She visits and stays a few months.

Find her at Evy Writes (https://evyjourney.net).

Her thoughts on art, travel, and food: Artsy Rambler (https://www.eveonalimb2.com/).

Her book reviews: Escape Into Reality (https://margaretofthenorth.wordpress.com/).

Also by Evy Journey

Sugar and Spice and All Those Lies
Chanterelles garnished with cream and mayhem.
Between Two Worlds
A series about negotiating separate realities. A family saga in three standalone tales of life and love

with a twist of mystery, the healing power of music, and international political intrigue.

Hello My Love, #1. A modern-day pastiche of Jane Austen novels.

Hello Agnieszka, # 2. A sequel/prequel hybrid. A raw tale of early love, rivalry and betrayal set in the seventies.

Welcome Reluctant Stranger, #3. A multicultural, interracial love story.

Margaret of the North

A sequel to Elizabeth Gaskell's *North and South*.

Made in the USA
Middletown, DE
11 January 2021